The Bootlegger's Confession

A SAM KLEIN MYSTERY
THE BOOTLEGGER'S
CONFESSION

BY ALLAN LEVINE

RaveN
STONE

The Bootlegger's Confession
© Allan Levine 2016

Published by Ravenstone
an imprint of Turnstone Press
Artspace Building
206-100 Arthur Street
Winnipeg, MB
R3B 1H3 Canada
www.ravenstonebooks.com
www.turnstonepress.com

FSC
www.fsc.org

MIX
Paper from
responsible sources
FSC® C016245

Turnstone Press gratefully acknowledges the assistance of the Canada Council for the Arts, the Manitoba Arts Council, the Government of Canada through the Canada Book Fund, and the Province of Manitoba through the Book Publishing Tax Credit and the Book Publisher Marketing Assistance Program.

This novel is a work of fiction. Names, characters, places and incidents are either the product of the author's imagination or are used fictitiously, and any resemblance to actual persons living or dead, events or locales, is entirely coincidental.

Printed and bound in Canada by Friesens for Turnstone Press.

Library and Archives Canada Cataloguing in Publication

Levine, Allan, 1956-, author
    The bootlegger's confession / Allan Levine.

(Sam Klein mysteries ; 4)
Issued in print and electronic formats.
ISBN 978-0-88801-599-0 (paperback).--ISBN 978-0-88801-600-3 (epub).--
ISBN 978-0-88801-601-0 (mobi).--ISBN 978-0-88801-602-7 (pdf)

        I. Title.

PS8573.E96448B66 2016   C813'.54   C2016-904714-8
                                              C2016-904715-6

For my mother, Bernice,
who has faced life's challenges with courage and strength

Author's Note

From the 1850s to the 1930s, the consumption of liquor was paramount. In one corner were the "wets," individuals who favoured choice, widespread availability, and a minimum of government regulations, if any at all; and in the other were the "drys," devoted crusaders who fought for prohibition and regarded alcohol abuse as one of the great threats to men, women, and children. Supporters of each side fought for their positions with a passionate conviction and believed they were championing progress and modernity.

In the United States, only slavery divided Americans more than liquor. In Canada, it was just as contentious. The dry side appeared victorious in Canada in 1915–16 when, for about six years, most provinces—including Manitoba—adopted some form of prohibition. Then, more significantly, in 1919 the Eighteenth Amendment to the US Constitution instituted Prohibition, along with the Volstead Act that regulated and enforced it, though poorly.

Prohibition in both countries was a failure. Too many loopholes were the problem in Canada. Provinces could shut down saloons and restrict the flow of liquor, but provincial governments could not stop interprovincial trade which was a federal responsibility. And the federal government was slow to respond to the issue on a national level. As a result, inventive businessmen found a way to sell whisky from one province to the other via mail order. Physicians and pharmacists were also able to prescribe booze for "medicinal" purposes. As humourist Stephen Leacock noted, to obtain a bottle of "medicinal" whisky in Ontario, a person had only "to go to a drugstore ... and lean up against the counter and make a gurgling sound like apoplexy. One often sees these apoplexy cases lined up four deep."

In the United States, Prohibition, which lasted from 1919 until it was repealed in 1933, was a fiasco from the start. Demand for liquor never stopped, nor was it policed properly. All of this made it extremely lucrative for Canadian liquor dealers, who were not breaking any Canadian laws, to sell their product to American bootleggers and gangsters who would smuggle it across the border and distribute the alcohol to speakeasies across the US. Organized crime, murder, theft, and gangster wars were the most serious consequences of this controversial trade. Some of this mayhem took place in small, isolated border towns in Manitoba and Saskatchewan, where it was easy to avoid American patrols.

This is the story at the heart of *The Bootlegger's Confession*.

Like the previous Sam Klein Mysteries, this is a work of fiction. The events described in this book did not happen, nor are the major characters real people. There are however references to real Winnipeggers of the era such as John Dafoe, editor of the *Winnipeg Free Press*, Police Chief Christopher Newton, and Rabbi Herbert Samuel, among a few others.

The Bootlegger's Confession

Prologue

Saturday, June 10, 1922
Vera, Manitoba

The warm and breezy wind did not let up all evening. Each time another customer came into Roter's General Store to buy some groceries or merely to share in the town gossip, another blast of air brought more dust and grime. And like clockwork, Rae Roter shouted at the latest visitor, "*Oy gevalt,* please shut the door, *fershtay?*"

Rae, a five-foot-three beauty rounded at the hips—*zaftig* was how her husband Max affectionately described her—was generally oblivious to the fact that she and Max and their two young children, Mira and Isaac, were the only ones in the town who spoke or understood Yiddish. In fact, they were the only Jews in Vera, period, just like the Jewish storekeepers and their families in dozens of other Manitoban towns. From Flin Flon to McCreary and all points in between, you could count on three things in any half-baked village and town in Manitoba and Saskatchewan: a grain elevator, a Chinese café, and a Jewish general store merchant.

3

Still, ever since Max and Rae had relocated over two years ago at her brothers' heeding from Winnipeg to this sleepy town ten miles from the North Dakota border to operate the store, Vera's other 773 citizens had become used to Rae's Yiddish rants. Within months of their arrival, many of them had even picked up a few phrases. It was not uncommon to hear Vera's Gentile farmers, cattle buyers, and shopkeepers—even Fred Lum who ran the laundry and Chinese food café—peppering their conversations with Yiddish expressions. Sometimes customers entering Lum's laundry were startled to hear Fred complaining that one of his clients was *kvetching* about the starch in his shirts.

During the weekdays, the store was open from eight in the morning to seven in the evening. But on Saturdays the hours were extended, when everyone in town it seemed came by to shop, browse, or socialize. Close to midnight, Max Roter, forty-one, tall, muscular, and as handsome a storekeeper as there was on the prairies, ushered out the only customers remaining in the store, his next door neighbours Mr. and Mrs. Smythe.

"Still blowing strong," said Jack Smythe, the manager of Vera's lone grain elevator owned by the Standard Grain Company.

"Sure is," replied Max, fussing with the diamond stick pin on his jet black tie. "Supposed to be calmer in the morning." He opened the door wide, staring Jack Smythe right in the eye.

"I guess we'll see you in church tomorrow..." Jack said, roaring with laughter.

"Honestly, Jack," interrupted his wife, Joannie. "Rae and Max don't attend church services." She was a striking redhead and in the unbiased opinion of the daily gathering of male coffee-drinkers at Lum's, the most alluring woman in the town.

Jack's jovial demeanour abruptly vanished. He glared at his wife, whose face turned pale. Then, just as quickly, he started laughing again, slapping Max on the shoulder. "Of course, dear. I was just *kabootzing*."

Max brushed Smythe's hand away. "I think you mean *kibitzing*," he said, rolling his eyes.

"That's it exactly," said Jack with a loud snort.

Joannie's face flushed. She looked at Rae behind the counter, lifting her shoulders. Rae smiled warmly and shrugged.

Once the Smythes finally left, Max shut the door and turned to his wife. "*Meshuggina goyim,*" he muttered.

"I like Joannie," said Rae. "She's probably the most pleasant woman in Vera. Never has a bad word for anyone."

"Maybe. I always get the feeling she's either unhappy or hiding something. I know you've heard the gossip about her, about them."

"I don't want to talk about that right now. It's none of our business. Isn't that what you've said?"

"It's a husband's prerogative to change his mind. And as for it not being my business, that's funny coming from you. Everything in this town is *your* business!"

Rae chuckled, playfully pushing Max's shoulder.

"He's a fool and besides, I don't especially trust him," said Max. "You know that expression, *a nar bleibt a nar*? He's a fool and will always be one!"

"Now who's being a *meshuggina*. Whatever Jack may have

done, I think deep down he's a decent man, though definitely not a perfect one. Who is? Not me or you, that's for sure. All I know for certain is that Joannie always pays her bill on time, unlike some of the others around here."

"They'll pay, don't worry, my darling," said Max, grabbing his wife around her waist and pulling her close. "You let Helen go home. I'm sure she's exhausted from looking after the *kinder*. And I'll close up." He gave her a peck on the cheek and his right hand glanced over her rump. "And then I'll be home to keep you company, if you know what I mean," said Max, raising his eyebrows.

Rae pushed his hand away. "I've been married to you for ten years, Max Roter. I *always* get your meaning."

Max chuckled and then looked at the store clock. It was half-past twelve. His smile abruptly vanished. "Go, dear. I promise I'll be home soon."

Rae tidied the counter, tied down the spring claw that was used to bring down boxes of cereal and cans of tomato juice from the top shelves—earlier in the day she had permitted Mira, about to turn ten, to practice using the contraption—and hung up her smeared white apron. She fixed her hair bun, smoothed her navy skirt, and prepared for the short walk to the family house, a large, white home perched on a mound at the end of Main Street.

"You be careful tonight," said Rae, rubbing her husband's back. "I really wish you didn't have to conduct this business so late."

Max said nothing. He opened the door for Rae and urged her out into the night.

Finally alone, Max opened the register and gingerly removed a wad of cash. He leafed through it and tucked it away in a green canvas bank bag. It had been another profitable Saturday. Farmers from the Gretna area often visited, stocking up on supplies and bartering with live chickens that Max kept in a henhouse outside at the back. There wasn't much you could not buy at Roter's. Besides groceries, there were hardware, pots, pans, shoes, spices, clothing, and knickknacks of every type and variety. The money was decent and from the store alone, Max and Rae made a good living.

Still, truth be told, Max hated this one-horse town, which was literally in the middle of nowhere. Not to mention that it was no treat using an outhouse in the middle of January when the temperature froze the hair in your nostrils in seconds. The town's one redeeming feature was the dirt road to the US border. Immediately on the other side was Hampton, North Dakota, as pathetic and isolated as Vera, perhaps more so. Yet that was the point. Or that was how Rae's brothers, Lou and Saul Sugarman, explained it to him when they convinced, actually coerced, him and Rae to move out here.

Lou especially had been good to him when Max arrived in Winnipeg a dozen years ago. The journey from Kiev had been arduous but Max knew he had no choice. There was no way he was going to be conscripted into the Russian army. His father had paid a trustworthy farmer sufficient funds to ensure Max got all the way to Warsaw. From there, Max had made his way to Hamburg and then took a miserable week-long voyage across the Atlantic to New York. He would have stayed there, except he had promised his father that he would travel on to Winnipeg in Canada where his third cousins, the Sugarmans, lived.

"They have money," his father had assured him. "They're *machers*. Own some hotels. They will give you some work." So like the obedient son he was, Max headed north.

Greeneh, or greenhorn, did not quite describe him back then. He couldn't speak a word of English and he had only a few dollars in his pocket. Lou had met him at the CPR station, taken him home, fed him, and given him a place to sleep. A cleaning job at the Prince Edward Hotel on Main Street, one of three the Sugarmans owned, was next. Max worked hard, learned English quickly, and before too long was working behind the desk and supervising the bar where the real money was to be made. He and Rae Sugarman had also fallen in love. Lou was thrilled; Saul, the elder brother, was less pleased, but he eventually came around. In Max's view, Saul had no sense of humour; he was all business, each day, every day. Nonetheless, Max was impressed by Saul and Lou's success.

Since those foolish and moralistic Americans had brought in prohibition two and a half years ago, the flow of cash to the Sugarmans was non-stop. "We're doing nothing illegal," Lou had reassured Max many times. "Just taking advantage of a business opportunity." And as far as Max understood the law, Lou was right—at least technically.

By 1922, even Max could see that the US ban against booze

was a farce. In Chicago, New York, even in Washington DC, where gossip had it that President Warren Harding served bootleg liquor to his dinner guests, demand was never higher. The Sugarmans quickly figured out a way to take advantage of this without violating Manitoba's Temperance Act, which was poorly enforced, at any rate. They bought and stocked warehouses full of liquor near the American border and waited for US customers to find them. And the more isolated the warehouses were, the better. It didn't take long for a booming cross-border business to develop.

Hence, Max and Rae found themselves in Vera, Manitoba on the pretext of running a general store, but the real money derived from the barn behind the store—a warehouse crammed with whisky, rum, and gin. Corby, Seagram, Canadian Club, Booth's Dry Gin were a few of the brands on the shelves of Max Roter's "boozorium," as everyone in town called it. A lot of the liquor was also homemade, as strong as 65 percent overproof alcohol, though watered down. Admittedly, it was a greedy, perhaps even foolish trick, but it worked. Lou slapped fictitious labels on the bottles—Old Highland Scotch, Shea's Irish Whisky, and Lion's Gin—and their thirsty American clientele were happy. Or, so they believed.

There were two things that Saul and Lou had not accounted for. The first was that from what Max had recently heard, the provincial governments in Manitoba, Saskatchewan, and Alberta were growing increasingly uneasy with this liquor trade and the booty it was generating for the likes of the Sugarmans. For the Canadian politicians, it was not so much that the Americans were upset about the flow of booze from places like Vera to towns in North Dakota, but rather that such money-making was morally repugnant. The second was that since a bottle of Scotch that used to cost three dollars was now being sold in New York speakeasies for as high as sixteen dollars a quart, the liquor trade attracted a lot of unsavory characters.

As Max learned, a few months after the General Strike, the Sugarmans sent Lou's friend, Sam Klein, a bit of a celebrity in the Winnipeg Jewish community for his detective skills, on a journey south. Lou later told Max that Klein had made contact with Fritz Michaels, a bootlegger in Minneapolis. Michaels had then sent him to New York to deal directly with Irv Rosen and Leo Forni. As the Sugarmans soon found out, however, these men were not to be toyed with. Business was everything to them but if you crossed them, swift and deadly punishment was meted out. There were no questions asked first.

Max reached for his pack of Player's Navy Cut, took a cigarette out, struck a wooden match against the counter, and lit it. He inhaled sharply, fiddling with his gold ring, and waited. He knew he had a problem that was not going to be easily resolved. And he dared not broach the subject with Lou or Saul, heaven forbid. He was certain that neither of them would be all that understanding. And who could blame them? If anyone was playing a dangerous game, it was him. He took a long drag of his cigarette and blew a puff of smoke upwards.

Other than a few howling dogs and the squeal of the Smythes' tomcat always on the prowl, Vera was silent. Max stared outside wondering yet one more time how it was he lived in this *chazerei* of a town. And from his perspective, that was putting it nicely.

He heard the roar of a Packard in the distance. Opening the door of the store, he was nearly blinded by the powerful spotlight Frankie Taylor had affixed to the car. He held his hand above his eyes as Taylor came to a screeching stop.

"That six-cylinder is purring tonight, Frankie," said Max, throwing his cigarette down and butting it with the heel of his shoe.

Taylor's luxurious Packard Twin Six was dark red. The auto's white-walled tires shimmered in the moonlight and there was a gleaming silver tiger ornament affixed to the top of the hood. An extra layer of steel had been attached to the bumpers in case Taylor ever had to break through a police roadblock.

Taylor, husky, dark-haired, and ornery, exited the vehicle, and as he did so Max caught a glimpse of his shoulder holster and gun. "Sure is, Roter. But I haven't got time for talk. Where's the shipment?"

"Where it always is," said Max, easing himself into the soft red leather passenger seat. "Drive around to the back and I'll load you up."

Taylor got back in the car, fired up the engine with the wondrous electric starter, and they were off. Taylor drove half a block down Main Street then turned right into a dirt alley that led to a barn at the back of Roter's General Store. Max hopped out of the car and pulled a set of keys from his jacket pocket. First, he opened the padlock that held the iron bar firmly across the warehouse door, and then the series of heavy-duty locks on the steel door itself. Once inside, he lit two lanterns and the building was quickly illuminated. There were ten wide, sturdy shelves from floor to ceiling. On each were stacked wooden crates of whisky and other liquor. There was hardly room for a person to move.

"I want the good stuff, Roter," barked Taylor. "None of that watered down shit the Sugarmans have been selling. No one was happy about the last shipment I sent them."

"You mean, Rosen?" asked Max.

"You know that's exactly who I am talking about. Now stop talking and let's load up the car so I can get the hell out of this fucking town."

Within twenty minutes, Max and Taylor had stocked twenty crates of booze into the back of Taylor's Packard. The rear seat had been removed so that there was more space for the precious liquid cargo.

"That should do it," said Max, carefully placing the last crate inside the car.

Taylor surveyed the haul. "Looks good. They'll be pleased."

"Assuming you get across into Hampton, of course."

Taylor flipped his hand. "When have I ever not been able to do that? Besides, this time of the night no cops or feds will be around. But just to be safe, give me a hand with these chains."

Max grabbed the two thirty-foot steel chains and helped Taylor fasten them to back of the spare tire. The chains, as he knew, stirred up a heavy cloud of dust so that even if some nosy federal agents were monitoring the border, they wouldn't be able to see him as Taylor sped away.

With the chains on, Max cleared his throat.

"Yeah, I know what you're waiting for, Roter. Always the Jew, right?" Taylor snickered.

Max ignored the taunt. "It's business, that's all."

Taylor pulled an envelope filled with cash from his inside jacket pocket and handed it to Max. "You gonna count it?"

"I trust you," he said, taking the envelope.

With that, Taylor was back in his car. He slowly eased his way back to Main Street and then accelerated. As he did so, a whirling dust storm flew back towards Max who ran for cover inside the store.

Max opened the envelope and shuffled through the bills. There was $7000 in total; Lou and Saul would be pleased. He placed the money back in the envelope, grabbed the bank sack with that night's take from the store, and moved to his small office at the rear where he kept a safe. He began to turn the combination dial when he heard a knock at the front door. Who the hell was that at this hour, he wondered.

He left the money on a table and began moving towards the door. He was nearly there when there was a crash and then flying glass shards. Max looked up to see a sawed-off shotgun through the broken window. "What the…"

The person holding the gun fired. The shell struck Max in his chest. He crumbled to the floor in a pool of blood. Calmly, the perpetrator reached through the window and opened the door.

The person touched Max's neck, ensuring that he was dead. He was. Max's tie clip and ring were removed. The murderer then walked to the rear office, snatched the envelope of cash and the bank bag, turned around, and quietly left the store.

1

Wednesday, June 14, 1922
Winnipeg, Manitoba

The distinct aroma of freshly brewed coffee wafted through the small, two-storey house on Cathedral Avenue. The bitter yet appealing smell roused Sam Klein from a deep sleep. He gradually opened his eyes, only to find his three children standing quietly at the foot of the parlour couch staring at him.

"Yes," he said softly. "Want something?"

The youngest, three-year-old Mel, smiled and waved at his father. His two older sisters, Freda, eight, and Bernice, five, were more glum.

Klein sat up and as he did so, little Mel jumped into his outstretched arms. He gave his father a big hug. "Why so sad, girls?" asked Klein tossing Mel around. The three-year-old let out a loud giggle. "Freda, don't you have to get ready for school?"

Bernice fidgeted but said nothing. She deferred to Freda, as she usually did.

With her angular face and long nose, Bernice, or Niecee to

the family, was the spitting image of Klein. Freda, taller, with long, reddish-brown hair was definitely Sarah Klein's daughter. She had her mother's high cheekbones, long legs, soft look, and unmatchable style that his wife still had at the age of thirty-four. Sarah was a "looker," as Klein liked to say. She had that *something* that made most men stop and gaze at her, whether it was at the grocery store or the park—which was exactly the reason he was sleeping on the chesterfield again, and had been for the past two weeks.

Freda cleared her throat. "Why are you in here, Daddy? Don't you love Mommy anymore?"

From the mouths of babes, thought Klein. "Of course I love Mommy, *bubeleh*. I just wanted to sleep by myself last night. You shouldn't worry about such things."

Freda raised her eyebrows. "Estelle's father was sleeping on the chesterfield and now he doesn't live with Estelle and her mother anymore."

Klein shook his head. "Where do you get such ideas? No one is going anywhere. Now go get ready for school and take your sister and brother with you."

"Is Mommy going bye-bye again?" Bernice piped in.

"Yeah," said Freda. "Mommy isn't leaving on another holiday, is she? We missed her. She was gone a long time."

"Mel, give me those cigarettes." The little boy did as he was told. Klein took one out, removed a match from the Eddy box beside him, and lit it. Mel's eyes widened as he watched his father's every move with great interest. Klein inhaled sharply. "Mommy isn't going anywhere, and neither am I. Freda, upstairs.

That goes for you too, Niecee, and Mel. Now, or we'll ship you off to the orphanage. Then you'll learn what life's all about."

"Oh, Daddy," said Freda, giggling. "You'll never do that. But I'm glad you still want to live with us." She took Mel by the hand and led him up the stairs to the second floor of the house. Bernice trailed behind them.

Klein stood up and straightened out his suspenders. He was still wearing his black pants from the night before and a white undershirt. He took another strong drag on the cigarette, pulled out his gold pocket watch, and checked the time. It was seven thirty. He had an hour and a half before he was meeting downtown with Lou Sugarman at Dolly's Café.

He had not lied to his children, though he may not have told them the entire truth either. He had had another restless night of sleep. The fact was, he had not slept well in more than a month, ever since his and Sarah's bitter argument. But he wasn't going anywhere. Hell, they had only moved into this house at 411 Cathedral Avenue six months ago.

The white stucco two-storey with the iron banister, electricity, and gas stove was about two blocks from Salter Street. He and Sarah had saved the fifty-dollar down payment so all that they owed was another $3,450. Klein thought his connection to his friend Alfred Powers, a respected lawyer, would get him in the door at the downtown banks. Then Alfred had dropped dead a few months ago from a heart attack and the bankers didn't consider a Jewish immigrant—and a self-employed private detective at that—as a particularly sound risk. Alfred's son Graham, a crown lawyer who had treated his sister Rivka so abysmally during the big strike a few years back, was of no help either. He didn't care much for Klein's "kind," as he wasn't hesitant about telling him.

With no other options open to them, Klein listened to Sarah and spoke to Lou Sugarman. Lou, in turn, sent him to see his brother Saul. The Sugarmans gave the Kleins the mortgage they needed. The interest was fair and the twenty-five-dollars-a-month payments doable. It would probably take twelve to fifteen years, but they would pay it off eventually.

On the other hand, dealing with Saul Sugarman left Klein uneasy; there was something about him that rubbed Klein the wrong way—and now, with what had transpired between Sarah and Sugarman, even more so. Maybe it was his expensive, custom-made suits or his monogrammed, pristine white shirts that he had shipped in from Maurice Rothschild's in Minneapolis? Or the thick roll of cash he always had in his pocket? Or, maybe, it was the way he eyed Sarah, like a hungry wolf stalking its next meal? Whatever it was, Klein detested the man. If it wasn't for the fact that Klein was genuinely fond of Lou Sugarman, the polar opposite of his brother, and that he and Sarah genuinely required financial help, he would have told Saul to take his money and shove it up his arse.

Klein made a decent living, averaging about a thousand dollars a year, but month-to-month his cash flow fluctuated. There were times recently when he had more clients and cases than he could handle—husbands and wives checking up on each other, businesses investigating their employees, missing persons, and a handful of suspicious deaths which he investigated, usually much to the annoyance of the police—but the work did slow down as well. In those months, he was thankful Sarah had her dress and cosmetics shop. Yet she, too, had her good and bad months. Since early 1920, there had been a noticeable downturn in the economy. Prices had increased; the grey suit, from Scotland no less, which Klein had recently purchased at Ralph's for $24.70 would have cost about fifteen dollars in 1916. To make matters worse, the rise in prices was not matched by a corresponding increase in wages. So, of late, there seemed to be a lot more bad months for both of them than good ones. In Sarah's case, many of her regular customers simply delayed buying new dresses and hats and purchased only the absolute minimum supply of cosmetics. On top of this, she was being outsold by Eaton's, the Hudson's Bay Company store, as well as Holt Renfrew.

This was the main reason some months ago Sarah had reluctantly accepted Saul Sugarman's offer to invest in her shop. She and Klein had discussed and argued about it; did they really want to be further indebted to the Sugarmans? Wasn't the loan from them on their house sufficient? But they also could not stand by and watch the dress shop go under. Klein knew the shop meant a lot to Sarah; it had given her the respectability she had craved and, in his view, deserved. And they needed any money it brought in. In the end, they both agreed that there was no other choice but to hold their noses and accept Saul Sugarman's money. What Klein did not expect, however, was how this transaction was to so seriously impact their marriage.

Klein sauntered into the main floor kitchen, helped himself to a mug of hot coffee, and lit another cigarette.

"You don't look so rested, Shailek," said Sarah, using Klein's Yiddish name. "I don't know why you felt you had to sleep on the chesterfield again." She was standing at the stove, stirring a pot of porridge for the children.

He stared at her, but said nothing. Her long, dark hair dangled on her shoulders while the thin straps of her white, lace nightgown slightly protruded from the top of the red, flowery housecoat she wore. Though Klein hated to admit it, she was as beautiful and alluring as ever. There was no denying it.

"What, you're not talking to me again, Shailek? How many times do I have to apologize?"

Klein took a drag on his cigarette and slowly exhaled it. He pushed his way past Sarah, cut a slice of bread, and spooned on some strawberry jam.

"You're an asshole, Shailek. Do you know that?"

"I'm an asshole," said Klein. "I'm an asshole. That's funny, Sarah. Who's the one who ran away? Not me. I was here alone with the kids. Where the hell were you?"

Sarah shook her head. "I've told you a thousand times, but I'll say it again. I just needed a few days to be alone. That's all. I know it was wrong. I regret it more than you can imagine. I have explained what I did to the children. I have apologized to them. I think Freda, at least, understands that I was not abandoning her or Niecee or Mel. My God, I never would leave them or you. You must know that in your heart."

Klein pursed his lips. "All I know for certain is that you stayed at Melinda's, for Christ's sake. At a whorehouse. Aren't you past that yet?" As soon as the words came out of his mouth, he realized he shouldn't have said them. He was being deliberately mean and he knew it.

Sarah's eyes widened and she touched her forehead with her right hand. "How can you ask me that? I just needed a place to sleep and there weren't many other places to go. Melinda's always been good to me, and to you, too, by the way."

"What if someone we knew or one of your customers saw you there or heard about it?" asked Klein, raising his voice slightly.

Sarah's body stiffened. "I don't know when you got so high and mighty. But as I recall, you used to sleep with a lot of the women at Melinda's in the old days."

"Exactly: old days. I don't make apologies for anything I've done to get ahead. And I've thanked Melinda many times for helping me when I needed it. And I still do. But to my mind, I've moved on. I'm not sure you have."

Sarah sighed. "That's ridiculous and you know it."

"Is it? What about that damn Sugarman?"

"You're kidding. We've been over this again and again. I told you how sorry I was. It didn't mean anything. Can't we move on? Please, Shailek, if not for me then for the children?" Sarah's eyes welled up. "I love you…"

"You kissed another man!" yelled Klein, slapping his hand hard on the kitchen table. "And then you lied about it. How am I supposed to ever trust you again? Can you tell me that, Sarah?"

"It didn't mean anything. It was a stupid, stupid mistake. I don't know why I did it…"

"I have an idea…" muttered Klein.

"What does that mean?" asked Sarah, her voice louder. Tears

ran down her face. "What, because I used to work at Melinda's? Is that what you mean?"

Klein said nothing.

"God damn you, Shailek. You're impossible. Go to hell. Just go to hell." She stormed out of the kitchen. As she did so, she nearly ran over the three children who appeared. Bernice was in tears and Freda looked like she was about to cry as well. Only Mel, who was dragging his raggedy stuffed bear in his right hand, was oblivious to the commotion. Sarah put her arms around the trio.

"Mommy, Daddy, what's happening?" Freda asked, her voice breaking. "Please stop yelling at each other."

"We were just having an argument," said Sarah softly. She picked Mel up. "It's nothing. You go to school, Freda."

Freda eyed her mother suspiciously and then looked at Klein.

"Listen to your mother," he said. "I have to be somewhere." He pushed his way past his family and climbed briskly up the stairs.

Ever so carefully, Saul Sugarman brushed the lint off the jacket of his new suit. It was navy, pinstripe wool and double-breasted. Abe Palay, his personal tailor, had done another superb job on the jacket, vest, and pants.

Sugarman was of medium-height with a slight paunch and dark, greased-back hair tinged with grey. He had deep-set eyes, a thin nose, and a European charm that some women found attractive. He also made no apologies for his wealth and expensive taste.

Taking a step back, he surveyed his fifth-floor Boyd Building office. There was his solid, hand-crafted oak desk, a swivel, high-back leather chair, deep mahogany shelves filled with books he admittedly had never read, and a hand-stitched carpet he had shipped in from the Orient. And outside on the street, in front of the building in his reserved parking spot, was his brand new, cream-coloured Rolls-Royce. The automobile cost him $12,000—pocket change really, and seeing the look in Sarah's eyes when she rode in it was worth every penny.

That was what life was all about, Sugarman thought; the finer things that money could buy—and at the moment he could pretty much buy anything his heart desired. Except, that is, the one thing that he coveted above all else: Sarah Klein. The thought of her close by, in her shop on the main floor of the building, excited him. Lovely, sensuous, desirable; the memory of her soft lips touching his was as powerful as any he had ever had. That she was the wife of another man and the mother of three children was beside the point. Saul wanted her and he aimed to have her—a fine trophy to add to his catalogue of fine possessions, and there would be little her self-important husband Sam Klein could do about it. They didn't call Saul Sugarman the "Rockefeller of Winnipeg" for nothing.

Sugarman spun his chair around and slid open a panel directly behind him revealing a hidden wall safe. He deftly turned the combination, lifted the lever, and pulled open the safe. Inside were neatly stacked bills of all types: piles of one hundred dollar bills from the US, an assortment from the Northern Crown Bank, mostly twenties and fifties, and several wads of $500 and

ALLAN LEVINE

$1000 Dominion of Canada bills. And this was merely a tiny portion of the month's take so far.

The Sugarmans truly could not keep up with the demand for booze. Saul and Lou had hired even more agents to man their warehouses along the Turtle Mountain hill. In the city alone, they now had on staff three chemists and four tinsmiths to construct the gallon cans they required for their homemade brands. They also had contracts with several bakeries in the city as well as in Edmonton and Vancouver for their sugar supplies. In fact, Lou had just purchased another warehouse on Logan Avenue near McPhillips. Business, as they say, was booming.

Problems, of course, arose from time to time. Nosy cops and customs officers had to be paid off and placating the likes of Rosen required patience that Saul did not always have. And now, admittedly, there was this mess with Max Roter, his late pain-in-the-ass brother-in-law. He felt terrible for his sister Rae and her children. Yet, if anyone was the architect of his own fate, it was Max. He had a big mouth and was greedy. There were some people you just did not cross. Max, unfortunately, either did not understand this, or, more likely, merely ignored it. Sugarman had warned him more than once that his actions would have consequences. But Max was as stubborn as a mule.

Over the past few days, the murder in Vera had garnered headlines and there had been several references to Max's family and business connections to the Sugarmans. Though, in Saul's view, the damage had been minimal and he had his man at the *Tribune* ensure that any liquor or gangster references were kept out of the story. But he knew he had enemies at the paper as well. The *Free Press* was also a problem, though thankfully John Dafoe, the paper's editor, wasn't as keen on sensational booze and crime stories.

Sugarman figured he had one other thing working in his favour. A month ago, Colonel John Rattray, the commissioner of the recently revamped Manitoba Provincial Police, had failed to halt a brazen bank robbery in Brandon, even though his men had been tipped off about the crime. The government immediately dismissed Rattray and two of his top men. They appointed as interim commissioner Detective Bill McCreary, who had been seconded from the Winnipeg Police Department.

McCreary was a tough, no-nonsense cop, but he also never turned down a drink from Sugarman, even since prohibition had been technically enforced in the province during the past six years. Saloons on Main Street might have been shut down, but you could drive a team of horses through the various loopholes in the Manitoba Temperance Act. Given that you could import liquor from Ontario or Saskatchewan, get a medical prescription—and many physicians and pharmacists were eager to help out for a price—or buy booze from the small army of local bootleggers in operation in and around Winnipeg, few Manitobans, McCreary among them, went wanting for whisky or beer. McCreary showed up frequently at Saul's office, parched and in need of a glass of Scotch. From Sugarman's point of view, the only strike McCreary had against him was that he and Sam Klein were on fairly good terms and had worked together on cases in the past. Perhaps, thought Saul, he could take advantage of that.

Sugarman had not had time to read this morning's paper, but stories in yesterday's *Tribune* and one from the day before noted that Max had been killed in what appeared to be a robbery at his general store. Saul had already dispatched one of his trusted fixers, Sid Sharp, to take charge of the matter. Sharp was as tough as any ruffian in the city, yet he had brains and was usually obedient. Sugarman was certain he could clean things up, because there was far too much at stake.

Meanwhile, Lou was helping Rae with the arrangements to ship Max's body back to the city for the funeral. She was arriving with the children and the casket early that afternoon.

Sugarman pulled out his watch from his vest pocket and checked the time. Saul knew that Lou was meeting with Klein in a matter of moments. His brother, ever sentimental, had not wanted to drag the detective into this. But Saul, as he usually did, had convinced him that it made perfect sense. Klein could be useful in this matter and that's all that counted. And though he had not said anything about this to Lou, Saul had personal reasons for keeping Klein busy and out of the way. He would be occupied with the case and most likely would have to travel to Vera and Sarah would be alone and vulnerable.

There was, too, the stolen $7000 from the liquor sale to Taylor. The money belonged to Saul. It wasn't all that much, but that was beside the point. A Yiddish expression his father had once told him always stuck in his head: *Gelt tsu fardinen iz gringer vi tsu halten*. It's easier to earn money than to keep it. He wanted what was rightfully his back. How perfect that Klein would solve this problem for him as well. The irony was too good for words.

There was a knock on the office door. "Excuse me, Mr. Sugarman," said Miss Shayna Kravetz, his secretary.

"What is it, Shayna? I thought I told you not to disturb me."

"I'm very sorry, sir," said Shayna, a tall, twenty-two-year-old brunette in a tight-fitting skirt. "But I am pretty sure you'll want to see this right away. The delivery boy just brought it upstairs from the newsstand."

"All right, bring it here and shut the door on your way out."

Sugarman grabbed the newspaper from her and glanced at the headline. Outside in the reception area, Shayna heard the distinct sound of a glass ashtray hitting the wall and shattering.

2

Klein hoped that the brisk walk from his house to the corner of Cathedral and Main, nearly four blocks, might clear his head. It was a warm and sunny June day, one to be savoured, especially when in five months or so there probably would be frigid temperatures and snow on the ground. That was the harsh reality of life every Winnipegger lived with and why enjoying the summer and early autumn took on a real meaning in the city, different than in many parts of Canada.

But it didn't work. As Klein boarded a downtown streetcar in front of the Merchants Bank, he was still in a foul mood. He truly hated having another shouting match with Sarah and upsetting his children. He just didn't know how else to react to everything that had transpired in the past couple of months. When he thought more about it, he wished that Sarah had not told him anything. She could've kept it from him. That's what he had done. He knew deep in his heart that he was a hypocrite, because he had done exactly the same thing as Sarah. The difference was he had chosen not to compound what was a minor transgression by telling her about it.

Four years ago, during the General Strike and the messy business with that Bolshevik Metro Lizowski who had wooed his misguided sister Rivka, Klein had become close, a little too close, to policewoman Hannah Nash. He and Hannah had a moment. Someone had taken a shot at them. Neither of them was hit or hurt, but in the danger they were vulnerable. In the heat of the moment, they had dropped their defences and kissed—one kiss, that was it. Both of them had enjoyed it, Klein could not kid himself about that, yet it had been a mistake and it never happened again. He had never told Sarah about it, nor would he. What would have been the point? She, on the other hand, had chosen to tell him about her encounter with Saul Sugarman. Why? What good had it done, other than to drive a wedge between them? They had fought; she had become so upset that he knew she had acted out of character: she had left him and the children for a few days. Nonetheless, when she returned, the wall between them remained erect.

Klein removed his grey flat cap and loosened the top button of his shirt. As soon as the streetcar stopped at Dufferin, more passengers boarded. Sitting near the back of the car close to the conductor manning the fare box, Klein was soon surrounded by businessmen in suits and fedoras with their noses in the morning newspapers and chatty women whose loud conversations were peppered with various mixtures of English, Polish, Ukrainian, and Yiddish. Out of the corner of his eye, he recognized Mrs. Appelbaum, an old neighbour from Flora Avenue, though he had no desire to speak with her. A bead of sweat formed on Klein's brow. It was too late; Mrs. Appelbaum saw him. Then, without any warning, the motorman hit the brake hard. When he did so, the conductor in the rear vestibule flew forward as did Mrs. Appelbaum. Seeing this, Klein leaped up and grabbed both of them, preventing what would've been a nasty collision.

"Mrs. Appelbaum, are you okay?" he asked her.

She was breathing heavily. "*Oy vay iz mir. Oy vay iz mir.* I thought I was done for, Sam. You're a good boy. Always have been."

Klein feigned a smile and helped her up. "Here, Mrs. Appelbaum, please take my seat."

The conductor was able to get up by himself. He replaced his cap which had fallen off and also thanked Klein.

"Apologies, folks," the motorman yelled out. "There's been another accident." A collective sigh echoed through the streetcar.

Standing on the wooden floor in the long aisle that separated the rows of seats on both sides of the car, Klein bent down and peered out the window to see what had happened. It appeared that a gentleman who was driving a Model-T Ford had accidently bumped the back of a horse-drawn delivery wagon. And the irritable wagon driver and his horse were not happy about it. A constable was already there preventing the altercation from escalating.

The number of horse-drawn vehicles on Winnipeg streets had been dwindling in recent years—as well as, thankfully, the amount of manure that had to be cleaned up each day—but there were enough of them that occasionally there were accidents like this one. Between the electric streetcars, rising number of automobiles, horse wagons, and the heavy traffic of pedestrians in this prairie metropolis of nearly 180,000, the streets of Winnipeg, especially in the vicinity of Portage and Main, were congested eight hours a day or more. Klein didn't mind the hubbub—as long as everyone stayed out of his way, that is.

Bidding the still distraught Mrs. Appelbaum farewell, he exited the streetcar on Portage Avenue and headed past Garry Street. In front of the Paris Building, he flipped a nickel to one-eyed Jimmy and grabbed a two-cent copy of the *Tribune*.

"Hot off the press," said Jimmy. The veteran of the Great War had a noticeable scar that stretched from his left ear to his mouth, the result of a nasty saloon fight at the Maple Leaf Hotel during the 1916 soldiers' riot.

"Thanks, Jimmy," said Klein, flipping him another nickel. "Lunch today's on me."

Jimmy doffed his cap, but said nothing.

Klein stopped for a moment and stood to the side of the walkway buzzing with the morning rush of grain men, executives, clerks, and secretaries dutifully marching like ants to their respective office buildings and shops. Standing back from the crowd so as not to get trampled, he perused the front page. The story headline in bold, block letters was impossible to miss. "Rum–Runners in Murder Plot." The provincial police believed that a "band of desperados" involved in rum-running across the border may have robbed and killed Max Roter. And the provincial police investigating the crime in Vera confirmed that Roter was also dealing in liquor as well as running the town's general

31

store. The last line of the story noted that "Max Roter was married to Mrs. Rae Roter, the sister of Saul and Lou Sugarman, Winnipeg businessmen, known to be involved in the liquor trade."

Lou and especially Saul won't be happy with this, thought Klein. It was petty, yet he had to admit that the idea of Saul Sugarman aggravated and squirming over this story made Klein feel better. He knew the brothers had worked hard to keep their names out of newspaper articles dealing with rum-running or bootleggers—though it was common knowledge in Winnipeg that nothing could be further from the truth. He and Lou had spoken of this recently. But Saul, that *mamzer*, was kidding himself.

Klein called it "playing ostrich," and he'd seen it a hundred times. Otherwise intelligent men of wealth and power had their proverbial heads in the ground, just like an ostrich, by convincing themselves that something so plain to everyone else around them was not true. High and mighty Saul Sugarman in his custom-made suits sauntered up and down Portage Avenue as if he was a grain baron with a mansion on Wellington Crescent. When, in fact, he was known as a Jew hotel and liquor man, and more recently as that "Hebe bootlegger," who was reaping in a treasure from brazen flaws in American Prohibition regulations. From what Klein had heard, the Sugarmans had earned something in the neighbourhood of five million last year, an astronomical sum that he and most of the other 15,000 members of the city's Jewish community found impossible to fathom.

Klein continued onward, making his way to Dolly's Café at

the corner of Portage and Hargrave, directly opposite Eaton's. Looking across the wide avenue, Klein could see that the popular department store's window awnings were pulled down. The June sun shimmered off the navy coverings, casting a shadow onto Portage. By nine o'clock in the morning, half an hour after opening, a small army of women shoppers were already admiring the latest cotton dresses, pongee blouses, "cool" crepe summer hats, and serge and tricotine dresses for their daughters. Klein observed, too, that like every shopping day when the weather was mild, mothers had parked their baby carriages on the sidewalk in front of the store. As was the custom, the women left the sleeping infants in the baby buggies while they ran in to purchase an item. The mothers didn't give it a second thought, knowing that their children were as safe as anywhere in the city.

"Sam, over here."

Klein looked in the direction of the voice coming from the back left corner of the café. Lou Sugarman stood tall even at five-foot-eight. He had a receding hairline, protruding ears, and a distinguished, lean nose. He stood up, extending his right hand towards Klein. Lou and Saul resembled each other in height and facial features, though as Lou readily conceded, no one was ever going to mistake him for a Scot or Brit. He was a "Hebrew" through and through, and unlike his brother, was proud of it.

If Saul was the brains behind the brothers' hotel and liquor enterprise, a business by 1922 with interests from towns in rural Manitoba to Montreal, then Lou was the heart. Saul and Lou had arrived in the city in 1905. Saul then was twenty-five and Lou twenty-two. Soon after, they were able to purchase their first hotel in Dominion City, the Star. As the well-known "Sugarman legend" had it, a story Klein had heard repeatedly told in Selkirk Avenue cafés, Main Street saloons, and North End synagogues, the brothers somehow amassed $3,000, some of it borrowed from friends, and the balance of $8,000 on the property came from liquor store merchant Mathew Sigurdson and Timothy O'Callaghan of O'Callaghan Brewery in Winnipeg. Though the Star was not much more than a rickety wooden structure with a few dingy rooms for boarders, it was the hotel's saloon, perpetually smelling of stale booze and rancid tobacco juice, which proved to be a bonanza—especially when a railway construction team stationed nearby made the Star's bar their home away from home. After that, the brothers purchased one hotel after the other—in Emerson, Plum Coulee, Holland, and finally the Prince Edward in Winnipeg. In 1912, the Prince Edward showed a profit of $32,000 and the Sugarmans were wealthy men.

Klein shook Lou's hand and took a seat. Before he could say anything, Dolly Smith, the café's short and plump proprietor set down a mug of steaming coffee in front of Klein. "Bread and jam are coming in a moment," she said with a smile.

Klein nodded and looked at Lou. "How's my sister?"

Lou smiled. "Rivka. She's as feisty as ever. Says she's going to make a socialist out of me yet."

Klein laughed. "Of all the people in this city to court, you and Rivka are about the last two I'd ever have imagined. A radical leftist and a capitalist liquor salesman, amazing."

"It's strange, I'll admit that," said Lou with a hearty laugh. "But we're good together."

"Yeah, like oil and water."

"More like salt and pepper, I'd say. We like to go to the theatre; you should've seen how she enjoyed the London Follies at the Walker a few weeks back. I even convinced her to join me after the show at the Dining Room at the Royal Alex. White tablecloths, low hanging lights, the murals on the wall. Can you believe it: Rivka, the radical, eating at the fanciest hotel in the city?"

"I can't," said Klein with a smile.

"Well, we have a good time together. That's all that matters."

"And the future?"

"No idea," said Lou, chuckling. "You don't have to worry about her, Sam. Rivka can handle herself."

"That's for damn sure. But you didn't invite me here to talk about you and my sister."

"No, I didn't," said Lou. The smile on his face vanished. "I really need your help." He threw the latest edition of the *Tribune* on the table. "You see this yet?"

Klein reached into the side of his jacket pocket and pulled out a copy of the newspaper. "I have. I was sorry to hear about Max. I didn't know him that well, but from what I gather, he was a good man."

Sugarman waved his hand. "He was a *paskudnyak*, as ornery as they come, though I suppose in a good way. And Rae loved him, so what could we do about it? We couldn't let my sister and her children go hungry. Saul said we had to trust him. Trouble was Max let it all go to his head. You know the expression, *gelt brengt tsu ga'aveh un ga'aveh tsu zind*?"

Klein nodded, lit a cigarette, and took a sip of his black coffee. "I know it. Money causes conceit and conceit leads to sin."

"Exactly," said Lou. "Max was in over his head, and I'm not even certain I have the whole story. Which is why, my friend, I called you."

"Why? You don't think the *Trib* has the story right? That Max was robbed and killed by rum-runners?"

"I'm not certain, Sam. Saul told me that the man Max met the night he was killed, a guy named Taylor, picked up his booze, gave Max an envelope of cash, and left. Less than twenty minutes later, Max was dead and the money gone."

"What do you know about this Taylor?"

"He's friendly enough … for a bootlegger, I suppose. I told Saul we'd have trouble once we started with this business. First, a few years back, it was the mail-order business. Then Saul bought the Voyageur Liquor Company in Montreal. Then the Western Drug Company."

"That made you some cash," said Klein.

"It was good while it lasted, I can't argue with you. Prohibition in the province has been *narishkeit*. Just stupid, plain and simple. Blame the feds for allowing pharmacists to sell booze for medicinal purposes. Can you believe that? So I got the wholesale druggist license and overnight we had hundreds of customers whose doctors had prescribed them whisky for what ailed them. We got rich, Sam, but now my sister's husband is dead because of our business."

"You want to give it up, Lou?"

"I didn't say that."

"Feeling guilty about it?"

"I suppose."

"You didn't force Roter to go out there. He was more than willing. Isn't that true?"

Lou nodded.

"So what about this band of desperados the paper mentions?" asked Klein.

"They don't exist. At least, that's what Saul says."

Each time Lou said his brother's name, the hair on the back of Klein's neck stood up. "I'm not sure I can help you, Lou."

"Sam, I know you're angry with Saul and you have every right to be. I don't know what's got into him. He should never have disrespected you and Sarah the way he did. But it's done, over. And I have to agree with Saul that there's too much at stake here."

Dolly arrived with a thick piece of bread and her famous homemade strawberry jam, which she placed before Klein. He thanked her, ripped off a piece, dipped it in the jam, and took a bite.

"You hear me, Sam?" Lou repeated. "There's a lot at stake. We've got half a million dollars of stock ready to move and we can't have the provincial police snooping around our stores and warehouses near Vera or anywhere else. And we don't want any more trouble. And..."

"And what, Lou?"

"Nothing. Just like I said, there's too much at stake. We need this resolved quickly. And, if I may say so, you do owe us."

Klein bristled. "And we are paying back our debts on the

house and the store every month with interest. So please don't throw that in my face."

Lou waved his hand. "I shouldn't have said that, Sam. I apologize. You know I was more than happy to help you and Sarah with the house and, whatever you think about him, Saul was more than willing to help Sarah with the shop."

Klein's face reddened. "Seriously, Lou, you think that your brother was just being nice? I know exactly what he was doing." Klein steadied himself; he had no desire to lose his temper in Dolly's. "In all honesty," he said more quietly, "I don't know if I can be involved in anything with that asshole. Things at home with Sarah aren't great at the moment."

"I'm truly sorry to hear that. You and Sarah are *bashert*. You were meant to be with each other. I know that. I've always been fond of your wife."

"Yeah, you and your brother," muttered Klein.

Lou sighed. "You have no idea how sorry I am about what happened. When I found out…"

"You did what?"

"I told him that he had no business near your wife."

"And what did he say?"

Lou shrugged.

"Exactly," said Klein.

"Look, Sam, this is none of my business…"

"So when has that stopped you?"

Lou smiled. "Sarah's a special woman. There're not a lot like her."

"Well, she'll never be one of those Hadassah ladies in River

Heights sipping tea and raising money for Jews in Palestine, that's for certain."

"That's so. You have to forgive her and move on. Think of your three *kinderlach*."

Klein threw his hands up. "Let's talk about the case instead."

"Why not?"

"You think someone might be trying to put you out of the booze trade? That possibly Max's killing was a message?" Klein rubbed his chin.

"That's occurred to me, yes."

"And Saul thinks so too?"

"He says I worry too much. But I don't think I do."

Klein took another gulp of his coffee and finished his cigarette.

"I'll triple your fee," said Lou. "And cover all of your expenses, of course."

"What expenses?"

"You or that kid you work with will have to take a train to Vera soon. Talk to some of the *goyim* there. Learn if anyone saw or heard anything. Aren't you pals with that detective McCreary?"

"We know each other, why?"

"He's heading the provincial police now."

"Yeah, I heard that. We don't see each other much."

"Well, maybe you can convince him to leave this alone."

Klein laughed. "Lou, as far as I know, no one, let alone me, has ever convinced Bill McCreary of anything. He looks and acts as mean as a snarly dog because he is one. But I could see what he knows. What else? What about speaking with Rosen?"

"You want to go to New York?"

"Don't know. A telegram or phone call might do it. If anyone knows what the hell's going on, it's Irv."

"He's a busy man. Personally, I wouldn't bother him."

"You not telling me something, Lou? Because if that's the case…"

"I'm telling you everything I know. I swear on my parents' graves. Please find out what happened to Max and who's behind it."

"For triple my normal fee, sure, I'll do it, Lou. But I don't want any questions from your brother about who I see, where I'm going, or how I conduct my investigation. That asshole so much as tries to interfere with me, I'm done. Do we have a deal?"

"Okay, Sam. It's a deal." The awkward look on his face, however, told Klein that Lou wasn't sure at all how he'd keep Saul from pestering him. That was his problem, however, not Klein's.

"The casket with Max is arriving later this afternoon at the CPR station with Rae and the children," said Lou. "The funeral is early Friday afternoon at the Shaarey Zedek. If you want, I can arrange for you to speak with my sister later that day or Saturday. Because of Shabbat, we won't be sitting shiva until Sunday, of course. It'll be at my house on Scotia."

"I'll get there, Max." Klein stood up.

"There's one more thing, Sam," said Lou, rising from his chair. "This could get ugly. So please, my friend, watch your back and be extra careful."

"I always am," said Klein with a slight grin.

"Booze and money have a way of making most men

meshuggina. They'll stop at nothing. As soon as you go poking around…"

"Rest easy," said Klein, lightly touching Lou's shoulder. "I'll be fine."

3

As was his custom when he embarked on a new case, Klein's mind raced a mile a minute. He made a mental list of all of the things he had to do and the order in which he had to do them.

Based on his discussion with Lou Sugarman, his gut feeling was that someone in the town had watched and waited for Max Roter to be paid off by this bootlegger named Taylor and then robbed and killed him. Perhaps, he reasoned, the murder was unintentional and committed in the heat of the moment. That seemed to make the most sense, though as Klein's past experience told him, logic did not always dictate crime and murder. The first item on his list was to send his assistant, Alec Geller, to Vera and have him poke around to see what he could learn. Though he was only nineteen years old, the kid was smart—smarter than Klein was when he was that age—and resourceful. Klein knew that one day he'd make a skillful private detective if he indeed wanted to follow in Klein's footsteps as he had said he did on several occasions.

This wasn't the case Klein particularly wanted. However, that was the business he was in. Besides, Lou's offer of tripling his fee was hardly something Klein could refuse, especially in this lousy economic climate. You only had to walk downtown to come across the gaggle of unemployed men. Many of them were Great War veterans who had saved the British Empire and now could not find decent full-time jobs. Even trying to get hired for the day on a road or construction gang, backbreaking work to be sure, was difficult to secure. It wasn't Klein's imagination; there were definitely more beggars on the streets and men as well as women seeking temporary shelter at Immigration Hall. Many of these impoverished souls had no choice but to stand in line for relief payments at the city's office. Yet like most Winnipeggers, Klein thought this was a grave error. Give a man a nickel and he'll want two. It was as simple as that.

Klein contemplated stopping at Sarah's shop at the Boyd Building, but then changed his mind. What was the point, he thought. He was angry and hurt and nothing she said this morning, or would say if he saw her now, would fix things. Sarah wanted to shove their problems under the rug; he was not prepared to do that—at least not yet.

Once Klein reached Main Street, he stepped into the telegraph office at the Canadian Northern Building. He grabbed a pencil and scribbled a message:

> To: Rosen c/o Ratner's, 102 Norfolk Street, New York, NY. Urgent. Information needed

on Vera. Please send details. Request from
brothers. Klein.

He handed the yellow paper to the operator behind the desk
with instructions to put it on the Sugarman account.

Klein was fairly certain that the quickest way to reach Irv
Rosen was at the speakeasy that he and his volatile partner Nate
Katz ran in the back room of Ratner's Kosher Restaurant in the
Lower East Side. The eatery, as Klein recalled, was a few steps
from the daily chaos of Delancy: a constant parade of street ped-
dlers, handcarts, and horse-drawn wagons, merchants shouting in Yiddish, hawking dresses, hats, and squawking caged
chickens, kosher eateries offering pickles, borsht, knishes, and
chopped liver, students and religious scholars arguing loudly
about the Talmud, and young children playing hooky from
school and stickball in the streets. Klein had always thought
that the Selkirk Avenue bazaar of clothes and food shops was
frenzied, but it was tranquil compared to what he had witnessed
in the Lower East Side.

He had been to Ratner's only once on his visit to New York
on behalf of the Sugarmans last year. The blintzes at Ratner's
alone were worth the trip. The secret bar at the back—which
wasn't so secret at all—was classy: red plush furniture, stunning,
wood-panelled walls, and a magnificent and well-stocked bar.
Klein was impressed.

Rosen was not a big man. He might have even been mistaken
for a typical Lower East Side or North End peddler. Yet when
he spoke, always looking at you right in the eye, he did have a

particular aura about him, even for someone only twenty-five years old. From the moment Klein had met him, he knew that Rosen was not a man to be taken lightly.

As soon as Prohibition was implemented, Rosen, as head of the "Nate and Irv Mob," had already set up an extensive operation to obtain booze from Canada and ship it as far west as Minneapolis. There were even plans to set up an export business—"Rum Row" is how Rosen referred to it—more than three miles off Long Island and beyond US jurisdiction. That way, Rosen and his men could ship booze from Canada and Europe literally anywhere they wanted.

Though Klein got along with Rosen, he wasn't as enamoured with his young, wise-ass partner, Nate Katz. He was a good-looking kid with sparkling blue eyes and a penchant for fancy suits, and he obediently did whatever Rosen told him to do. But Klein had heard about Katz's nasty temper. For forty dollars, Katz would do just about anything—including murder. At least, that's what the gangster gossip was. The two were also partners with Leo Forni, an Italian bootlegger, though Klein did not meet him on his visit. About the only problem Rosen, Katz, and their gang had was dealing with Willie "the Boss" Amari, who didn't think too much of the two Jewish punks attempting to move into the liquor and gambling business. And Willie the Boss was not someone to be taken lightly. But Rosen had assured Klein that he had everything under control and that he was happy with his arrangement with the Sugarmans.

As Klein proceeded to his office, it dawned on him that maybe Max's murder was not a local matter after all, but connected to gangster trouble in New York that had reached Manitoba. Anything, he supposed, was possible.

"Niecee, keep up. I'm going to be late," said Sarah sternly. She was moving briskly down the south side of Portage Avenue, pushing Mel in a carriage and dodging other pedestrians as she walked.

Aggravated by her husband's pig-headedness, Sarah was in no mood for her daughter's tardiness. She glanced at her new Longines wristwatch and sighed ever so slightly. The watch was another fib to Sam. She told him it had been a gift from a customer. In fact, Saul Sugarman had given it to her weeks ago, before she had told him that nothing further would happen between them. One part of her knew that she shouldn't be wearing it. Yet, as a woman who had always appreciated fine jewellery and clothes, the slender Swiss watch was too lovely to pass up. There were likely only a handful of women in the city that had one. However, that watch was the reason for her troubles.

She had replayed it over and over again in her head. She had not planned to tell Klein what had happened. Saul had given her the watch and then in a foolish moment of weakness, she had kissed him. She didn't know why. It just happened. And then she had only made matters worse when, wracked by guilt, she told Klein what she had done—though leaving the part about the watch out. She told him the kiss had meant nothing and that it had merely been a momentary lapse of judgment. But, of course, he was furious and who could blame him? At the same time, she was not about to let this stupid mistake break up her marriage or family. Her children needed both her and Sam together, not living apart. She had seen with one of her friends, Anita Margolis, how upset Anita's two children had been, when Anita's husband Mitch had divorced her. Sarah didn't know how to repair her relationship with Sam yet, but she was determined to do so, one way or the other.

It was 9:30 a.m. Mrs. Kingston's appointment at the shop was in about fifteen minutes. Sarah knew that it would be a lucrative meeting and one she could definitely not afford to miss.

Betty Kingston, the young wife of Nicholas Kingston, president of the Winnipeg Grain Exchange and the owner of the Standard Grain Company, had taken a liking to Sarah and more importantly to the stock of New York dresses Sarah had acquired through a dealer in Montreal. No other store, not even Holt Renfrew or Hollinsworth, one of her neighbours at the Boyd Building, had such fine fashions coveted by the likes of Mrs. Kingston, a vivacious woman of impeccable taste—at least from Sarah's perspective.

Betty powdered her nose, wore brash but tasteful sweaters, fringed skirts, multi-coloured scarfs, blouses with Peter Pan collars, and low-heeled "finale hopper" shoes. She was what the newspapers were now calling a "flapper," a modern woman who was not shy about smoking in public, using cosmetics, or expressing herself, and in a vernacular that was akin to a secret language. She was no "tomato," that was certain; she was beautiful yet had brains to go with her sleek look. Best of all, from Sarah's view, she had an indulgent and wealthy older husband.

The society columns had been bursting with news of their

47

nuptials. It was deliciously scandalous when forty-six-year-old Nicholas Kingston, a widower with two teenage children and the scion of an old, moneyed Winnipeg family, took as his bride twenty-three-year-old Elizabeth "Betty" Scanlon from Toronto, the daughter of a stockbroker with a less than scrupulous reputation. Betty played her part as the wife of the most important grain executive in the city—but in her own unique way.

And now, because Sarah's regular babysitter, Molly Jacobson, was detained because of something to do with her grandmother's missing cat, the girl would not be able to watch Bernice and Mel until later in the afternoon, before Freda returned from school. Sarah was genuinely fond of Molly, a pretty young woman who usually looked like she had stepped out of an Eaton's catalogue. She lived with her parents on Bannerman Avenue and Sarah had met her by chance soon after the Klein family moved into the house on Cathedral. She was pleasant enough and Freda, Bernice, and Mel instantly took a liking to her. Last year, when she decided to leave St. John's Tech after grade ten, Sarah offered her a part-time job as a babysitter. Her one real flaw, apart from being infatuated with movie magazines, was her interest in young men. But Sarah could hardly fault her for that.

Today, however, Sarah had no choice but to bring the two children to the shop. She had no idea how she was going to get through the day, a day that at nine thirty in the morning was already too hectic for her liking.

"Coming, Mama," Bernice shouted. The five-year-old was skipping along, petting every stray dog and cat she came across and picking up twigs and other junk strewn along the sidewalk. "I'm thirsty."

"There's water at the shop, Niecee. Now please, hurry up. I'm going to be late. Be a good girl for Mama, please."

Bernice ran ahead and grabbed hold of the carriage. "I want to push."

"Not now. I'm in a rush." Sarah's tone was firm, though not especially angry.

Yet it did not take much for Bernice to cry. "I want to push Mel. Me," she said through the tears.

Sarah calmed herself down. She knew there was no point in yelling at her further; that would only make her cry harder. She gently took her daughter's hand and wiped away her tears. Instantly Bernice stopped crying. Sarah and the children crossed Edmonton Street. Betty Kingston was standing outside the shop waiting for her.

"Mrs. Kingston, my sincere apologies," said Sarah. "My sitter didn't show up today, and as you can see, I had to bring the children to the shop…"

Betty Kingston smiled. "First, Sarah, my dear, call me Betty. And never mind it. I was just cutting myself a piece of cake."

"A piece of cake?" asked Sarah, scrunching her eyebrows.

Betty giggled. "That's flapper talk for waiting patiently."

Sarah shrugged. "I see. Here let's go in." As soon as she unlocked the shop door, Bernice obediently held it open so her mother could wheel in the carriage.

Sarah stooped down so she was at eye level with her daughter. "Niecee, Mama needs you to be a big girl right now. Can you do that?" Bernice nodded. "I'm going to take you and Mel to the back room. There's something for you to drink there, and then you can watch Mel for a few minutes while I talk to this nice lady. Can you do that?"

Bernice nodded again and a broad smile crossed her face.

Sarah planted a kiss on her cheek. "Excuse me for one moment, Betty, while I settle them."

"You take however much time you need. I'll just look around. You know your shop's the cat's pajamas?"

"Okay," said Sarah, wrinkling her eyebrows again. "Is that a good thing?"

Betty laughed. "Yes, very good."

Sarah pushed the carriage to the back of the shop and parked it in a small alcove where she kept her cash books and supplies. There was also a sink with running water and a small icebox that Klein had bought for her at Oretzki's on Selkirk. She poured Bernice a glass of slightly murky water and gave both her and Mel a handful of Arrowroot biscuits. "Now be good and let Mama work."

"You can count on me, Mama," declared Bernice.

Sarah smiled. "I know I can," she said, kissing her daughter's forehead.

From the front of the shop came the sound of a loud laugh. Sarah peered around the corner and her eyes widened. Standing beside Betty Kingston was Saul Sugarman.

Sarah left the children and marched towards them. Her eyes never left Sugarman.

"I was explaining to your friend here that he's what I call a sharpshooter. He says he's a good dancer and that he likes to spend money! Nothing better in a man than that."

Sugarman grinned.

"Is that so?" asked Sarah. Her body tightened and her eyes narrowed.

"He also likes my bob," said Betty, brushing her bangs. "You should try it, Sarah. Giselle's Salon on Carleton Street, that's where I go. You see how nicely she did the fingerwaves." She pointed to the S-shaped waves on the side of her hair.

"They do suit you," said Sarah as politely as she could muster.

"I just love these new, slim-fitting, cream dresses you have, and with such wonderful beadwork," said Betty, holding up the knee-length, sleeveless dress against her. "With rolled stockings and black Mary Janes with a bow, I'll look like a real brooksy, classy, you know what I mean?"

"You will indeed," said Sugarman. He bowed slightly and kissed the top of Betty's right hand.

Betty whistled. "Aren't you fluky?"

Saul shrugged.

"May I speak to you outside, please," Sarah said to Sugarman.

At that moment, Bernice came running up. "I want another cookie, Mama."

"Niecee, Mama's busy. Go back to the room and I'll be there in a moment."

"Here, young lady, how about this?" Sugarman handed Bernice a quarter.

Sarah immediately grabbed it away from her. "She doesn't need that. Niecee, back in the room. Now."

Tears welled in Bernice's eyes, but she did as her mother said, waving to both Sugarman and Betty as she departed.

"She's a darling, Sarah," said Betty.

"If you'll excuse me for a moment, Betty."

"Take all of the time you need. I'm not going anywhere."

Sarah followed Sugarman out the door of the shop. As soon as she reached the walkway, she reached for Sugarman's left shoulder and spun him around.

"How dare you. How dare you come into my shop unannounced like this. What are you doing here, Saul?"

"I just came to check on my little investment."

Sarah shook her head. "You have no idea how much I regret taking that money from you."

"Well, if you didn't, my dear, you wouldn't have your shop, now would you? You know I only want good things for you."

"I'll pay you back every penny. I swear it."

"I'm sure you will. I see you're wearing the watch."

Sarah undid the strap of the watch and threw it at him. "I don't want this ... Saul, did I not make myself clear? I don't need this and I don't want anything more from you."

Sugarman picked up the watch and stared at her. "You are beautiful. You do know that?"

"Saul, stop please," she said, her voice rising. "There's nothing between us." Several passers-by took notice. "It was a mistake, what happened. You must accept that and move on. Please. I have a family and a husband."

"Yes. Your daughter's precious. It's like this, Sarah," he said with his eyes narrowed and a wolfish smirk. "I always get what I want. And I want you. And I will have…"

Sarah's right hand slapped him hard across the face. Stunned more than hurt, Sugarman's face turned a deep red. "You shouldn't have done that. But I suppose I'd expect nothing less from a woman like you."

Sarah ignored the taunt. "Leave me and my family alone." Her voice was shaking. She pushed him to the side, ripped open the door, and entered the shop.

4

The streetcar ride back to the North End was uneventful save for a stray hound which wandered onto the tracks and nearly got run over. Sitting again at the back of the car, Klein hardly noticed the dog's yelp or the other few passengers. He tried hard to focus on the Sugarman-Roter case, reviewing the various permutations and combinations of possibilities. Yet the truth was, he could not get Sarah out of his head. The two of them had been through a lot together, but this seemed the worst. He loved her, he knew that. He just wasn't certain he could ever trust her again.

He got off the streetcar when it reached Selkirk in front of Elliot and Hazel's grocery store.

"Here's a few apples for you, Sam," said Hazel Brown, the store's always-cheery owner. She handed Klein a paper bag.

"How much do I owe you?"

"Next time, Sam. For those adorable kids of yours."

Klein thanked her. He dashed across Main and headed about

a block down Selkirk, passing the usual crowd. They were either waiting for the Royal Bank to open or patients coming and going from the office of Dr. Frank Rodin, who'd repaired Klein more times than he cared to remember. Next to Dr. Rodin's office was the headquarters of the *Israelite Press,* or *Dos Yiddishe Vort,* which covered all things Jewish in the city. Its feisty editor, Mark Selchen, was not shy about criticizing the community's many *machers*, who, in Klein's opinion, believed they were the self-appointed rulers of their own prairie fiefdom.

Next to the newspaper office was the Queen's Theatre, one of Sam and Sarah's favourite haunts. In fact, many years ago, Klein recalled, Sarah had first enticed him with an invitation to accompany her to the Queen's. There was nothing quite like seeing a Yiddish play at the theatre, despite the constant commotion throughout most performances. Members of the audience rarely refrained from talking loudly and eating everything and anything—including full course dinners of roasted chicken, kugel, and knishes.

Two months ago, before things had become tense at home, Klein and Sarah had attended the play *Mirele Efros*, otherwise known as "the Jewish Queen Lear." The play by the New York-based Yiddish playwright Jacob Gordin was admittedly sentimental, but even Klein was moved by the depiction of the mother, Mirele, and the hardships of Jewish life in the New World she experienced. It brought back fond memories of his mother, Freda, gone now so many years. The family home on Flora Avenue had permanently had the exquisite aroma of Freda's delicious chicken soup.

Just past the Queen's, at 249 Selkirk Avenue, Klein entered Isaac Badner's sign shop.

"G'd morning, Klein," Badner grunted. Bald, short, and stocky with a full beard, Badner was busy cutting a piece of plywood.

"Isaac, how's the day going?" asked Klein with a nod.

"Same as yesterday." It was the response that Badner offered nearly every day.

"Geller here yet?"

"You think I keep track of that kid's comings and goings? I got work to do."

Badner was never one for small talk. Two years ago, Badner's youngest son, Abe, a gambler and all-around pain in the ass in Klein's view, was accused of killing a Point Douglas bookie by the name of Krask. Young Badner claimed he had been framed. He swore that he was miles from Krask's house on Euclid Avenue when the murder had occurred. Nevertheless, the police arrested him. Detective Bill McCreary had assured Klein that Abe Badner was guilty. Isaac had refused to believe it and urged Klein to look into the case. Sure enough, with the able assistance from his old boss, Madam Melinda, Klein proved to McCreary's satisfaction that the real culprit was Lucy Jackson, a prostitute who worked at a brothel close to Melinda's. Krask had hit her one too many times and she claimed she stabbed him in self-defence. Isaac was so grateful to Klein that he offered him rent-free the use of a small office at the back of his shop.

"Alec, wake up," Klein said loudly as soon as he was in the small room.

"What? Oh, Sam. Sorry. I was out late last night. Just dozed off."

"Well sleep on your own time," said Klein. "No doubt you were courting Miss Kravetz."

A wide grin crossed Geller's face. "What can I say, Sam? I'm smitten. It doesn't matter what she says or does, I can't seem to take my eyes off of her. Smart as a steel trap, too."

Klein whistled. "You're head over heels in love, Alec. She works for Saul Sugarman, doesn't she?"

Geller nodded. "I know what you think about him. But she says he's good to her. Pays her $1.25 an hour. That's close to fifty dollars a week, ten times more than she'd get working twelve to sixteen hours a day at a sewing machine for Jacob & Crowley, Hurtig, or the Freeds."

"You're beginning to sound like my sister. However, your sweetheart may prove useful on our new case."

Geller removed his tweed flat cap, exactly the same type that Klein wore, and sat upright. "I wouldn't want Shayna to get in any trouble. She needs that job. But, tell me about the case. What's going on?"

Klein smiled at Alec's eagerness. He genuinely liked Geller. Just under six feet tall, lean and muscular with a rugged look that young women found attractive, Alec had spunk. In fact, the first time Klein met Geller was in 1918 and he was in the middle of a scrap. Some neighbourhood kids had decided to pick on another kid from the Jewish orphanage, a regular occurrence in the North End—except that day they picked on the wrong orphan. Geller knew how to handle himself. He had a bloody

57

nose from that altercation, though as Klein recalled, his antagonists looked a lot worse.

Alec was then fifteen years old and had been at the orphanage only a couple of months. His father had died when he was five and his mother, Sylvia, had died in the spring of 1918 during the influenza epidemic that had gripped the city and country. That year, there likely wasn't a Winnipegger who didn't lose a parent, sibling, or friend to the ravaging virus. For a time, Klein's daughter Freda had shown symptoms. She came down with a high fever, terrible headaches, and had pains everywhere. Then, a week or so later, her fever broke and she miraculously recovered. Sam and Sarah thought they were going to lose her. Geller wasn't so lucky. His mother, thirty-six years old, died three weeks after becoming ill. The family had no relatives or friends who could take Alec in, so he ended up in the orphanage.

Located in the three-and-a-half-storey house on Matheson east of Main Street, the orphanage wasn't quite a military camp, but it was close, as Alec had told Klein on many occasions.

"Every day, we were up at 6:45 a.m. Tardiness was not tolerated and there were loud bells and shouting for those who failed to get out of bed quickly enough," Geller had related. "Breakfast was porridge except on Thursdays when we received Red River cereal with a dash of honey. One of the few meals I enjoyed. On Saturdays, because it was the Sabbath, there was only cold food since cooking was not allowed."

Alec had attended St. John's Technical High School where all the male orphans were referred to by the other students as "Abie." Geller did not tolerate that either and a few too many fist fights landed him in trouble with the school's principal, Alexander Campbell.

After Klein broke up that scrap on the street, young Alec started following Klein around like a puppy dog. Sam brought him home for dinner one night and Geller never really left. After he turned eighteen and was old enough to leave the orphanage, he boarded with an elderly woman on Magnus Avenue. She was not only known in the North End for her strong bootleg whisky, but as fate would have it, she was also Shayna Kravetz's grandmother—which was how the two met.

To pay the ten dollars room and board, Geller started doing odd jobs for Klein. First, it was fetching coffee, and then tidying up the office. Finally, Klein had him discreetly track a husband, whose distraught wife had hired Klein to ascertain if her husband was cheating on her. Geller had done so without being detected and predictably discovered that the culprit in question, Eddie Goldstein, a shoe salesman, was indeed having an affair with his voluptuous next door neighbour Delores, who also happened to be the close friend of his wife, Stella. It was messy, though Alec acted like a real professional. Since then, he had become Klein's assistant, working on a contingency basis; he was paid fifteen per cent of Klein's fee and twenty if it was more than five hundred dollars—which was rare.

"You're taking a train ride to Vera, Alec," said Klein. "You ever hear of that?"

Geller shook his head. "Where the hell is it?"

"About eighty miles due south, close to the North Dakota border."

"And I'm going there, why?"

Klein filled Geller in on the details of Max Roter's murder, who he was, and why Lou Sugarman had hired Klein to investigate his death.

"It's all about booze," said Klein. "Money and booze, a very dangerous combination. Go to Vera. Talk to Roter's neighbours and see what you can find out. There might be a chance that this bootlegger Taylor, Roter's last customer, had nothing to do with this, or any other bootlegger for that matter. Perhaps this was a simple case of a robbery gone wrong. Someone found out about the payoff Roter was getting that night and decided to steal it from him."

"Sounds likely," said Geller, trying very hard to be nonchalant about his first out-of-town assignment

"There's a train leaving from the CPR station late tomorrow morning you can take. But I need your help right now. At about one o'clock Max Roter's widow is arriving with his body for the funeral being held on Friday morning. I'd like to be there, maybe have a quick word with her. Meet me in the middle of the rotunda in an hour and a half—at twelve thirty. I want you to stand back and determine if anything's not right when Mrs. Roter and her children arrive."

"Not right?" asked Geller, his eyes widening.

"Easy Alec, just taking precautions. That's all."

Any time Klein entered the imposing CPR station on Higgins Avenue, he felt as if he was entering a European cathedral. The power of the Almighty was clearly evident as soon as you passed through the three sets of wooden doors. Klein paused for a moment, as he usually did, and felt genuinely humbled by the station's magnificent stone portico. The engraving held by the columns, "AD CANADIAN PACIFIC RAILWAY 1904," was a constant reminder of the CPR's dominating presence on the prairies. If Winnipeg was truly the "Gateway to the West," as the city's leaders boasted, then this was where it all began.

There was a time, before the Great War, when the stream of immigrants arriving at the station from all parts of Europe never let up. These newcomers reshaped the character of the city, though in ways Winnipeg's elite did not especially appreciate. Who needed more Poles, Ukrainians, Galicians, and Jews? Certainly not the barons at the Grain Exchange or the lords of Rosyln Road, who feared their city was under siege by the "scum of Europe," as Klein remembered the old *Winnipeg Telegram* putting it.

But that was more than a decade ago. Yes, Klein was still occasionally referred to as a "dirty kike" and his daughter Freda had been told more than once by the Gentile students at Luxton School that she had "killed Christ." Eaton's, the Hudson's Bay, and a dozen other stores still refused to hire Jewish clerks and Sandy Hook, the beach resort on Lake Winnipeg, promoted itself to prospective cottage owners as "a Jew-free area."

Nonetheless, things were changing, in Klein's view, and for the better. There were Jewish members of the Grain Exchange as well as Jewish doctors and lawyers. Klein had done some investigative work for Max J. Finklestein, known around the city as "MJ," a big-time lawyer. He was a Jew who had one foot in the Jewish North End and another in the WASP Winnipeg of Portage and Main. That was definitely progress. Jews had been elected to city council and Abe Heaps, one of the leaders of the General Strike—who had been arrested by the Mounties and locked up briefly in Stony Mountain Penitentiary—was now fighting for labour as a city alderman. The gossip on Selkirk Avenue was that Heaps was thinking of running for Parliament in the Winnipeg North constituency as an independent labourite. As a British-born Jew, Heaps did not speak Yiddish, but he was perceived positively among the North End Jewish community. His chances of winning a seat, Klein figured, were excellent.

Klein peered up at the station's ornate clock. It was twelve thirty on the dot. He looked in every direction. It was quieter than it used to be, that was certain. In the old days, the station buzzed with the steady arrival of newcomers. A babel of languages echoed through the grand station's rotunda fifteen hours a day. This multitude was generally disoriented, poor, and unable to speak English. Yet somehow, and with a lot of hard work, most of them persevered, adapted, and survived.

The war had put a halt to the immigration wave and even when the conflict ended and the country's gates opened again, the number of newcomers never reached what it was in 1912 and 1913. There were 9,000 Jews in Winnipeg in 1911 and only 6,000 more in 1921. Klein didn't pay much attention to these community issues. He took a more philosophical approach and always remembered an old Yiddish expression his mother used to tell him: *tsum glik, tsum shlimazel*—for better, for worse. Life went on.

"Sam, I'm here," said Alec Geller. He was fixing his hair and adjusting his shirt as he walked.

"You look like you just got out of bed, Alec. Where the hell were you?"

Geller grinned.

"You just came from Saul Sugarman's office, didn't you? You saw Shayna?"

Geller's grin widened. "What can I say? I can't seem to get enough of that woman."

"Alec, it's the lunch hour, for God's sake."

"You're getting old, Sam. When I arrived, Sugarman was in a foul mood and left the office. It was just Shayna and me there. The other office girl also went out to lunch. One thing led to another…"

"I get it. Let's leave it at that."

"I had to see her before I left and she's busy this evening," Geller smiled.

"Christ, Alec. You'll be gone for two days at the most. It's not like you're going back to the Promised Land."

Geller chuckled. "So what's the plan?"

"Head for the platform and stay out of sight," said Klein, glancing again at the clock. "I want you to watch the other passengers on the train with the Roters. And anyone else you see. If anyone doesn't look right, let me know immediately."

"What are you expecting, Sam?"

63

"Maybe nothing. Maybe something," said Klein, looking off into the distance.

Geller knew better than to question Klein's sixth sense. "Whatever you say, sir."

"This isn't the army or the orphanage, Alec. Just go now. You're worse than my kids," he said with a slight grin.

Geller raised his hand to his forehead in a mock salute and did as he was instructed.

A few minutes later, Klein heard a familiar voice. "Shailek, over here." He turned to see his sister Rivka accompanied by Lou Sugarman.

The spectacle of the two as a couple was still fresh and still peculiar. Lou reminded Klein of an affable old uncle, the type who showed up each Friday night with treats for the kids, while Rivka at thirty-eight had matured into a handsome woman with both style and intelligence. Still as radical and stubborn as ever, she had improved her life. A year and a half ago, she quit her job as a seamstress at Moses Asner's garment factory, where the days were twelve to sixteen hours and the pay was barely five dollars for a six-day week. She was now teaching at the IL Peretz School, which was in the process of moving into its new home on the corner of Salter Street and Aberdeen Avenue. Pertez School offered a Yiddish-based and more secular curriculum than the mainstream Talmud Torah. "The Jewish child for the Jewish people," as Rivka put it. To this end, she was also spearheading a fundraising campaign for the Kulture Kreiz's Jewish Public Library—the Yiddishe Folk Bibliotik—that was to be located in the basement of the Peretz School. It was all very exciting in Rivka's sheltered world. That Rabbi Israel Kahanovitch, the esteemed Chief Rabbi of Western Canada, had publicly denounced radicals like Rivka as "Godless" merely reinforced her commitment to work towards a Jewish socialist utopia.

All Klein had to do in order to get a rise out of his sister was to hint that the Talmud Torah's Hebrew education was more beneficial for Jews in Canada than that offered by the Peretz School. Then, he sat back while Rivka embarked on a tirade about the socialists' noble cause and the curse of capitalism. She liked to spout her philosophy about the "struggle of the proletariat" to Freda and Bernice, even Mel, though Klein attempted to keep such indoctrinating of his children to a minimum. He could not understand how Lou Sugarman, a capitalist if there ever was one, could tolerate such propaganda. But as Klein also knew from his many experiences, love sometimes could truly trump all. This was one of those times.

Rivka gave Klein a light peck on the cheek. "I'm glad you came, Shailek. It's just terrible what has happened. Poor Rae. How will she manage?"

Lou lightly touched her shoulder. "She'll be taken care of. Don't you worry, my dear."

"I'm sure she will," said Klein. Rivka noticed his sarcasm, yet said nothing.

The clock struck one and the sound of the arriving train on the outside platform echoed through the station. Lou led the way and Rivka and Klein fell in behind. As soon as they did so, Klein spotted Geller through the billowing smoke from the

ALLAN LEVINE

steam engine. He was sitting reading a newspaper on a bench and far enough away that Rivka and Lou would not see him.

Rae and her children were in the third car from the engine. Gone was her usual jovial spirit. Dressed in black, her eyes were red and hollow. As soon as she saw her brother Lou, she crumbled. He grabbed and held her tightly. Rivka took hold of the children, Mira and Isaac, and gave them both a hug. Klein watched the other passengers climb down. He wasn't sure what he was looking for, only that he felt uneasy.

"It was the liquor, wasn't it, Lou," said Rae, her voice shaking. "This is because of that damn booze." She looked around her. "I see that Saul's not here."

"He had a meeting," Lou mumbled. "I know he wanted to..."

"Stop, Lou, please. You and I both know that the only thing that matters to Saul is money, money, and more money. That mattered to Max as well. And now look what happened to him." She glanced at Klein. "Mr. Klein, isn't it?"

Klein nodded.

"Lou's told me that you've agreed to help us. You'll find out who did this horrible thing to my Max, won't you?"

"I'll do my best," said Klein. "Can we talk soon?"

"Of course, but after the funeral. I can't speak of it until then."

A porter walked up to them. "Ma'am, if you'll come with me we can unload the casket."

Rae, with tears in her eyes, and her children walked towards the rear of the train. Lou and Rivka followed them. Klein held back for a moment and noticed Geller standing, pointing in the direction of the train on the track directly across from them that had just pulled in from Minneapolis.

Disembarking from the first passenger car were two burly men in dark pinstripe suits. Both wore white fedoras. The shorter of the two men had a black patch over his right eye and the taller one carried a small case. Neither of them looked especially friendly or happy to be arriving in the city. Klein watched them and for a split second his eyes made contact with the taller man. A cold chill rippled through his body. Dangerous thugs, thought Klein, like the ones he had seen with Rosen in New York. The man quickly looked away. He whispered to his partner. The two men stopped. They crossed the dusty platform and started walking slowly towards where Rae and her children and Lou and Rivka were standing.

Klein immediately moved in their direction. The two men were about ten paces in front of him. Klein could see four porters lifting the casket off one of the cargo cars. Lou had arranged for a flatbed Ford truck to take the casket to Simpson's mortuary on Main and Redwood, which often prepared Jewish bodies before burial. Lou, among other Jews in the community, found this situation unacceptable and efforts were underway to raise funds for a Jewish community funeral chapel that would assume responsibility for this. The truck was parked at the end of the train, accessible from Higgins.

The porters carefully carried the casket to the truck. Rae held Mira and Isaac's hands and walked behind them. The two thugs began to move more quickly. The man with the eyepatch reached into his suit pocket. Klein froze for a moment. What the hell, he thought. Then the man pulled out a black object that looked like a pistol.

"Everyone down," Klein shouted.

Lou and Rivka looked back at Klein. "What is it, Shailek?" Rivka asked loudly.

"Get down, all of you…"

The words were barely out of his mouth, when there was the distinct sound of a gun firing. The shot came from behind where Geller was standing. Alec dropped to the ground. Then, another shot. Klein also ducked for cover behind a wooden bench. His eyes scanned the area and it seemed to him that the hidden gunman, who was perched on top of a nearby shed, was not firing at Rae, Rivka, or Lou, but at the two men. The thugs kneeled and the man with the patch, who indeed had a pistol in his hand as Klein had suspected, began firing in the direction of the shooter.

"Stay down, Alec," yelled Klein.

Abruptly, the gunfire stopped. Klein slowly stood up. The two thugs were gone. When he was certain that the danger had ended, he ran towards his sister and the others.

5

Within thirty minutes, the CPR station was filled with Winnipeg police constables, all properly attired in their dark blue uniforms adorned with gold buttons. On their heads they wore tall bobby-style helmets held in place by a black chinstrap. Several officers were swarming around Rae Roter and her children as well as Lou Sugarman and Rivka, firing questions at them.

Klein stood back and watched quietly, puffing on a cigarette. From the frustrated look on the constables' faces they were not getting the answers they wanted.

Before the brigade of police had arrived from the Central Police Station on Rupert Avenue a few blocks away, Klein had ensured that no one was hurt. The Roter children were naturally upset, as was everyone else.

"I think that was meant for me," said Lou, shaking. Rivka held his hand tightly.

"I don't know what to think," said Klein. In his mind, the

shooter had aimed and fired at the two thugs, who were nowhere to be seen. Klein wasn't one to second-guess himself, but maybe Lou was right. On the way up the business ladder, Lou and Saul had made a few enemies—not the least of whom was the high-minded preacher, Reverend John Vivian, a moral crusader whose declared life's purpose was to single-handedly shut down the liquor trade in Canada.

As Klein was aware, Vivian had about ten to twenty young, devoted followers who heeded his every word and did his bidding. The reverend, dubbed "the battling preacher" by Winnipeg journalists, and his men frequently carried clubs as well as guns. Despite repeated warnings from the police, they had wielded their revolvers on more than one occasion. Just last month, Vivian and his "gang," as the *Free Press* called them, had literally carried out a military-style assault on a notorious illegal saloon on Jarvis Avenue, whose greedy operator had been selling homemade brew to the neighbourhood children. It was possible that Vivian was behind today's attack, thought Klein. The reverend had been quoted as denouncing the Sugarman brothers as the "devil's sinners who were destined for Hell."

"Klein, what a surprise to find you in the middle of this," said a familiar voice. There was no disguising the mocking tone.

Klein turned and came face-to-face with Detective Bill McCreary, decked out in his trademark three-piece, grey, loose-fitting sack suit and derby. Klein liked to kid McCreary that he hadn't purchased a new suit since the blood libel-Rabbi Davidovich murder trial from 1911—Klein's first official case. "Why spend the money when you don't have to," was McCreary's standard explanation.

Another taller plain-clothes detective stood silently beside him. Klein did not know him, but he did look familiar. Like McCreary, the detective sported a thick moustache. Except while McCreary's moustache was flecked with lots of grey, this officer's thick whiskers were as dark as his deep, penetrating eyes.

"McCreary, you still on the job? I heard you retired," said Klein with a wisp of a smirk.

"Interim Commissioner of the Provincial Police, if you haven't heard," said McCreary, puffing his chest forward.

"Yeah, I've heard," said Klein. "So if that's the case, what brings you down here? Isn't this a matter for the city police?"

McCreary motioned in the direction of Lou Sugarman. "Anything involving those two Jew liquor traders, the Sugarman brothers, I'm involved in. Those were my orders from up high."

Klein was used to McCreary's rough language and ignored the taunt. "So who's your new partner?"

"Name is Thomas Allard," the detective said, extending his right hand to Klein. "McCreary's told me all about you."

Klein stared at him for a moment. He seemed friendly enough for a cop, Klein thought, but was as rigid as a slab of wood. "Allard. Aren't you that sniper who won all those medals during the war?" he asked, shaking his hand.

"That's him," McCreary said before Allard could reply. "He's also the first half-breed on the force."

The stoic expression on Allard's face was firm. "I am Métis, grew up in Fort Rouge," he said. "But, yes, Mr. Klein, you're correct about me."

Klein had read the feature story about Allard in the *Tribune*. His father, Joseph, was a fireman on the Canadian Northern Railway and the family was much better off than many of the Métis in Winnipeg, some of whom lived in abject poverty in tarpaper shanties in Rooster Town, the bush slum located south of Corydon Avenue and Wilton Street. Allard had attended St. Ignatius Catholic School and eventually joined the Canadian Expeditionary Force. The marksman was credited with killing close to 389 enemy soldiers at Passchendaele, Ypres, the Somme, and the other bloody battlefields of Europe where he served. For his bravery, he was awarded the Military Medal with two bars, the highest honour awarded to a Métis or Indian soldier.

"Honestly, I didn't think it would work, hiring a half-breed, but Allard has skills," said McCreary, speaking as if Allard was not standing beside him. "When I got my promotion a while ago, Chief Newton thought it would be a good idea to see how Allard works as a detective. Said it was a progressive move, whatever the hell that means. Next thing you know they'll be hiring Hebes like you, Klein."

"You'll have to excuse Commissioner McCreary," said Klein. His tone was sarcastic, yet mixed with a tinge of anger. "But once a boor, always a boor."

Allard waved his hand. "Never mind it. I've grown up with it. Like water off a duck's back, for me."

"I understand," said Klein.

Like most Winnipeggers, if Klein thought about Métis or

Indians at all—and to his mind there wasn't much difference—it was not in a positive way. "Drunken Indian," was the common refrain whenever an Indian from a nearby reserve ventured into the city—and it hardly mattered that some of the more industrious ones set up berry stands in the summer. The prevailing attitude among Winnipeg citizens, whether they were "old stock" Canadians or newcomers from Europe, was that the Indians were indolent beggars who needed to adapt and conform to a "Canadian" way of life. The Métis of St. Boniface who had more or less assimilated into the French community were tolerated. The same went for the Métis in Fort Rouge like the Allards who had decently paying jobs and owned or rented houses. But those who resided in Rooster Town without electricity or running water or who were squatting on other land beyond the city limits were reviled as immoral and condemned for living in squalor. Still, casting a glance at Allard, Klein could see right away that he carried himself with a professional dignity generally lacking in many of the city's cops he had encounted.

"If you two are finished," said McCreary, "can you tell me what the hell happened here, Klein?"

Klein proceeded to relate what had transpired, but left out a few details. He decided that he would omit any mention of the two thugs and whether they were the intended targets of the shooter. He wanted to investigate further and figure out who these two men were and why they were in the city. For the moment, there was no point involving the police; they would merely complicate things.

Seeing Klein speaking with the detectives, Lou Sugarman

walked over to where they were standing. "You need to find out who did this."

"Easy, Sugarman. The last thing I need is advice from the likes of you," said McCreary.

"My brother and I are honest businessmen trying to make a living…"

"Yeah, by selling booze to American bootleggers."

"It's not illegal," said Sugarman.

"Maybe so, but the province is not going to turn a blind eye to this profiteering forever," said McCreary.

"And when did you ever concern yourself about such things, McCreary?" asked Klein.

"You implying something, Klein?" McCreary's voice rose.

"You've stayed dry during prohibition in the province, McCreary? That's not what I heard, or saw, for that matter. Didn't you and I have a drink at a blind pig on Magnus Avenue a few months back?"

McCreary waved the back of his hand. "You don't know what the fuck you're saying, Klein. Like always."

"Mr. Sugarman, who do you think shot at you today?" asked Allard. "If, in fact, you were the intended target."

"Of course I was. Who else could it have been? My sister and her children? Klein's sister, Rivka? Trust me, I could've been killed and I know who it was."

"Is that so?" said Allard.

"What's your thinking, Lou?" asked Klein.

"That crazed preacher, John Vivian. It had to be him."

"That's bullshit," said McCreary.

"Did you see him here?" Allard asked Sugarman.

Lou shook his head. "In the past few months he's sent at least a dozen threatening letters to me and my brother about how he's going to put us out of business permanently. Refers to us as the 'evil sinners' and 'the manufacturers of immorality and depravity.' Don't you think that's enough?"

"Maybe," replied Allard. "Seems hard to believe that the reverend would go as far as to hire someone to try to kill you and in such a public place."

"Yeah, well, I disagree," said Sugarman. "That man's the real menace, not us."

"I think you should talk to him, McCreary. It makes sense," said Klein.

"Well, you're not a cop, are you, Klein? If I had to make a guess, I'd say this has to do with the murder of your brother-in-law in Vera, Sugarman. And I intend to get to the bottom of that very shortly. However, don't let it ever be said that Bill McCreary does not investigate every angle carefully..."

"No, of course not," said Klein, shaking his head slightly.

"As I was saying. Allard will question Reverend Vivian and we'll see if he knows anything about this."

"Good," said Lou. "Now, if you'll excuse me, I have to help my sister-in-law with the funeral arrangements."

"I thought you and Saul Sugarman were on good terms, McCreary," said Klein after Lou had rejoined his family and Rivka.

The detective glared at Klein for a moment. "You ask too many questions, Klein. You always have."

"My aim is to keep you honest, McCreary, as impossible a job as that is," Klein said coolly.

That comment elicited a hint of a smile from Allard.

"So you do have a sense of humour, Allard?" Klein asked.

Before Allard could respond, McCreary, muttering to himself, walked towards the group of constables searching for evidence beside the railway shed. "I want a report, now," he said loudly.

Sarah's sitter, Molly, had finally shown up at the store at two thirty in the afternoon and offered to take the children back to the Klein house. Sarah was slightly annoyed with the sixteen-year-old girl and did not have the patience to listen to her convoluted story about her grandmother's missing cat. She kissed Bernice and Mel as they left with Molly, instructing the girl to give the children milk and biscuits when they got home, and returned to her work.

It had been as profitable a day as she had anticipated. Betty Kingston had purchased two suits, a new navy blue piquetine and pebble-grey tweed. The outfits, fifty dollars each, were not entirely to her taste—"too blaah," as she had put it—but she said that she required them for the various social engagements she had to attend with her husband. In addition to the dresses, she bought three skirts, a white cloche hat, and an assortment of powders, vanishing creams, pan sticks, lipsticks, and mascaras. In total, her bill came to nearly $200, more than Sarah usually sold in a week.

Betty then insisted that Sarah join her for tea and cake at Eaton's elegant Grill Room.

"I just can't close the store in the middle of the afternoon, Betty," Sarah had pleaded.

"Nonsense, my dear. Who's to say anything about it? Thanks to me, or rather my Nicholas, have you not had a profitable day?"

Sarah laughed. "Yes, I have."

"So what's the problem, then? Come, we need to talk," Betty said, taking hold of Sarah's arm.

Fifteen minutes later, the two women were on the fifth floor of Eaton's department store seated among the other ladies enjoying mid-afternoon tea and Dundee cake. This was not a dining room Sarah frequented. Everything about the Grill Room—its oak-panelling, wrought iron chandeliers, well-appointed carpeting, crisp white tablecloths, and formally attired waiters— gave the distinct impression that this was an establishment which catered to Winnipeg's wealthy elite, and definitely not the wife of a Jewish private detective who lived in the North End. Even though she was with Betty Kingston, Sarah's face flushed. She immediately felt as if various sets of eyes were staring at her.

"Ignore them," said Betty, lightly touching Sarah's arm. "They're actually looking at me, rather than you. I'm what you call a gold digger. You should hear the gossip about how I tricked innocent and naïve Nicholas into marriage. The story would make a wonderful play, though I can't decide if it would be a tragedy or a comedy."

Sarah smiled. "I can assure you, I've never thought anything about it. And trust me, if either one of us has a past to conceal, it's definitely me!"

Betty chuckled and patted Sarah's hand. "I know all about you, my dear. I think you're very brave."

"Yes, there's no escaping it. I worked in a brothel and I kind of enjoyed it. Until Sam gave me a new life, that is. I owe him everything."

A waiter with a thin moustache and tailored black suit interrupted the conversation. He set down a silver teapot and served each woman a slice of Dundee cake filled with raisins and topped with almonds.

"You'll enjoy this," said Betty. "If we were here for dinner, I'd have the chicken pot pie. Simply delicious."

"I hope you don't mind me saying so, but you are curious," said Sarah.

"How so?"

"You're young and beautiful, lively and funny..."

"So why did I choose to marry a stuffed-shirt like Nicholas, a man more than twenty years older than me with teenage children?"

Sarah grinned. "I suppose that's the question, yes."

"I grew up in a nice neighbourhood in Toronto. My father's a stockbroker. He was out of the house each weekday at eight o'clock and home after six. My mother, who died in the flu epidemic, had his dinner on the table. She lived her life for me and my younger brother. I can't say that she wasn't happy, but that's the way it seemed to me. Life, I think, has to be more than a bunch of dinners on the table and the occasional social outing.

Life has to be gay and filled with exceptional moments. Not just hard work and sitting there waiting for your husband to come home."

"And Nicholas Kingston was your answer?" asked Sarah.

"Hard to believe, I know. But he has a marvelous sense of humour and he adores me for who I am. He promised never to try to change me and he hasn't yet. I only had to agree to be at his side for balls and pageants and other society affairs and in exchange I can spend an afternoon purchasing what I choose at shops like yours. And besides…" Betty paused and glanced in every direction. "The sex is wonderful," she whispered, giggling.

Sarah smiled. "I can understand that."

"After three children, you're still in love with your husband?"

"I am, yes."

"Not wishing to pry…"

"Well, go ahead, I did."

"Why that loud argument with that gentleman who visited us earlier?"

"You could hear?"

Betty nodded. "Hard not to."

"I apologize for that. It's a very long story and so far does not have a happy ending."

"I have all the time in the world," said Betty, sipping her tea.

"I made a foolish mistake and for the life of me, I can't tell you why. Or, perhaps, it will make perfect sense to you. The so-called gentleman is Saul Sugarman. I'm sure you've heard of him."

"Yes, Nicholas has mentioned his name, but not in a pleasant way," Betty said, lowering her voice. "He's quite the business-man, I hear. Involved with the liquor trade."

Sarah nodded. "That's putting it lightly. Saul and his brother Lou, a much kinder man, are very wealthy. They first owned hotels and later began selling whisky. They've done very well. Maybe I should be selling liquor too. For some months, business at the shop has been slow, like everywhere else in the city. I wish I had a lot more customers like you," she said with a smile, "but unfortunately that's not the case. Things were not good. When it appeared I might have to close, in walked Saul. His office is also in the Boyd Building. He and I exchanged pleasantries, and, I must admit, I flirted with him. We got to talking and then, much to my surprise, he offered me a deal: an investment in the shop. I would pay him back without interest whenever I could afford it. Sam warned me about him. We argued about it, though in the end we both finally agreed that I had no choice but to accept Saul's help. At the time, I told Sam he was wrong. That Saul was genuine in his desire to save the shop. Yet now I know I misjudged his intentions. Several weeks ago, I was working late, restocking. Saul showed up with a bottle of whisky. I was tired. He was charming. We had a drink and then another one. I honestly don't recall exactly what happened. I have replayed the scene in my head many times. We were laughing and he gently rubbed my cheek. And then before I could do anything, he leaned in and kissed me. And, for moment, I kissed him back. But I quickly pushed him away and asked him to leave, which he did."

"Sounds innocent enough to me," said Betty.

"I don't know. A few days went by and I was troubled. Sam kept asking me what was wrong. I kept saying nothing and then…"

"You didn't tell him, did you?" asked Betty, shaking her head.

Sarah shrugged. "He wouldn't stop, so I told him."

"From what I know of your husband's reputation, I imagine that didn't go well."

Sarah sighed. "No, not at all. He's been angry ever since. There was so much yelling that I just left for a few days. It was impulsive and foolish, I know that. Worse, I didn't tell him where I was, which naturally made him angrier. I've tried to explain it to him, but he won't listen."

Betty sat back in her chair. "Men are stubborn and pig-headed, though I'm sure I don't have to tell you that."

"You don't!"

"Do you still love him, Sarah?"

"I do, of course."

"Then don't give up on him. He'll come round."

"I hope you're right. I can't lose Sam," said Sarah, her eyes welling.

Betty patted Sarah's right hand. "Now, now dear, let's finish this cake and then order another piece."

By eleven o'clock in the evening, the only people out on the streets of Winnipeg were stragglers from the last theatre and movie performances of the day and the usual motley collection of drunks, beggars, men making their way home from the Point Douglas brothels, and would-be thieves and muggers.

Bill McCreary, as irritable as he normally was after a long day of work, turned onto Portage from Donald Street, pushing out of his way a trio of young drunks who had the misfortune of being in his path. One of the dishevelled young men went crashing to the sidewalk, while his two friends abandoned him, running in the opposite direction as fast as their wobbly legs could carry them.

"Damn fools," bellowed McCreary. "Where's a cop when you need one?" He left the drunk lying on the sidewalk and continued on his way.

When he reached the Boyd Building, he banged on the front door and the night watchman jumped up from his desk and let him in. McCreary mumbled hello, proceeded to the elevator, and rode it up to the fifth floor. This time of the day, there was no elevator operator so McCreary had to pull the cage door shut and work the lever himself. A few minutes later, he found Saul Sugarman alone in his office.

"I was hoping that secretary you keep around here, the blonde with the legs, might still be here," said McCreary, sitting down in a leather chair opposite Sugarman's desk.

"You mean Miss Kravetz?" asked Sugarman with a chuckle. "She's gone home long ago. You're old enough to be her father, by the way."

"Yeah and…"

"And nothing. I know she's a choice bit of calico." Sugarman opened a panel on the wall behind his desk, took out a bottle of Gooderham & Worts Special Rye Whisky, and poured two glasses. "Here, have a swig of this, McCreary," he said, handing the detective a shot.

"It's not that panther piss that your brother concocts."

Sugarman smirked. "Lou's homemade brew has not been bad of late. Not like that famous first batch he tried that turned purple. Just try this. Very smooth."

McCreary grabbed the glass and gulped down the whisky. "You're right, Sugarman. It's smooth, and I needed that. I presume you've heard from Lou about the shooting at the station today."

Sugarman nodded. "Of course. My sister and her children were nearly killed," he said, his voice rising. "It is nonsense! How could something like this have happened? It's not part of the plan, that's for damn sure. Do you think it was that pain-in-the-ass preacher Vivian? That's what Lou thinks."

McCreary removed a thin cigar from his inside jacket pocket, took a wooden match from a silver container on Sugarman's desk, and lit it. He took a deep drag and blew a puff of smoke upward. "Might've been. I have a man trying to find him. He wasn't at his home. But we'll find him by Friday at the latest, I promise. You know Klein was there?"

"Yeah, I heard. I told Lou to hire him. It's fine. He could prove useful, but not for the reason he thinks."

"I sure hope you're right. I have my men in Vera on the lookout for that young Jew who's working with him. Geller, I think his name is."

"Yes, it's Geller. He's young and inexperienced. There's nothing to worry about. But I have a man there, too: Sid Sharp. I've already sent a wire to him with instructions to keep an eye on the kid."

McCreary took another drag on his cigar and stared at Sugarman for a moment. "You shouldn't underestimate Klein, Saul. He's capable and he knows how to solve a case. I can vouch for that. His problem is that he thinks no one else is as smart as he is. He saw something else at the station, but didn't tell me about it. Still thinks I'm an idiot. But I know all about it."

Sugarman opened a sterling silver cigar box on his desk, took one out, chopped off the end with a silver cutter, and lit it. He handed one of the cigars to McCreary. "Here, this is a lot better than the cheap tobacco you're smoking."

McCreary took a whiff of Sugarman's cigar, smiled, and put it carefully into his jacket pocket.

"So what did Klein see?" asked Sugarman.

"You won't like it."

"I don't like it already."

"Two of Rosen's men might be in the city and from what my source tells me, the shooter might have been aiming at them rather than your brother."

"Is it reliable?"

"The conductor on the Minneapolis train. I've been dealing with him for years, an old guy named Pete Buchelle. The two men were on his train. Swears he saw the whole thing unfold."

"God damn it." Sugarman banged his hand hard on his desk. "Who does he think he is?"

"Irv Rosen, that's who," said McCreary, pouring himself

another shot of whisky. "He doesn't answer to you, me, or the American government for that matter."

"So who the hell was shooting at them?"

"I have some thoughts on that, too, but let my men look into that further."

"There's a possibility," said Sugarman, scratching his chin. "Seems unlikely, however."

"You want to tell me what the hell you're talking about?"

"Not right now, McCreary. But, here, I have a gift for you in honour of you being named head of the provincial police." Sugarman opened his desk drawer and pulled out a brown envelope. He slid it across the desk towards McCreary.

The detective opened the envelope. Inside was a stack of bills. "That's generous of you, Sugarman … but…"

"But what?"

McCreary finished his whisky and helped himself to another of Sugarman's cigars. Without saying another word, he stood up, tucked the envelope in his jacket, and walked out of the office.

6

One by one, the men marched silently into the small house. George Dickens had not been physically fit enough to fight in the war because of a bad knee, but now he truly felt like a soldier. An office clerk for the Standard Grain Company, he had a mission to rid Winnipeg and the world of alcohol, the evil drink and the cause of misery, poverty, and wrecked marriages. He owed this renewed sense of purpose to one man, his "General," Reverend John Vivian, "the battling preacher."

Like the other men, Dickens had been sent instructions yesterday: he was to report to 1774 Belmont Avenue at eleven o'clock on Thursday morning. And he was to bring his hunting rifle. He had been forced to call in sick at work, but such was his loyalty to the reverend. His wife, Maggie, as much or more of a supporter of the anti-liquor crusade, had encouraged him to do so.

The isolated, white, wood cottage on the corner of Belmont and Salter was about a mile from Bannerman Avenue and civilization. Dickens had initially wondered why the reverend had chosen this rural location as opposed to the more comfortable confines of the house on Sherbrooke Street near Ellice Avenue where the group usually convened. But Dickens understood that when Vivian gave an order, he was to be obeyed, no questions asked. The war on drink demanded it.

There was hot coffee on the wood stove in the kitchen and Dickens poured himself a cup. So, too, did several of the other men.

"Anyone know what's going on?" Dickens asked the man with the neatly trimmed moustache standing beside him.

This older gentleman also poured himself a mug of black coffee and motioned for Dickens to follow him into the cottage's parlour. There, standing in the middle of the modestly furnished room, was John Vivian.

No matter how many times Dickens saw the Methodist preacher, his heart always skipped and his palms instantly became sweaty. The reverend had a definite presence. To Dickens, Vivian exuded the wisdom of a Biblical prophet: calm, measured, righteous, and unwavering. A towering figure in a time of increasing depravity was how Dickens frequently described him.

Vivian surveyed the room, staring intently at each of his men. As his piercing gaze landed on Dickens, he could feel the hair on the back of his neck tingle. Dressed in a stylish, three-piece black suit with a white shirt and a black tie with small, white speckles in it, Vivian at first said nothing. His thick, short, auburn hair was parted almost in the middle. He had high cheekbones and deep-set, brown eyes. His jaw was firm like that of a boxer. He was both a handsome man and a determined one. Twenty years ago, after his older brother, while hunting near Lake of the Woods, had been accidentally shot and killed by an intoxicated hunter, Vivian dedicated his life to halting the trade in liquor and shutting down as many saloons as he could.

"It is prosperity against poverty, sobriety against drunkenness, honesty against thieving, heaven against hell," Vivian declared.

Several of the men in the parlour nodded.

"Who is to blame for this tragedy? This calamity that is destroying otherwise good men and women everywhere?" He did not wait for a reply. "The saloon owners and the liquor profiteers. And the worst of these sinners are the Sugarman brothers, Jews, of course, who live off the weakness of others. They have no interest in humanity, only in the almighty dollar. They now are lawbreakers, sending their vile liquor across the border. They deal with the criminal element."

Dickens and the other men shouted, "Yes!"

"The Sugarmans and others of their ilk must be stopped, one way or the other! Are you ready to stand with me? Are you ready to do the Lord's bidding? To do what is necessary?"

"Yes!" the men said loudly again.

"Come, now let us pray," said Vivian.

The preacher and those in attendance bowed their heads, while Vivian recited the Lord's Prayer.

Once the meeting had ended, Vivian motioned for Dickens

to join him in a small alcove of the parlour to the back of the house.

"How are you, George?" asked Vivian.

"I am well," replied Dickens, rubbing his sweaty hands. "How may I serve the cause today?"

"You've heard what happened at the train station yesterday?" asked Vivian, speaking softly.

Dickens nodded. "I've heard conflicting reports."

"The police are searching for me. They believe I was responsible. That I sent someone to kill Lou Sugarman."

Dickens's eyes widened slightly, though he remained silent.

"Do you want to know if that's true?" Vivian continued.

"No, no. I'd never question you…"

The preacher put his hand on Dickens's shoulder. "There's nothing to fear, my son. If the Sugarmans are to die for their sins, then it's God's will."

"That must be so," said Dickens.

"I plan to visit the police soon, however."

"Do you need me to accompany you?"

Vivian smiled. "Thank you for asking. But it is probably better if I go alone. I have nothing to hide. George, you trust me in all things?"

"You know I do."

"Yes, of course. In a few days, I may require your services. You must do as you are told without any questions or hesitation. Can you do that?" asked Vivian. His voice was steady and self-assured.

Dickens stood at attention. "I am your servant, always," he said, staring straight into Vivian's eyes.

"That's good, George, very good. I knew I could count on you," Vivian said, grasping Dickens by the shoulders.

Alec Geller stared out the window at an endless vista of pasture, cows, and forests of trees—a panoply of maples, oaks, cottonwoods, and jack pines. All he could think about was Shayna Kravetz and his rendezvous with her at her office yesterday afternoon. He knew that they were being careless, that she surely would have been fired had they been caught by her boss, Saul Sugarman. Nevertheless, the image of her sleek body was imprinted on his brain and it excited him. As the coal-powered train meandered south of Winnipeg towards Emerson at thirty miles an hour, Geller shook these thoughts and momentarily dozed, only to be jarred awake as the train jerked to a stop first in La Salle and then in Osborne, Morris, and Gretna before turning west towards Vera.

He nodded off again and nearly missed his stop when the train rolled into Vera. Leaping from his seat, he pushed his way past the conductor and jumped from the car just as it started moving again.

Standing on the wooden platform in front of the small station, he got his bearings. To his right, close to the platform, was the towering Standard Grain Company elevator, the most important structure in any prairie town. To his left was Vera's bleak Main Street, the same as a hundred other "main streets" in a hundred other Canadian towns. There was the requisite post office, telephone exchange office, livery stable, drugstore, bakery, barbershop, Chinese café, and Presbyterian Church, by far the grandest building in the town. Across from the church, he eyed Roter's General Store, closed because of tomorrow's funeral.

Klein had told him to contact a friend of the Roter family, the grain elevator manager named Jack Smythe, with whom Rae Roter had entrusted the keys to the store and liquor warehouse. Alec planned to remain in Vera until Friday evening, staying the night at a rooming house operated by a Mrs. Tillsdale on Railway Avenue. He could then take the six o'clock train back to the city. Klein had given him five dollars for his room and food expenses. He wasn't sure what he'd find, perhaps nothing, but he prided himself on his ever-expanding abilities as a private detective—a Sam Klein in the making, as Geller liked to joke with Shayna. At least she was impressed.

Geller stepped off the platform onto a cement sidewalk. This surprised him as he was certain that Vera would still have wooden walkways. That's progress, he thought to himself, further inspecting the hard surface.

"You won't find anything down there, boy."

Geller looked up to see a broad-shouldered man in a dark suit and high boots with a black Stetson that matched the shade of his thick handlebar moustache and unbroken eyebrow. "Maybe not," Geller said, standing up. The man was about a head taller than he was.

"You know who I am?" the man asked.

Geller stood back and cockily looked the man up and down. "I'd guess that you're a provincial cop."

"That's exactly right, kid. Sergeant Duncan Sundell."

"Sergeant, a pleasure to meet you," said Geller, extending his right hand.

Sundell pushed it away. "Listen, kid, I know why you're here. You work for that Hebrew detective, Klein. Name is Alec Geller. That so?"

"That's so. And what of it?"

"I was told you were coming."

That hardly surprised Geller. He knew of Klein's relationship with McCreary. "Your new commissioner let you know, I suppose?"

"You mean Interim Commissioner McCreary."

"That's right," said Geller, momentarily looking downward. "He doesn't much care for my boss."

"I wouldn't know anything about that. But I do know that you're here to poke around about the Jew storekeeper's murder," said Sundell, moving closer to Geller so that the two men were only inches apart.

He may have been young, but Geller was not easily intimidated, even by a burly provincial police officer. He stood his ground and looked straight ahead, directly into Sundell's eyes. "Maybe. Maybe I'm just visiting. Never been to Vera before." He knew that response was bound to goad the sergeant, but in that moment, he didn't care.

Sundell flinched first and took a step backward, tipping the front of his hat up. "You think you're as clever as your boss, don't you? Listen, I have my men here. We're doing all the investigating that needs to be done. There's no mystery. No need for you to be bothering the good folks here. This was a robbery and shooting, almost certainly by the bootlegger who gave the storekeeper…"

"Mr. Roter," interrupted Geller.

Sundell stared at Alec for a moment, his singular eyebrow furrowed. "Yes, Mr. Roter. As I was saying, we believe Mr. Roter met with a bootlegger from Hampton…"

"I believe Taylor is his name," said Geller, his tone matter-of-fact.

"… That he met with a bootlegger named Taylor who gave him money for a shipment of liquor and that Taylor later returned to steal his money back. The case, as they say, is closed—or will be shortly."

"Interesting theory, Sergeant, but as I said, I'm only visiting."

Geller began moving past the officer when Sundell grabbed him hard by his left arm. "That smart-ass mouth of yours will get you in serious trouble one day, Geller."

"I've been told that," said Alec, trying to wiggle free.

Sundell tightened his grip. "Now listen to me, boy. I'm going to say this once and once only. You're free to visit Vera, this is Canada after all, not Revolutionary Russia. But if I find out that you're anywhere near the crime scene or get any complaints that you're bothering anyone in this town, I'll put you on the next train myself. And it won't be a pleasant trip back to the city."

Geller pushed back as hard as he could and was able to escape from Sundell's clutches. "Why's that exactly?" he asked, catching his breath. "Why won't it be a pleasant ride home?"

"Because you'll be black and blue," Sundell retorted, pushing

Geller to the sidewalk. "We'll be watching you." The officer turned and marched back down the street.

Geller picked himself up. He was shaken, though not injured. Admittedly, his pride was more hurt than his body. He had always been able to take care of himself—at the orphanage and on the street. This tough cop was something else, however.

Nevertheless, it was curious, he thought, dusting off his trousers. One important piece of wisdom that he had learned from Klein was to put yourself in your opponent's shoes, to think like he did. Why would Sergeant Sundell go out of his way to antagonize him? Why not just ignore him? Surely, Sundell didn't really believe that he could frighten him enough so that he'd run back to Winnipeg with his tail between his legs? Either Sundell was a foolish cop or there was more to this murder than he was letting on. And Geller's initial impression was that Sundell was not a stupid man.

Shaking off his encounter with Sergeant Sundell, Geller found his way to Mrs. Tillsdale's home on Railway Avenue. The house, like most in the town, was compact but comfortable. There was no electricity or running water, but the kitchen was bright and inviting and there was hot, strong coffee warming on the wood stove. Mrs. Tillsdale offered him cup and though Alec had other business to attend to, he sat for a few minutes. In that brief time, he learned that the small and slight grey-haired woman's first name was Grace and that she had lived in Vera for most of her life. She had been a widow for about five years, since her husband Cecil died in a farm accident.

As he gulped down his coffee, Geller listened politely to Mrs.

Tillsdale's stories. When he asked her about the death of Max Roter, all she could do was shake her head in disbelief. "A tragedy," she said, adding that there had not been a murder in Vera for a decade, ever since Norman Fielding had mistakenly shot and killed his son-in-law, Ed. "They were both stone-cold drunk. Nothing worse than the bottle," Mrs. Tillsdale said. "Now poor Mrs. Roter has to suffer because of liquor as well."

Geller thanked Mrs. Tillsdale for the coffee and told her that he'd return for dinner around six. She promised him a hearty meal of roast beef and potatoes. Leaving her house, he headed back to the railway station. His destination was the Standard Grain Company office and a visit with Jack Smythe.

The sun was hotter now. Alec removed his jacket and walked slowly down the dusty street, saying "hello" or "good afternoon" to every person in Vera who crossed his path. It was much friendlier here than on the streets of Winnipeg, he thought, where it was usually best to avoid eye contact with strangers. The warm weather that improved his mood also made him oblivious to the fact that an unsavoury-looking character with a dark beard and bowler hat had started following him the moment he left Mrs. Tillsdale's.

Alec moved past the station and up the three stairs leading to the Standard Grain office, about twenty feet in front of the elevator. He was about to knock when he heard the shouting.

"God damn you, Smythe! You're a thief and always have been." The deep voice was loud and angry.

"You're a fool, MacGibbon. I've told you a hundred times, this is how it works. I'm offering you the best street price I can.

95

Now, if you don't like it, take your bloody grain and business somewhere else." The second voice Geller could hear was calmer but stern.

"You'll rot in hell like the rest of the speculators and leeches who suck us dry," said the first voice.

"Get out of my office, MacGibbon, now!" yelled the second man.

Geller gently opened the door and came face-to-face with whom he presumed was MacGibbon, a heavy-set man of medium height wearing dark blue overalls and a straw hat. When Alec did not move fast enough, MacGibbon pushed him out of the way, causing Geller to stumble to the ground.

"Hey, mister, what's going on?" asked Geller, picking himself up.

"You were in my way, kid. I don't have time for this shit."

"You need to learn some manners." But MacGibbon wasn't listening. He started his truck and immediately drove away. "Asshole," Alec muttered to himself.

"You don't know the half of it," said Jack Smythe. "You must be Geller? I was expecting you."

"Yes, I am. Sorry about that…"

"About calling Fred MacGibbon an asshole? Don't worry, that describes him perfectly," Smythe said with a chuckle. "He's just another farmer who has no clue as to how the grain business works. He thinks because cash wheat is trading at the exchange in Winnipeg for a dollar and twenty-five cents a bushel, that's the price he should receive. That's impossible. There're shipping and storage costs. I offered him a dollar-ten instead, really about five cents higher than I should've, and he thinks I'm trying to rob him. You might've heard that farmers like him have got the federal government to undertake another official inquiry?"

Geller did not follow the grain business news and said nothing.

"Like everyone at the Winnipeg exchange, farmers like Mac-Gibbon think that the banks and railways are all out to fleece farmers," continued Smythe. "It's bullshit, always has been. But, my apologies Geller, I know you didn't come all the way to Vera for a lecture about the grain trade. Come in and sit down."

Smythe's office was dominated by a large, chestnut-coloured roll-top desk. With the cover up, Geller could see that the slots on the back of the desk facing him were filled with letters and paper slips. Files and papers were strewn about and stacks of yellow newspapers tied with twine sat on the floor collecting dust.

"It's a mess. My wife has offered to tidy it up but, believe it or not, I like it just as it is. Now, I know you want to speak to me about poor Max."

"You were friends with Mr. Roter?"

"I was, yes. My wife Joannie and his wife Rae are dear friends. And if you live in Vera, there's nowhere else to buy groceries than at Roter's General Store. Everyone has had to go to Emerson or Dominion City for food supplies. It's just a terrible tragedy, that's all I can say."

"When did you last see Mr. Roter?"

"That night when it happened, in fact. We were at the store, as we usually are on a Saturday night. We were having a good time. We bid goodnight to Rae and Max and that's the last time I saw him."

"Do you have any idea what happened to him?"

Smythe sighed. "Connected to that liquor business, I'd wager. I know that's what the police think, at any rate."

"Yes, I've met Sergeant Sundell."

"He's a decent enough officer. Does a good job in these parts."

"Let me ask you, Mr. Smythe. The sergeant seems to think that it was a bootlegger named Taylor who might be involved in the robbery and shooting."

"Yes, I've heard that. I wouldn't be surprised. Ever since the Americans started with prohibition, every Manitoba town along the border, Vera included, has had its share of trouble. Bootleggers with their big cars and guns showing up day and night. There's a lot of money to be made with booze. I tried to warn Max that it was a dangerous business, but he said he had no choice in the matter. Something about family obligations. I hope this helps you," said Smythe, standing up. "Now I must get back to work."

"No, of course. I apologize for taking up so much of your time. I was told you have keys for me."

"I do, yes." Smythe reached into a corner slot on his desk and pulled out a ring with several keys on it. "This smaller one will get you in the store. And the others are for the locks on the liquor warehouse in the back. Do you need me to escort you there?"

"No, that's kind of you, but I can look around myself and then return the keys. Probably best to go later this evening when there's less of a chance of anyone else around, especially the police. In my earlier chat with Sergeant Sundell, he made it clear that I was to stay away from the crime scene. Not that such a warning has ever stopped me before…"

Smythe smiled. "Let me have a word with Sundell. I'm sure I can assist you."

"I'd appreciate that," said Geller. "I'll return them in the morning before I return to the city." He shook Smythe's hand and left the office.

As soon as Geller was gone, Smythe opened a side door behind a large panel near his desk. "You can come in now, Sid. You know I don't feel good about this at all…"

Sid Sharp removed his bowler hat and stroked his beard. "Relax, Smythe. Sugarman's paying you for your time." He pulled out a handful of bills and threw them on Smythe's desk. "I heard the whole conversation. You did just fine. Just leave the kid to me."

For about an hour and a half, Geller walked up and down Vera's Main Street. He spoke to just about everyone of importance in the town: Mr. Richardson, the undertaker and reeve, Fred Lum at his Chinese café, and Joe Hendricks, the owner of the hardware store. Everyone liked Max Roter. They expressed the same concern Smythe had about the dangerous liquor trade. And not one person had anything to add about the crime.

At Linda's dress shop, he was introduced to Joannie Smythe. Geller was immediately taken with Joannie's striking appearance, though he found it odd that she was wearing a blue and white floral, long-sleeved dress on such a warm day He chose not to ask her about it and instead told her what he was doing in Vera. She insisted on speaking to him further, naturally devastated by what had transpired, and mentioned to Alec that she was taking the Thursday evening train to Winnipeg so that she could attend Max's funeral on Friday afternoon. Her husband, she added, was unable to accompany her due to business obligations. Klein had taught him to be thorough so he decided to probe further about the Roter's marriage. At first, Mrs. Smythe was aghast and reprimanded Geller for his impertinence. But when Alec explained that as an investigator he had to explore every angle, she was more receptive.

"Max and Rae adored each other," she explained. "They loved their children and any idea of impropriety on either of their parts is entirely unthinkable."

Geller listened closely and though he believed what she was saying, there was something about Max Roter's all-too-perfect life that gnawed at him. Maybe he was being overly suspicious? Or perhaps he was merely hoping to find something that would impress Klein. He wasn't sure. He just had this gut feeling, which he honestly could not explain, at least not yet, that there was more to Max Roter than he had been led to believe. He readily conceded that it didn't make sense considering what everyone in the town had told him about Max. Still, he wanted to consider this further before he said anything to Klein about it.

Geller spent an hour having dinner at Mrs. Tillsdale's; the roast beef and potatoes were as delicious as she had promised. He had to endure her stories about Vera in the years before it became a bootlegger depot, and he heard more, much more, about the day her husband Cecil lost control of a tractor, crashed into their barn, and ultimately died from his injuries.

Around ten o'clock, after his second serving of blueberry pie, Geller excused himself. It was nearly dark. "Just need to stretch my legs for a few minutes," he said.

"Not one for walking around this late myself. But I guess with you city folk, it's different. Just make certain that you watch out for foxes and coyotes," Mrs. Tillsdale cautioned him. "They like to lurk around the garbage."

He assured her that he would take precautions. It wasn't foxes and coyotes he was concerned about, however, but Sergeant Sundell and his men. Leaving Mrs. Tillsdale's house, Geller checked in every direction to ensure he was not being followed. He quickly reached Main Street, glanced around again, and did not see a soul. He proceeded to Roter's General Store, not certain what he was searching for but hoping that perhaps there was something the police missed.

Reaching the front door, he used the key Jack Smythe had given him to open it. The dwindling light outside coming in the repaired front window was sufficient for him to make his way around the store. He could make out a patch of dry blood on the floor where Roter had been shot. Everything else seemed to be in its place. He sidestepped a barrel filled with straw brooms and some wooden boxes of canned goods.

As he moved towards the rear, the light faded and he gingerly groped his way through the dark. He reached Roter's small office. There was a kerosene lamp hanging nearby. Figuring he was far enough inside that no one would be able to see the light, he lit it. The office was quickly illuminated. There were files and order forms scattered around the desk. A can of tobacco was half-open and beside it was a half-empty bottle of Shea's Irish Whisky. Alec was certain that the bottle was full before Sundell's men started guzzling it. He was about to take a swig, but thought it might be best to leave it alone.

Geller planted himself in Max Roter's office chair. Other than the sound outside of chirping crickets, it was eerily silent. He saw Roter's safe. It was open and empty. There was nothing here, he thought, nothing unusual. And he doubted he'd find anything in the liquor warehouse as well. He wasn't sure why Klein had sent him here.

Pushing the chair back slightly, he saw that the desk had two drawers on its right side. He opened the bottom one. There were black, leather-bound accounts books stacked on their sides, marked for 1920, 1921, and 1922. Geller leafed through one, but all he found were columns and numbers. He placed the ledger back, shut the bottom drawer, and opened the top one. Inside was an assortment of pencils, paperclips, and bottle caps. He was about to shut the drawer when he noticed a small piece of paper jutting out from a back corner. He reached in and immediately felt a small wooden handle. He pulled it and eased it open. Inside the compartment was a small bundle of paper tied together with twine.

His heart raced slightly. Maybe he had indeed found something significant that the police had missed. He pulled the papers out and placed them on the desk when he heard the distinct creak of a floorboard.

He stood up and looked into the store, but the light from the lamp made it difficult to see much. He stepped around the chair and moved forward. At that moment, a figure lunged at him, striking him hard on the head with a wooden club. Before Alec could say another word, his knees buckled and he fell hard to the ground.

7

Klein slept on the parlour chesterfield again Wednesday and Thursday nights and Friday morning he once more opened his eyes to find his three children staring at him. Freda looked more distraught at this situation than she had two mornings ago. But before Klein could offer a word of explanation or reassurance, Sarah appeared and quickly took charge of the situation. She ushered the children into the kitchen for breakfast and then did something quite unexpected: she kissed Klein's cheek.

"Good morning, Shailek. Sleep well?"

Taken aback, Klein did not know what to say.

"Mommy kissed Daddy," shouted Bernice gleefully. Freda smiled and little Mel started running around the house like an excited puppy.

"In the kitchen, now, you three," ordered Sarah. "There's coffee when you want it, Shailek."

Klein feigned a smile. He knew how his wife operated. She was trying to wear him down and win him back. And it was working, though not for the reason she might have imagined. Even with Wednesday's events at the railway station, Klein's guilty conscience in recalling his encounter with Hannah Nash had been on his mind. How could he punish Sarah for committing precisely the same mistake he had? Deep down, he knew that he had to forgive her. The alternative was to break up his marriage and his family over this transgression and that he could not do. He had to find it in his heart to forgive Sarah and move forward.

He shaved and dressed and made his way into the kitchen. Sarah handed him a cup of steaming coffee.

"Thanks," he mumbled, taking a sip. He sat down at the table in the chair beside Freda. His daughter smiled warmly at him.

Sarah smiled too, but said nothing. She knew then that all would soon be well.

Klein lit a cigarette just as the telephone rang, as exciting an event as there was for the children. Only listening to the radio eclipsed the elation of answering the telephone from the children's perspective. And that was recent. Klein had only purchased a crystal radio set and headphones for sixteen dollars a few months earlier after the *Free Press* inaugurated radio broadcasts.

The black rotary candle-stick phone, on the other hand, was more functional. The phone stood on a small half-desk with an attached chair outside the entrance to the kitchen. Beside it was a bound telephone book with local numbers. And above the telephone was a torn piece of paper Sarah had affixed to the wall. It was entitled "Winnipeg Automatic Service at Your Finger

Tips!" and had instructions on "How to Operate the Automatic Telephone." It was a reminder that if the number started with the letter prefix A or N, you could dial the number directly without the assistance of the operator—the city's "Hello Girls." Sarah found the new telephone somewhat challenging but as long as she remembered to pull the dial to the right until her finger struck the finger stop and then release it before she dialed the next number, she was miraculously connected. "What will they think of next?" she usually said.

As Klein walked briskly to answer it, he had to be careful not to step on Bernice and Mel who raced ahead of him.

"My turn," said Bernice.

"I haven't got time for this, Niecee," said Klein.

"My turn," she repeated.

"Okay, okay, quickly, pick up the receiver."

Carefully, Bernice jumped up on the chair and lifted the receiver. She handed it to her father with the same care she had cradled Mel in her arms with a few years earlier.

Klein took it from her and picked up the phone by its long stem. He held the receiver to his left ear and spoke into the mouthpiece.

"Hello … Yes, this is Klein … Detective Allard, what can I do for you?… All right, I will be there within the hour."

Klein replaced the receiver and put the telephone back on the table. He was surprised. He had only met Allard, yet the detective had decided for some reason to keep him informed on developments. In Klein's experience, that was rare for members of the Winnipeg Police Department. He had learned many times in his dealings with McCreary that sharing information was not something the city's cops did willingly—especially with him.

"Anything important?" asked Sarah.

"I have to go down to the police station before the Roter funeral."

"I would like to be there with you and to pay my respects to Lou, at least. And a wife should be with her husband at such a sombre occasion. I'll close the shop and meet you there."

Klein shook his head. The last thing he wanted at the moment was to be at the synagogue when Sarah would likely encounter Saul Sugarman. "It's really not necessary," he said, trying to be as polite as possible. "But thanks for the offer. Can you manage with the kids?"

"I always do," said Sarah, who was also trying hard to be as agreeable as she could. "Shailek…"

Klein interrupted her. "Let's talk later," he said, lightly touching her hand.

"I would like that." She reached for his forehead and gently pushed his hair from his eyes. He took her hand and kissed it. Ten minutes later he was out the door.

As Klein approached the three-storey Central Police Station on Rupert Avenue and Martha Street, he could see that at the main entrance two constables were struggling to control a man wearing a flat, grey cap and a torn jacket. This particular individual was twisting and turning in a futile attempt to free himself from their grip.

"I'm going to tell you one last time, Novak, stop jumping around," said one of the constables.

"I've done nothing. You must let me go," the man pleaded.

"That would be for the judge to decide," the second constable said. "Now, you'll only make this more difficult on yourself."

"What's wrong, I ask you? A man is entitled to make a living."

"Not by being a thief, you shit," said the first constable.

"I do nothing wrong," said Novak. He stopped fast in his tracks, dropped to his knees, and with all the power he could muster, threw both constables forward. They went crashing to the steps and their bobby hats went flying. Novak stood up, turned around, and began running towards where Klein was standing.

"Stop, you Bohunk, so help me…" yelled one of the constables, wildly waving his billy club.

Novak attempted to push Klein aside, but as he did so, Klein moved to his left and stuck out his foot. Novak tripped and went tumbling to the sidewalk. That was all the time both constables needed to recover and grab him. They whacked him several times with their clubs, further incapacitating him.

"Get the hell to the station," one of them ordered.

"Klein, isn't it?" the other constable asked.

"It is, yes…"

"Michaelson … Thanks for your assistance."

"I'm always ready to help the Winnipeg Police Department."

"Interfering again in police business, Klein?" McCreary was standing at the station entrance with a bemused look on his face.

"Sir, Mr. Klein helped stop this man," said Constable Michaelson.

"Well, Michaelson, he wouldn't have to if you and James knew how to handle a suspect," barked McCreary.

"Of course, sir," said Michaelson. "We should've done a better job. Won't happen again, sir." He tipped his helmet to Klein and he and his partner dragged Novak into the station.

"You're being a little hard on them, McCreary," said Klein. "As I recall, you've lost a few suspects in your day."

"You're full of shit, Klein. So what the hell are you doing here? I told you that I'd let you know if I found anything about the shooting."

"And I thought you were running the provincial police. So why are you involved in a city crime?"

McCreary waved the back of his hand at Klein. "If it involves the Sugarmans and booze, it involves me."

"Fair enough."

"You still didn't answer my question."

"What am I doing here?" asked Klein. "I'm here for the same reason you are, to hear what Reverend John Vivian has to say."

"How do you know about him coming in this morning?"

"You're really asking me that?"

A wry smile crossed McCreary's face, though just for a moment. "Newton will never allow you to be in the room."

"Actually, I've cleared it with the chief," said Detective Allard, who appeared behind McCreary. "I invited Mr. Klein. I thought he might be useful in speaking with Reverend Vivian and the chief agreed."

"Is that so?" asked McCreary, narrowing his eyes.

"That's so," said Klein, pushing past him.

"The reverend is in a room on the second floor, Mr. Klein. Follow me," said Allard.

At ten in the morning, the station's second floor was as noisy and bustling as usual. Klein found himself in a cacophony of ringing telephones, clattering typewriter keys, and the general mayhem of a squad room before a weekend. He noticed the suspect Novak, now with a small trickle of blood on his forehead, slumped in a chair in the corner. He was handcuffed to a steel pole and still yelling that he had done nothing wrong.

Klein doubted that very much. He had seen too many like him: newcomers just off the boat and looking for any way to make money quickly. Perhaps he was merely hungry and desperate? He certainly wasn't the first immigrant to resort to stealing to sustain himself.

At the back of the squad room, Allard was standing by a door leading into an interrogation area. The detective made eye contact with Klein, beckoning him. Beside Allard, Klein could see two more cops: McCreary, who had a scowling look on his face, and Edward "Big Ed" Franks, the morality inspector. Franks, as his nickname implied, was a broad-shouldered and robust man. Everything about him was "big": his hands, feet, ears. The little hair he had left on his head and his full, round face made him seem even more imposing. He was one of the first detectives Klein had met when he was working as a minder and bouncer at Melinda's. And he knew from his past dealings with him that he was as solid as a brick wall and a cop not to be taken lightly.

As Klein reached the trio, only Allard offered a friendly nod. "As I told you, Klein, I'm happy to have you sit in on our meeting with Vivian. And it's only a meeting for now. He hasn't been arrested. But I'd appreciate it if you would stay quiet. We can talk privately when the questioning is over. Agreed?" said the detective.

"Agreed," said Klein.

"Ha. Sam Klein keeping his mouth shut," snorted McCreary. "That'll be a first."

Klein ignored the jibe. "Inspector Franks," he said, extending his hand. "Always a pleasure to see you."

"I doubt that," said Franks, firmly shaking Klein's hand but only for a moment. "You're still the snot-nosed punk who got in my way at Melinda's. I don't care how famous you've become. You and your kind are the reason I have to do what I do: uplift the morality in this community."

"My kind?" said Klein. His voice dripped with sarcasm, though he knew what Franks was implying.

"Yeah, your kind. From what I hear, you still associate with that troublemaking whore, Melinda. For more than ten years, she's done nothing but pull this city down into the depths of depravity. And then there are the Sugarmans, flouting the law and distributing booze far and wide. Whatever happens to the Sugarmans, it's their own damn fault."

"Even more so I imagine because they're Jews like me. Isn't that what you mean, Inspector?"

"You said it, Klein, I didn't. But if the shoe fits…"

"Gentlemen, please," implored Allard. "Inspector, I realize anything to do with the liquor trade is your jurisdiction. And Klein, I asked you here and Chief Newton agreed to my request because we both felt you might have some insight into this case. But let's keep this dignified, please."

"Fine by me," said Klein.

Franks nodded. "Let's get this over with. I got work to do."

McCreary chuckled. "Everywhere you go Klein, you're trouble."

Klein was about to reply to that taunt, but stopped himself. Allard opened the door of the interrogation room and entered. Klein followed him in as did McCreary and Franks.

Seated at a chair, straight and erect, at the table in the middle of the room was Reverend John Vivian. Sizing him up, Klein figured that in any boxing match he would be a difficult opponent even for someone as tough as Franks.

There were three wooden chairs on the opposite side of the table. Allard immediately sat down in the middle one and McCreary and Franks in the other two. Klein stood back against the wall. He stared at Vivian's face and as he did so, his eyes momentarily locked with those of the reverend. Try as he might, Vivian could not disguise his moral superiority or disgust for everyone else in the room. A chill went down Klein's spine.

"Reverend, I want to thank you for voluntarily coming to the station to answer our questions," said Allard.

"I didn't really have a choice, did I? I know Detective McCreary and Franks, of course. Detective Franks and I have much in common in fighting the devil that will bring ruination to this city. 'Uplift' is your motto, sir, is it not?" asked Vivian, looking directly at Franks. "Do you and the members of your morality division not keep watch on persons of good character and admonish them if you believe they have strayed off the path of righteousness? You do everything possible for them so that they will continue to be useful members of society?"

Franks nodded. "That's so, Reverend, yes. But, of course, I do my work as the law permits. I don't arm a gang of vigilantes with clubs and decide when and how justice should be meted out."

"'And the disciples, everyone as he was able, made a decision to send help to the brothers living in Judaea.' Acts, chapter eleven, verse nine. In short, each of us must do what he can, in the way that is open to him."

"Does that include sending someone to shoot at the Sugarman family at the CPR station?" Allard asked, leaning across the table.

"Before I answer that question, I have one for you," said Vivian, gesturing with his right hand. "What is Mr. Klein doing here? Is he now a member of the Winnipeg Police Department?"

That comment brought a slight smile to Klein's face.

"He's not," scoffed McCreary.

"He's here at my request," explained Allard.

Vivian was silent for a moment. He stared at Klein and then at Allard. "I see," he finally said. "Fine, then. Have it your way. I've nothing to hide. What would you like to know?"

"Where were you Wednesday afternoon?" Allard asked.

"Working at my office on Sherbrooke. I am leading a parade

down Main Street in three days to protest the liquor and brothel trades. For too many years, this city has been as close to Sodom and Gomorrah as is possible. Public drunkenness is an abomination and fornication in the name of greed is rampant. Families have been ruined. It must stop."

McCreary rolled his eyes, but said nothing.

"So you didn't send one of your men with a shotgun to the railway station?" asked Allard.

"I most certainly did not. However…"

"However … what, Reverend?" said McCreary sharply.

"If I may continue, Detective, without being so rudely interrupted?"

"Continue, please," said Allard, glancing at McCreary.

"I was going to add that if some calamity has befallen one of the Sugarman brothers, then it is God's will."

"It's God's will for young children to be shot at?" said Klein. "Is that what you think?"

"Klein, please," said Allard. "We had an agreement."

Vivian waved his hand. "No, no harm done, Detective. I'm happy to address Mr. Klein's question. Of course, I would never condone violence against children. As I said, I had nothing to do with what took place. But the liquor trade is evil and so are its practitioners. If anything terrible happens to anyone, even a child associated with the Sugarmans, then those two bear the full responsibility for that calamity."

Allard held up a piece of paper that was sitting on the desk. "You did call them 'the devil's sinners who were destined for Hell.' It's right here from a newspaper article."

"That's accurate and I stand by those words."

"So perhaps you tried to make this happen?" asked McCreary.

"Gentleman, I have answered all of your questions," said Vivian, rising from his chair. "I have absolutely no knowledge of the shooting at the CPR station. Am I free to go? Or do I need to summon my lawyer?"

Allard looked at McCreary and Franks. "Any other questions for the reverend?" Both detectives shook their heads. Allard turned to Vivian. "Very well, Reverend. I would ask you to remain in the city in case we have to speak to you again."

Franks stood up to face Vivian. "Though I support your intentions, Reverend, I am concerned about your methods. You're free to hold your parade on Monday, but tell your men to leave their clubs and shotguns at home."

"There will be no trouble from us," said Vivian. "I will guarantee it."

"I've heard that before," mumbled Klein.

Vivian left the room and Allard shut the door.

"What do you think?"

"He knows something," Klein said. "He's not told everything."

"As much as I hate to admit this, I have to agree with Klein," said McCreary. "He's hiding something."

Allard turned to Franks.

"As I said, the reverend's intentions are sincere," said Franks. "He truly does want to uplift this city. But he's a zealot and in my experience, zealots can be dangerous, very dangerous."

A knock at the door interrupted the conversation. "Ah, yes,

that must be my guest." Allard stepped to the door and opened it. Klein's eyes widened and his face flushed.

Standing in the entrance was policewoman Hannah Nash.

8

Alec Geller felt like he had been kicked in the head by a horse. He was in pain; there was no mistake about it. His eyelids flickered before he gradually opened them, yet everything was blurry. All he could make out was the outline of a face, an elderly woman's face. She was smiling at him.

"Where am I?" he whispered.

"Easy, Alec. Try not to move. You'll be okay. The doctor has checked you and you'll recover," said Grace Tillsdale. She gently squeezed Alec's left hand.

Behind Mrs. Tillsdale, Geller could now see two men. The first he did not know. The second man he recognized immediately as Sergeant Duncan Sundell of the provincial police. His face was firm, tight, and tense. Geller looked back at the woman. "Mrs. Tillsdale, right?"

"Yes. You have had … an accident. You're in my home now and safe."

"Geller, I'm Doctor Lewis," said the first man. He was bald

with a thin beard and was wearing a brown suit. A stethoscope hung around his neck. "You've been hit very hard on the head. Frankly, had Sergeant Sundell not found you as quickly as he did, you might've succumbed to your injuries."

"Died?" exclaimed Geller.

"That's right, son. Now, you need to rest for a few days at least."

"Thanks, Doc. But I have to get back to the city."

"I wouldn't advise that for at least seventy-two hours. By then, I think you'll be strong enough to travel. But you should see your own doctor in Winnipeg as soon as you return. Do you understand?"

Geller shook his head. "Three days. It's a long time to do nothing."

"I'll keep you company, Alec," said Mrs. Tillsdale. "And you won't believe some of the comings and goings in this town."

"Good, so that's settled," said Dr. Lewis, packing his bag. "Now I have to leave you. Rebecca Johnson is about to go into labour and it's a twenty minute auto ride to her farm. I've left Mrs. Tillsdale with everything she needs to nurse you back to health. Take a Bayer tablet of Aspirin twice a day and drink half a teaspoonful of sal volatile in water and you should feel much better. And if those fail, then try this," he said, pulling a bottle out of his black kit. "Hean's Tonic Nerve Nuts. These will enrich and purify your blood and nourish your nervous system. A shot of whisky once or twice a day also gets the blood flowing again. And, of course, rest. My fee is five dollars, which you can leave with Mrs. Tillsdale."

"I'd like to speak with Mr. Geller alone," said Sundell once Dr. Lewis had departed.

"Of course," said Mrs. Tillsdale. "But be kind, Sergeant. Alec has been through a lot."

Sundell forced a smile. "I wouldn't think of upsetting dear Alec."

As soon as Mrs. Tillsdale left the bedroom, Sundell shut the door. He sat down at the chair close to Geller. "Didn't I tell you to stay away from Roter's store?" As Sundell spoke, he tightened his fists.

"The store, yes," said Geller, his voice rising. "I remember now."

"What do you remember? Tell me exactly."

"Very well. I obtained the keys to the store and warehouse from Mr. Smythe."

"Yes, I know that already. I've discussed this with Mr. Smythe. He says that he was just carrying out the wishes of Mrs. Roter. But go on."

"It was dark by the time I arrived there. I let myself in and looked around the store. Then…"

"Then, what? What happened?"

Geller paused for a moment. He remembered quite clearly what occurred next. That before he was attacked, he was in Roter's back office and that he had found a bundle of papers. Klein had taught him that it was usually best to keep certain facts to yourself until you could figure out what they meant. Sharing information with the police, therefore, had to be considered carefully. Wiser, he thought, to not say anything about the papers just yet.

"I walked to the back of the store and then I must have been hit on the head," said Alec.

"That's it?" asked Sundell. "That's all you recall?"

"Yes. I'm afraid so."

Sundell's eyes narrowed and he leaned even closer to Geller. "Think about this, please. When you were in the store, did you hear the sound of a car engine—one that was powerful?"

"It's all kind of hazy. But I don't think so. Why?"

"Someone else mentioned it to us. I believe that this American bootlegger named Taylor may have returned last night. And he might have been the one who nearly killed you. He was the last known person to see Max Roter alive. That much I'm certain of."

"Why would he attack me?"

"Why indeed, Mr. Geller. That's the question, isn't it? And be assured, I will find out the answer one way or the other."

"I have some tea for you, Alec," said Mrs. Tillsdale, knocking on the bedroom door.

"I'd love some," said Geller, beckoning her to come in. "And I'd love to hear some of those stories about the town you promised to tell me."

Sundell abruptly stood up. "Tea and stories," he mumbled. "You'd better watch yourself, kid." He tipped his hat to Mrs. Tillsdale and marched out of the bedroom.

"Mrs. Nash, I'm so glad you've arrived," said Detective Allard. "You know, Detective, I mean, Commissioner McCreary…"

"Interim Commissioner," McCreary barked. "But it's good to see you again, Mrs. Nash."

Hannah smiled. "From you, I will take that as a very big compliment."

"It was actually McCreary who recommended I contact you," said Allard.

"Is that so?" said Nash.

"As much as I hate to admit this Nash, no one knows as much about the bootlegging business as you do," said McCreary.

Nash mockingly touched her heart. "Commissioner McCreary, I'm touched. You've changed for the better."

"And this is Detective Edward Franks, the department's efficient morality inspector. And I don't know if you are acquainted with Sam…"

"Yes, we know each other," said Nash. Her face was as flushed as Klein's. "In fact, we worked together a few years ago during the Strike. That nasty business with Metro Lizowski … Sam, how are you?"

Klein was rarely speechless, but he was truly stunned to see Hannah. His heart was pounding and his palms were sweaty. Images of that evening three years ago when they kissed bombarded his head. She looked better, if that was possible. Her brown, curly hair that she had worn short was now somewhat longer. Her eyes were still dark and large, but her slender figure was more inviting than he recalled. In his view, she had not aged a day in three years.

"I'm good," he finally stammered. "It's a pleasant surprise to see you again."

A hint of a smile crossed her face and her eyes widened. Klein then smiled as well.

Without being too obvious, she glimpsed at his face. He was still as captivating to her as he ever was. He was lean and fit and it immediately struck her that he exuded an even more seasoned demeanour than he had when she first met him.

"If the introductions are now out of the way, maybe we can get down to business," said McCreary. "Allard, I haven't all day here."

"No, of course not. My apologies. Mrs. Nash, please have a seat for a moment."

Nash sat down in the chair that had been occupied by Reverend Vivian and joined Allard, McCreary, and Franks at the table. Klein again stood with his back against the wall. He watched Hannah intently—the way she pushed a strand of hair away from her face, her delicate cheekbones, and, above all, her moist and full lips.

"Gentlemen, owing to an agreement with the Calgary Police Department, where, as you know, I've been a detective since I moved to Calgary in 1919, I've been with the Alberta Provincial Police for about a year now. My assignment was to work with the APP to stop as much as possible the shipment of Canadian liquor across the border to the US."

McCreary snorted. "Not bloody likely."

"I agree. So far we've failed. Mostly, it's the fault of the Americans. They put prohibition into effect but have refused to spend much money to police it. As you well know, along the border, especially in the more isolated towns here and in Saskatchewan and Alberta, it's a return to the Wild West. And I don't say that lightly. Rum-running on the Great Lakes has also been a terrible problem, though that, thankfully, is someone else's headache. I can tell you that the federal government is screaming about this, not so much because of the booze traffic, but because the rum-runners are returning to Canada with cheap American clothing and tobacco and literally millions of dollars in custom duties are not being paid to the treasury. From what I understand, corruption in the Customs Department is rampant. There's a rumour that the Chief Preventive Officer in Quebec has a house in Vermont and a bank account with two million in it. Not bad for a guy making less than fifteen hundred a year. But as I said, this is not my or your immediate concern. What is, however, is that in the past fourteen months in prairie towns close to the border, there's been a spate of robberies and four murders, five now with the one in Vera last week."

"Any pattern in these crimes that you can share with us?" asked Allard.

Nash nodded. "Yes. At least five of the robberies involved American bootleggers, usually rival ones, robbing the Canadian liquor salesmen of money paid to them by other bootleggers. And that's also the case in three of the other murders. One in Carway has not been solved yet, but I'm quite sure there's a bootlegger in Babb, Montana who's involved. We're working with US Federal Prohibition Agents on this case and I'm confident the culprit will be apprehended shortly. However, it's clear to me that Canadian liquor sellers have been caught up in a bloody gangster war. And it will only get worse. What can you tell me about the robbery and murder in Vera?"

"McCreary, you want to answer that?" asked Allard.

"Sounds possible," said McCreary. "This morning I received a telegram from an MPP sergeant in charge of the investigation. He believes that a bootlegger named Frankie Taylor was most likely involved. Though in this case, it wasn't a rival thug. The view is that Taylor simply was greedy. He wanted his booze for free so he came back for his money and took it, killing the storekeeper. Here's a mug shot of him we got from the police in Minneapolis, when he was arrested for getting into a fight at a saloon some years back."

McCreary passed around a sheet. In the black and white photograph, Taylor was wearing a light-coloured suit with a vest and wool knit tie. His dark hair was slicked back, though it still stood up slightly at the front. But it was the gaze in his eye—angry and hostile—that everyone looking at the photo immediately noticed.

"Looks like a real charmer," said Allard.

Nash glanced at it for a moment and then passed it to Klein. "What's your interest in this, Sam … Mr. Klein?" asked Hannah, rubbing her hands together.

Klein looked at the mug shot, handed it back to McCreary, and cleared his throat. There was a tiny bead of sweat on his forehead. Despite his best efforts to remain calm and collected as he always tried to be when he was around the police, Hannah's presence definitely unnerved him. "I've been retained by the storekeeper's family to investigate. The family, I suppose, doesn't quite trust McCreary and his men to figure this out."

"That's bullshit, Klein, and you know it," retorted McCreary.

"McCreary, your language, please. There's a lady present," admonished Franks.

"That's fine," said Nash, smiling. "I'm quite used to Commissioner McCreary's colourful language."

"The fact is, Klein," Franks continued, "the storekeeper was married to the Sugarmans' sister and was doing their bidding in this filthy bootleg business. They have made thousands of dollars off this trade, and probably a lot more. You may be a skilful private detective, Klein, but I am in agreement with McCreary on this. Your clients are the real troublemakers and Max Roter was fully responsible for what happened to him. Why is it, by the way, that you people are mixed up in this? The only answer is money."

"That's quite enough," said Allard. "With all due respect, Detective Franks, there are many liquor traders who are not Hebrews. Is that not correct, Mrs. Nash?"

"That's true. I wouldn't go on blaming Jewish people alone for supplying bootleg liquor. I can tell you that there are Brits, Scots, and Irish men involved as well."

"So what would you suggest, Mrs. Nash?" Allard asked.

"Yeah, I'm all ears," said McCreary. As much as he accepted Nash's expertise in the liquor trade, permitting a woman, even a smart policewoman, to dictate strategy was difficult for McCreary to swallow.

Nash, who was used to dealing with obstinate men, paid no

attention to McCreary's remark. "If Mr. Klein can arrange it," she said, glancing at Sam, "I'd like to speak to one or both of the Sugarmans. They may know more than they think about the Vera murder."

"Klein, can you arrange such a meeting?" asked Allard.

"If you can wait a few days until the shiva ... the time of mourning is nearly done, I believe. I can bring in Lou Sugarman. His brother Saul, I don't know about. He and I are not on the best of terms."

"Figures," said McCreary. "How many enemies do you have in this city?"

"A few, but I'd wager your list is longer than mine," said Klein.

"Good, then we are settled. I will continue to investigate the shooting at the CPR station and keep an eye on Reverend Vivian. I presume, McCreary, you want to work on the Roter murder, so Mrs. Nash can assist you with that," Allard suggested.

"Glorious," said McCreary.

"That's a good idea. I plan to be in the city for about a week," said Nash. "And what of Mr. Klein?"

"Since Mr. Klein is not a member of this department, he's free to serve the interests of his clients as he sees fit," said Allard.

"That suits me fine," said Klein. "Not that I wouldn't have done that under any circumstances."

"Then it's settled. Does anyone have anything else to add before we adjourn this meeting?" Allard asked.

"As a matter of fact, I do," said McCreary. "Klein, this news is for you." He held up a telegram. "I suppose I should have told you this earlier. Sundell also reported to me regarding an incident last night in Vera. That kid who works with you…"

Klein's body stiffened. "Alec Geller, what of it? Did something happen to him?"

"He'll survive. But he was roughed up a bit last night. Got hit hard over the head. He's resting now. Sundell reports that the kid was found in the store where he was warned not to go."

"I'd better phone him at the rooming house," said Klein. "Does your man have any idea who attacked him?"

"Not certain yet, but it's possible this bootlegger, Taylor, our suspect for the Roter murder, might have been in Vera last night. I don't have all the facts yet."

Klein said nothing more. He walked briskly out of the interrogation room and through the squad room. He was at the top of the stairs when Hannah grabbed him by the arm.

"Sam, wait, please. I wanted to speak with you privately for a moment."

"I'm sorry, Hannah. I didn't mean to rush out. It's just that I'm responsible for that kid they mentioned and I want to ensure that he's all right. Probably foolish of me to have sent him to Vera alone."

"I understand. The bootleg business can be dangerous… It's good to see you again, Sam. You look well." Her face reddened slightly.

"And you. I'd be lying if I said I haven't thought about you many times," he said, lightly wiping another bead of sweat off his forehead.

"And I you, too," Nash said with a smile. She gently touched Klein's hand. "How are your children? You have three now?"

"They're a handful, that's for sure."

"And Sarah?" she asked gingerly.

Klein immediately took a step back. The last thing he wanted to do was discuss his recent troubles with Sarah with Hannah Nash. "She's fine. Busy with her store and the kids," he said in a matter-of-fact manner.

There was a momentary awkward silence. Nash could sense his discomfort. "Perhaps, before I leave the city again, we can have that coffee I think you promised me once."

Klein nodded and took a short breath. "I think that would be possible. Hannah, let me ask you, do you really believe that this bootlegger Taylor robbed and killed Max Roter?"

"I've only read the report, of course. But it does seem likely, yes. Why, you don't think so?"

"You remember Alfred Powers, don't you?" asked Klein, leaning up against the railing.

"Of course, I was sorry to read in the newspaper about his passing."

"He was a wise man. He taught me about Ockham's razor. You know what that is?" he asked, raising his eyebrows.

Nash shook her head. Her heart was pounding faster now. This was the side of Klein's personality she liked most: his passion, drive, and curiousity.

"Let me tell you, then. William of Ockham was an English philosopher who lived in the fourteenth century. As Alfred explained it, Ockham believed in simplicity. And that the simplest theory almost always makes more sense than the one that's complicated."

Nash settled herself. "I'd agree with that," she said, as if she was speaking to a fellow officer. "I can think of many cases I've worked on when the simplest explanation proved to be the correct one in solving a crime. Find a murdered woman and the odds are her husband or someone she knew killed her."

"Exactly," said Klein.

"So what's troubling you then, Sam?" she asked more cautiously.

"How do you know something is troubling me?" His body tensed up again.

Nash shrugged. "Just a guess. You don't think that this bootlegger is the one who killed Mr. Roter?"

"I suppose I don't."

"It's the simplest explanation."

"I know that, but there's something else going on here. Maybe it's connected to the shooting at the station. I'm not saying Taylor's not involved, but my gut tells me there's more to this. Ockham's razor just might not be the answer this time."

Klein was about to leave the station, when he heard someone calling his name. He turned around and saw McCreary standing in a secluded area of the hallway.

"What do you want?"

"I want to speak to you, Klein."

"Haven't we talked enough today?"

McCreary beckoned him to come closer. "There's one more thing."

Saul Sugarman touched the spot on his face where Sarah Klein had slapped him. The pain had vanished quickly, but his anger had not. No one, certainly not a woman with her past, he thought, treats a Sugarman like that—and in public. It was only his good fortune that no passers-by had seen the incident and told the newspapers. With yet another story in the morning paper about Max's murder being linked to bootleggers and the family's lucrative liquor business, he hardly needed a negative article about his personal life. But he also knew that this matter between him and Sarah was not finished. He wasn't about to let her have the last word.

"Mr. Sugarman, a telephone call for you," said Shayna Kravetz. "I know you're getting ready for the funeral. Should I take a message?"

Max's funeral. Sugarman detested attending synagogue at the best of times. At the moment, he had many more important things to do than listen to a rabbi go on about Max's so-called virtues. But for the sake of family peace, for Lou and Rae, he also knew he had no choice: he had to be at the Shaarey Zedek at two o'clock.

"Who's calling?" asked Sugarman.

"The operator says it's long distance from Mr. Sharp."

"Put the call through to my office and shut the door."

Sugarman picked up the telephone on his desk and unhooked the receiver. "Sharp, is that you?"

"Yes, it's me," said Sid Sharp, his voice soft and crackling.

"Well I can barely hear you so speak louder." At the best of times, telephone calls from outside the city limits were tricky.

And even if you could hear, the odds were the operator was listening in on the conversation. So Sugarman was well aware that discretion was required.

"My apologies," said Sharp, speaking louder. "There's been a development here."

"I already know about it, Sharp. What the hell happened? I was clear in my orders."

"It wasn't me, Saul. I had nothing to do with it."

"So what happened?"

"I kept an eye on him and Smythe gave him the keys and told him to go to the store in the evening like we told him to."

"But you weren't there to manage this problem? Why the hell not?"

The line was silent.

"I got distracted."

"You got distracted?" repeated Sugarman. "What does that mean? What were you doing?"

"I made a mistake. I wasn't watching the time and I was … let's say I was meeting with someone else."

"For God's sake, I pay you good money." Sugarman knew exactly what Sharp meant. The fool had found a woman in Vera. "So who were you 'meeting' with when you should've been watching him?"

"Can't say right now."

"You can't say… What about this Taylor? I've been told that he might have attacked the kid."

"I've heard that as well. To be honest, I'm not certain. Do you want me to stay here for a few more days?"

Sugarman thought about it for a few moments. "Do you think you can do your job there and not get distracted again?"

"I'm sure I can, Saul. It won't happen again. I'll give you a report in a day or two."

"Very well. But don't disappoint me, Sid, or you'll live to regret it. I have too much invested in this for you or anyone else to mess it up," said Sugarman, ending the call.

He should've known better than to send Sharp to Vera. Sid could never keep his dick in his pants and for some reason, which Sugarman could never fathom, women, especially married women, found Sharp's rough and swarthy demeanour appealing. He would give Sid another chance to figure out what happened to Geller, while he worried about the latest events in Winnipeg. Quite possibly the shooting at the CPR station was not perpetrated by that moralizing pain-in-the-ass Reverend John Vivian, as McCreary believed. The reverend may have had nothing to do with it. Saul decided to send a coded telegram to New York and await further instructions.

9

The Shaarey Zedek Synagogue on Dagmar Street stood proudly across from the magnificent Romanesque Carnegie Library. Both buildings had been erected before the Great War. While the synagogue was not as stately as the library, Klein always felt that the four columns guarding the synagogue's entrance emanated the power of the Almighty. Sarah laughed at him when he pointed this out, but that's what he sensed—and as just about everyone in the community knew, Sam Klein was by no means religious. If he attended Shabbat services five times a year, it was a lot. Nevertheless, he found the synagogue spiritual and haunting.

Wearing his finest black suit, a gift from Sarah on his thirty-ninth birthday last year—he later learned that she had spent nearly thirty dollars, a small fortune, at Ralph's on Main near Logan Avenue for the hand-tailored worsted suit—Klein stood on the walkway in front of the synagogue. Methodically, he scrutinized the faces and mannerisms of each person arriving for Max Roter's funeral, looking for anything out of the ordinary. But he was having trouble concentrating.

Life, he understood, took many twists and turns. The very same morning when he decided that reconciling with Sarah was paramount, Hannah Nash walks back into his life. It was like holding one ace in draw poker and drawing three more—twice in a row. It never happened. And while meeting Hannah again took him back to that night in 1919 when they had kissed, he also knew that it could never happen again. He might not have wanted to admit how hypocritical he had been earlier when he was angry with Sarah for her encounter with Saul Sugarman, but now there could be no more excuses.

In any case, he had come to pay his respects to Max and to ensure that his family as well as Lou, with Rivka by his side, remained safe. As everyone began to enter the synagogue, he noticed an attractive, red-headed woman walk up to Rae Roter and embrace her.

"Joannie, it's so nice of you to make the trip to the city for this. You're a good friend," said Rae, hugging the woman.

Someone from Vera, thought Klein. It might be worth his time to seek her out.

He was momentarily distracted by the sound of a vehicle pulling up on Dagmar. Looking behind him, he saw the cream-coloured Rolls-Royce and his body immediately tensed up. Saul Sugarman strode towards the members of his family as if he was King of England. He said nothing to Klein but stared at him with disdain in his eyes. Klein could barely contain his own resentment. He knew that such hostility was wasted and that his anger was only making him miserable. And to make the situation odder still, the target of his wrath was the person who was technically employing him at the moment. Nevertheless, if he could have wringed Sugarman's neck, he probably would have.

He wished Geller was with him. He could have used a second set of eyes and the kid always lifted his spirits. But he had spoken to Alec and he seemed to be recovering, which was great news. Geller had told Klein about the bundle of papers he had found before he was knocked out—despite the fact that the telephone operator may have been listening in on their call. It was unfortunate that Alec had not had a chance to examine the documents, Klein thought later. According to what Geller had told him, the attacker had taken the papers. Alec had smartly not said anything about them to the police, which in Klein's view was to their advantage. Clearly, whatever the papers contained, someone did not want Geller reading them. Whether they also had relevant information pertaining to Max's murder remained to be seen. As much as Klein did not relish the idea, a trip to Vera might be necessary in the near future. That red-head might be helpful in this regard.

Klein stood outside waiting for the last few stragglers to enter the synagogue and then he followed them in. The closed wooden casket sat on a black metal stand in the synagogue's small lobby. Two thick, white candles flickered on a table beside it. Tiny gobs of wax from the dwindling, dripping candles gradually hardened on its surface.

In the silence, Klein took a black silk *kipah* from a basket on a nearby shelf and stood for a minute contemplating the thin line between life and death. Max Roter had a loving wife and family and now he was gone. His involvement in the liquor trade had undoubtedly killed him, though a full accounting of that fateful night still had to be determined. Klein, however, couldn't decide whether his hostile feelings towards Saul Sugarman were impairing his detective instincts. If Frankie Taylor was indeed guilty of the crime as the police suspected, then Ockham's razor was applicable once again and there was nothing more to it. So why, Klein wondered, did he have a gnawing feeling that this case wasn't that straightforward?

Entering the sanctuary, Klein found a seat in a pew near the back and sat among the men. Like other Winnipeg synagogues, male congregants sat together on the main floor and the women were seated in the balcony on the second floor. The separation, so Klein had been taught many years ago as a student at after-school *cheder* lessons, dated back to biblical times and was essential so that true prayer could take place without distraction. In any event, this was the way it had always been, despite occasional protests from more progressive Jews who argued that men and women should be allowed to sit together. This, naturally enough, included his sister Rivka, whose voice had to be heard on every issue, big and small.

Klein acknowledged several of the men he knew, who shook his hand or nodded at him, and waited in the uncomfortable silence for the funeral service to begin.

Across the street, George Dickens, carrying a long canvas sack, stopped to admire the arched entranceway to the Carnegie

Library. Looking upward, he could see a carved pediment incorporating the crest of Manitoba with the distinctive Red Cross of St. George on a white background and below it, a graceful bison, which once roamed the Great Plains in great numbers. Above the archway, flanked on both sides by stone cartouches, were the etched words, "History & Literature" and "Arts & Science."

Dickens entered the grey limestone building and climbed the marble staircase into the library's main hall. He stopped and got his bearings. At the reference desk speaking to a female librarian he noticed Mary Turner, a busybody who lived with her husband Harold down the street from him and Maggie on Furby. His body immediately tensed up. He had no desire to speak with her, certainly not at that moment. He anticipated that there would be a polite exchange of greetings, followed by questions that he would not and could not answer. She waved at him and started moving in his direction. But he pretended he did not see her. It was rude, he knew, though necessary. He doubted he fooled her. Nevertheless, perhaps sensing his uneasiness, she stopped, pursed her lips, fixed her hat, and walked instead into the ladies' reading room, not looking at him again. A few seconds later, she disappeared from sight. His shoulders slouched again. He headed in the opposite direction to the large men's reading room, where he was certain that Mary Turner or anyone else would not bother him.

With his sack securely by his feet, Dickens sat down in a comfortable chair. From a tall stand, he removed a wide newspaper fastened to a decorative wooden stick. He scanned the library's latest copy of the *Illustrated London News*, dated May 30, 1922.

On the third page was a sketch of the recent trial at Old
Bailey of disgraced newspaper magnate and financier Hora-
tio Bottomley. Four months earlier, as Dickens read, Bottomley, who was also a Member of Parliament, had been charged
with twenty-four counts of fraud for the misappropriation of
an alleged £170,000 from his Victory Bonds Club. According to
the accompanying article, Bottomley had used club members'
financial contributions, funds which were supposed to be used
to purchase government bonds, to finance his own business
interests and lavish lifestyle. Predictably, Bottomley had denied
the charges, yet the jury had taken only twenty-eight minutes to
find him guilty on all but one of the charges. On May 29, he had
been sentenced to seven years of penal servitude.

Dickens was hardly surprised. Bottomley had a well-known
fondness for expensive champagne. It was the evils of drink
that really did him in, thought Dickens. Closing the newspaper,
Dickens took out his pocket watch and checked the time. Fifteen minutes later, he did it again. Fifteen minutes after that, he
popped up, checked to see that no one in the library was watching him, and headed back to the main staircase and up to the
second floor.

Out on Dagmar, a black McLaughlin Buick pulled up in front
of the Shaarey Zedek and parked behind Saul Sugarman's Rolls-
Royce. At the steering wheel and wearing his white fedora was
the tall man who had arrived on the train from Minneapolis.
And beside him in the passenger seat, also wearing a fedora

and a shoulder holster with a pistol, was the man with the black eyepatch.

"You sure that piece is necessary?" asked the taller man, Paul Backhouse, otherwise known as "Paulie the Plumber."

"Just takin' precautions," replied Richard Tazman, who was known far and wide as "One-eye Richie."

"The boss…"

Richie cut Paulie off. "I know what the boss said, but the other day we nearly bought it. I don't intend for that to happen again. You know I always follow orders, but this job is kind of nuts."

"Well, we do what he says. As long as the boss keeps paying me, I'll do whatever he tells me to."

Richie nodded. "I say that as soon as we see what they're up to today, we drive over to Rachel Street. There's a place run by a Madam Melinda that's supposed to have the most beautiful whores in this city."

Paulie laughed. "This is Winnipeg, for fuck sakes, Richie. You think you're going to find some baby vamps here like back in the City?"

"Maybe not, but it'll still while away the evening."

The mood in the synagogue was sombre. "We are here to remember the soul of Max Roter," declared Rabbi Herbert Samuel in his thick Oxford accent. He stood on the *bimah* or dais in the middle front section of the sanctuary. Close by, on the synagogue's eastern wall, stood the ark where the Torah scrolls were kept. Above the ark was a large white rendering of the Ten Commandments with black Hebrew lettering.

Samuel, who came from a long line of distinguished British rabbis, often spoke fervently about a Jewish homeland in Palestine, and was committed to introducing as many progressive rituals as his opinionated congregation would tolerate. He had been the synagogue's rabbi since 1914. Like usual, he was wearing a turned collar similar to the type worn by Anglican priests. He also sported a fashionable van dyke beard, which made him look a lot like Theodore Herzl, one of the founders of modern Zionism.

"Max was the loving husband of ten years to Rae and the beloved father of Mira and Isaac, a brother-in-law to Saul and Lou Sugarman, and a friend to many. In the town of Vera, no one was more respected and admired." Sitting in the front row of the balcony, Rae Roter let out a painful cry, as Rivka and Joannie Smythe comforted her.

"He has been taken from us far too young," continued the rabbi. "Max was a decent and hard-working man who was led astray." Saul Sugarman, who was barely paying attention to the eulogy, immediately raised his head, as a murmur of restrained voices echoed through the synagogue. "Had Max been content to operate his general store, things might have turned out differently for him," said Rabbi Samuel.

Now everyone in the sanctuary was hanging on his every word. Klein noticed Saul gesturing to Lou and neither brother looked especially pleased with the tone of the rabbi's remarks. "Instead, Max was led astray by the promises of riches that could be found in a bottle of whisky. And the consequences have been tragic."

Sitting in the front pew, Lou Sugarman stood up. "Rabbi, please, that's quite enough. You are upsetting my sister and her family and me as well." No one in the synagogue said a word. Saul Sugarman also had had enough of the rabbi's insults. Clenching his fists and clearly ready to explode with rage, he rose, stared at the rabbi, and marched out of the sanctuary. Only the sound of Rae's sobbing broke the uncomfortable silence.

Klein was stunned as well. He had attended many funerals and synagogue services and heard an array of eulogies and sermons, but he had never heard anything so pointed as the comments delivered by Rabbi Samuel.

Sensing the unease in the synagogue, the rabbi quickly finished the service with a chanting of "*El malei rachamim,*" the prayer for Max's soul. That seemed to bring everyone, except possibly Lou Sugarman, back to the reality of the moment. This was followed with everyone reciting the mourner's *Kaddish*, the prayer sanctifying God's name. Once that was completed, the pall bearers, Lou among them, left the synagogue first, stopping by Max's casket. Everyone else in the sanctuary, men and women, followed. The rabbi requested for two lines to be formed that extended out the front doors of the synagogue and the six pall bearers lifted the casket and carried it outside to the waiting hearse, a Reo Funeral Coach, which Lou had arranged for. Max's casket was to be taken to the Shaarey Zedek Cemetery, down Main Street, located in rural Kildonan, a mile past the city limits. Rae Roter and her children got into the Model-T directly behind the funeral coach. Both cars started moving towards William Avenue.

"Lou, what the hell was that?" shouted Saul Sugarman, as he stepped towards his brother. "How dare Rabbi Samuel be so disrespectful?"

"I know, Saul. I'm angry too, but not here. Think about Rae."

"I'm going to have him fired. Do you know how much money we've given to this synagogue?"

Hearing the commotion, Rivka approached them. "Lou, Saul, please, not here. Rae's car has already left. We have to get to the cemetery. Your sister…"

"Don't tell me what to do," said Saul, inching closer to Rivka. "Not ever."

"Or what, Sugarman? What will you do?" said Klein. He touched Rivka on the shoulder and gently moved her to his left.

"It's fine, Shailek. No trouble, not here," Rivka pleaded.

"Leave it, Sam. Let me handle this, please," said Lou.

How Klein wanted to pop his fist into Saul's face. Yet, he knew that all he would accomplish would be humiliating himself and Rivka. Keeping his eyes riveted on Saul, he slowly backed away.

"I have no idea why I let my brother hire you to do anything, Klein," said Saul. "The only good thing about you is your wife."

Klein's face reddened and his fists tightened. He wasn't sure how much longer he could restrain himself. Then, out of the corner of his eye, he noticed the Buick parked on the street. The driver looked familiar. It was the thug from the railway station. Looking more closely, he could also see the passenger; it was his partner, the man with the eyepatch.

Saul Sugarman, who clearly enjoyed taunting Klein, moved closer to him. Klein shoved him, moving past him. He took a few paces and then stopped, turning back around. The impulse to go after Saul was overwhelming.

"Shailek, stop, please," said Rivka, her voice shaking.

Her cry brought a group of people to where she was standing, as Lou put himself between Klein and his brother. "Saul, you had to start up with this *meshugas*? Here, now?" he said loudly enough for Saul to hear.

Saul Sugarman waved the back of his hand. "I'm not paying another cent to that bastard. Do you hear me, Lou?"

Lou walked to towards Klein and gently reached for his arm. "Sam, over here, please. I need to speak with you."

But Klein wasn't listening. He freed himself from Lou's grasp and began walking purposefully towards the men in the car.

"Shit, I think we've been made," said Paulie. He reached for his pistol inside Richie's shoulder holster.

"Easy," advised Richie. "Don't do anything stupid. We're just going to talk to him."

As Klein reached the vehicle, he scoured the area, looking in every direction. His first thought was that they might have brought more men with them. However, apart from a small group of neighbourhood children playing stick ball, Dagmar was quiet.

Klein cautiously approached the open driver's side window. He looked at Paulie and immediately saw that he was holding a gun. "I just want to talk to you. I'm not looking for any trouble and I don't have a weapon," said Klein.

"We don't want any trouble, either, at least not here, Klein," said Richie, leaning forward. He took the gun from Paulie and tossed it in the backseat. "See, we just want to talk, too."

"You have me at a disadvantage. You know my name, but I don't know yours."

Richie sneered. "Don't worry about it, Klein. It's not important."

"Okay. So I saw you at the railway station but you disappeared after the shooting. And now you're here again."

"You're observant, Klein. We're just visiting the city. Seeing the sites," said Richie.

"Is that so?"

"That's right," said Paulie. "We like Winnipeg."

Klein looked around again and then back at the two men. "What is it you want?"

"What we want is this, Sam. You don't mind if I call you Sam, do you?" asked Richie.

"Call me whatever the hell you want."

"As I was saying," continued Richie. "What we want is for you to stop poking around the Sugarmans' business. No more questions about what happened in Vera. No searching for Frankie Taylor. Just stop before someone gets really hurt."

"Do you know something about what happened in Vera? To Alec?"

"Klein, you have a nice family. A wife and a few kids. Why don't you worry about them? Stay out of the booze business. You've been warned. Let's go, Paulie."

From the second-storey window of a secluded corner of the library, George Dickens watched Klein's encounter with the two men. To their right, he could see the Sugarman brothers. Perfect, he thought. He untied the rope on the long sack and pulled out his shotgun. He cranked open the window enough for the barrel to poke through.

Reverend Vivian had been quite clear in his instructions: Do not hit or hurt anyone. Merely scare them, he ordered Dickens. This was the object of the exercise. It was unfortunate that this warning had to take place at a funeral, Vivian had conceded. But he pointed out that this way the Sugarmans would realize that they could never be safe as long as they continued to peddle liquor and defy God's will.

Paulie started the car and as he did so a shot rang out. He slammed the brake. Klein dropped to his knees and yelled at everyone behind him to get down. Several women screamed.

From the window of the library, Dickens's face turned white. He had not pulled the trigger. A second shot rang out and he saw Lou Sugarman grab his shoulder, falling to the ground and hitting his head. He scanned the area. The shots seemed to be coming from the attic of the house next to the synagogue.

"Shailek, Lou's been shot," cried Rivka. "There's blood…"

Klein looked to his right and then left. A third shot whizzed over his head narrowly missing the driver of the car.

"Go, now," shouted Richie. "Get the fuck out of here."

Paulie hit the clutch, shifted gears, and accelerated forward.

As he did so, two figures stood in front of him with their guns pointed at him and Richie.

"Stop or we'll fire," said Detective Allard, his pistol out. Beside him, Hannah Nash had her revolver aimed at Paulie's head. She had special permission to carry a firearm and was one of only a handful of policewomen in Canada permitted to do so.

"Sam, are you hit?" asked Nash.

"No, not me, but Lou Sugarman has been. The gunfire is coming from beside us. That house, the third floor window. I'm sure of it."

Nash turned to look and as she did so, Paulie shifted into reverse and hit the gas. The Buick jerked backward down Dagmar, barely missing the children on the street, who screamed. Allard fired one shot that grazed the front of car, but did not slow it down. Paulie backed up all the way to Bannatyne Avenue, stopped, shifted the gears again, turned right, and sped away.

Several more shots were fired at the crowd near the Sugarmans. By this time four other constables had arrived. Allard ordered them to the house where the shots seemed to be coming from. The officers could hardly hear from the screams and shouting in front of the synagogue. They stormed the house and ran up the stairs to the attic. But no one was there.

In the library, a thick bead of sweat ran down Dickens's face. He quickly put his shotgun back in the sack and pushed his way through the crowd of patrons who had now gathered near the library's main door. Damn, he thought. Between him and the main door was Mary Turner. He froze for a second. Then, there was another shout from the synagogue and everyone, including Mary, moved en masse towards a window in the main hall. Not wasting another second, he pushed open the door and exited the building. Just before he did so, Mary Turner, momentarily distracted, glanced at the main door. She saw Dickens leave and found it curious that he was carrying a sack used to hold rifles.

On the walkway, Dickens looked one more time at the chaos near the synagogue. Turning left, he walked as quickly as he could down William Avenue towards Isabel Street until the noise from the synagogue shooting faded. When a streetcar happened along, he boarded it. He took a seat at the back, still reeling from what he had witnessed.

10

An ambulance arrived to take Lou Sugarman to the Winnipeg General Hospital ten blocks away. Rivka, whose white blouse was soaked in Lou's blood, accompanied him. She was upset, but as solid as a rock—as she usually was in times of crisis. Klein always acknowledged that this was a trait that she had inherited from their mother, Freda. He, on the other hand, had to work hard at keeping his emotions in check, though not always successfully. The ambulance attendants had bound Lou's wound to stop the bleeding and reassured Rivka that Lou, who was slipping in and out of consciousness, would recover. Allard ordered two of his men to stand guard over Lou at the hospital in case the shooter returned to finish the job.

Klein stared at the astonishing scene in front of the Shaarey Zedek. There were distraught men and women, several of whom were sobbing. Dozens of police constables and plain-clothes detectives wielded guns and batons. Competing newspaper reporters methodically tried to elicit answers from mourners and police officers. And across the street, patrons from the library and neighbourhood stood watching the horrific scene unfold as if it was a rugby match. It wasn't quite the turmoil of "Bloody Saturday" during the 1919 strike, but at that moment, that's what it seemed like to Klein.

In his head, he analyzed recent events, trying to make sense of it all. Two shootings in three days; someone was after the Sugarmans. Of that, he had no further doubt. Yet questions abounded. Who were these two thugs who had arrived from Minneapolis? What were they doing in the city? And why was the mystery shooter seemingly after them as well? The gunman had deliberately aimed at their car as well, which meant that their lives were in danger. Klein needed to speak with them, and fast. He had an idea where he might be able to find them later in the evening.

The shooter, who Klein had to admit, was not the best of marksmen since he now had seemingly missed his targets on two occasions, was probably not going to stop until these men and the Sugarmans were dead. Once Lou recovered, he would need to speak with him again and determine if he knew more about this than he had told him. If that was the case, Klein was puzzled why Lou, a smart man, would have held back information that put his life and the lives of his family members in jeopardy. As for Saul Sugarman, Klein realized that he would have to leave questioning him to the police; the palpable hostility between him and Sugarman was too deep and bitter.

Close to the entrance to the synagogue, Klein saw Saul Sugarman having what appeared to be a heated discussion with

McCreary. Two provincial officers stood guard around them. In the midst of the confusion, Klein hadn't noticed when McCreary had arrived.

There was far too much noise for Klein to hear what Sugarman, who was doing most of the talking, was saying. All McCreary seemed to be doing was uncharacteristically nodding his head in agreement. After another minute or so, Sugarman angrily pushed McCreary out of the way and headed towards his car which happened to be in Klein's direction. Again, McCreary uncharacteristically did nothing.

"You know what's going on here, don't you, Sugarman?" Klein called out to him. "Who's trying to kill you and your brother?"

"I don't know what you're talking about, Klein. Nor do I have time to answer any of your questions. As of now, you're off the case."

"Well, your brother hired me and until such time as he tells me differently, I'm still working for him."

Sugarman stopped and moved closer to Klein. "You have no idea what's going on here. And I can assure you that this will only lead to trouble for you and your lovely, lovely wife and children. Now get out of my way."

As Saul began walking, Klein grabbed him by his arm. "What does that mean, exactly? What does this have to do with my family?"

Sugarman said nothing; he only sneered at Klein, who tightened his grip on Saul's arm.

"Let go of me, now, Klein," Sugarman barked.

Klein looked straight at Sugarman; his eyes were focused and his lips pursed. Without saying another word, he released his grasp and Saul stepped towards his car.

"Hold on, Mr. Sugarman, we have a few questions for you." Detective Allard and Hannah Nash blocked his path to his automobile.

"I've nothing to say to you, either. Other than I have no idea who's shooting at my brother or me. But I do know that I've had enough of all of this for today."

"You understand, sir, you are likely in danger. That the shooter will strike again," said Allard.

"That's my concern. You need not bother yourself with this."

"We'd like you to come down to the station. We believe you do know more than you are willing to admit." Nash's tone was firm, though somewhat friendlier and more respectful than Allard's.

"Look, miss. I don't know who you are, nor do I particularly care. I am not answering to any woman or anyone else for that matter. If you want anything further from me, then speak to my lawyer, Graham Powers. Now get out of my way ... please."

As Sugarman attempted to walk forward, Allard stood his ground. Klein could see Sugarman's face redden and his body stiffen. Had he been speaking with anyone else, Klein was certain that he would have exploded into one of his infamous rages.

"Let him go," said McCreary, who was now standing beside Sugarman.

"But he must be questioned," Allard insisted.

"You deaf, Allard? I said let him go."

Allard and Nash stared at each other and then McCreary for a long moment.

"What's going on, McCreary?" asked Klein.

"I don't have to explain myself to you or anyone else here for that matter," McCreary said, clenching his fist.

Klein's eyes widened. "You're on Sugarman's payroll, aren't you McCreary? That's it, isn't it?" said Klein.

"Watch it, Klein. You're asking for trouble."

"You're the commissioner of the provincial police, for Christ's sake. I thought your duty was to stop the Sugarmans' liquor trade, not abet it."

"I haven't time for this, Klein. Now stay out of my way or I'll have you arrested."

"You certain you want to do this, Commissioner?" Nash asked.

"No more questions," McCreary said sharply. "Get the hell out of the way! Now!"

At that, Allard and Nash parted and Sugarman moved passed them towards his car. As he was climbing in, he sneered at Klein a second time. A moment later, the Rolls-Royce pulled away.

When Sugarman was out of sight, Klein smiled at McCreary. "You like that line? Accusing you of being on the payroll?"

"Yeah, real clever," said McCreary with a laugh.

Allard and Nash looked at each other in disbelief.

"Would one of you please tell us what's going on?" asked Allard.

"Sugarman thinks he owns me. That's what's going on," McCreary said. "But he doesn't."

"After questioning the Reverend Vivian, McCreary and I spoke," Klein continued. "I told him about the two thugs who arrived from Minneapolis the day of the railway station shooting, who, as it turned out, he already knew about."

"You mean the two men who tried to run us over?" asked Nash.

"Exactly. We think they're working for Irv Rosen," said Klein.

"The other night, I tried to get Sugarman to explain to me what was going on, but he was cagey," said McCreary. "He did give me an envelope of cash for my troubles, however. Don't worry, Allard, the money is in a safe place. It'll be used in the case we're building against Sugarman. But all in good time."

"So what about these gangsters? Rosen's men, you say?" Allard asked.

"More than likely. But so far they've eluded my men," said McCreary.

"You both could've let us in on what was going on," said Nash.

"I suppose," said Klein, smiling warmly at her. "But what would be the fun in that?"

McCreary walked away to speak with one of his MPP constables who had been waiting patiently for him. The officer was standing off to the side, speaking with a woman.

There was a cry from the street.

"Shailek, Shailek, are you all right?" Sarah ran up to Klein and threw her arms around him. "I was told you were shot," she said, breathing heavily.

"I'm fine. Still in one piece," said Klein.

"I was in the store when Betty Kingston came running in to

tell me that she'd heard you'd been shot. I left her there and her chauffer drove me here," she said, pointing to a gleaming blue Lincoln parked on Dagmar with a uniformed driver standing beside it. "But I'm so relieved you're not hurt. I don't know what the children would have done. Or me." Sarah threw her arms around Klein again and hugged him. Then, noticing Allard and Nash watching them, she stood back. "I'm sorry, I've been rude."

"Not at all, Mrs. Klein," said Allard. "We're happy Mr. Klein has not been injured today as well."

"Lou Sugarman was shot, but not seriously, I think," said Klein.

"That's awful. Who would do such a thing?"

"We are attempting to determine that, ma'am," said Allard.

There was a.momentary pause. "You going to introduce me, Sam?" asked Hannah.

"Of course. My apologies ... I ... wasn't..." Klein turned to his wife. "This is Detective Hannah Nash. She's visiting us from Calgary. Assisting the MPP with this case."

"I see, very nice to meet you Miss, or is it, Mrs. Nash?"

"Mrs., but please call me Hannah, Mrs. Klein."

"It's Sarah."

Nash nodded.

"Is this your first time in the city?" Sarah asked.

"No, not at all. As a matter of fact, I used to work for the Winnipeg department."

"I'm sure I mentioned Mrs. Nash before," said Klein, rubbing his hands together. "She was the first policewoman in the city. She helped with the case during the strike involving Metro Lizowski."

"Yes, of course. Please forgive me Mrs. ... I mean, Hannah. I do remember. And my husband has spoken of you before."

"Has he?" Nash said with a tight smile.

Sarah returned the smile. Both women guardedly glanced at the other, while Klein fidgeted with his hands.

"Now that all the pleasantries are finished, can we get back to work?" said McCreary, who had returned. "Mrs. Sam Klein, always a pleasure to see you."

Sarah grinned. "It's been a while, McCreary. You're looking as spry as ever."

"Do you have some news?" asked Allard.

"I do." McCreary motioned for the MPP officer and the woman he was speaking with to come closer. "This is Officer Newhouse and Mrs. Mary Turner. Mrs. Turner was at the library and she saw something you might find interesting. Go ahead, ma'am, please."

Mary cleared her throat. "Yes, as I told the officer, I was across at the library before and after the shooting started."

"Yes, and what did you see?" asked Allard.

"A man I knew. He was carrying a sack large enough to hold a rifle. When the shooting ended, I saw him rush from the library."

"And who is this man?" Allard inquired.

"He's a neighbour. My husband Harold and I live on Furby near Westminster. He and his wife, Maggie, and their son, Charles, live about six houses away."

"His name, ma'am, please," said Allard.

"George … George Dickens."

"He's one of Vivian's men," said McCreary.

With McCreary in the passenger seat and Klein and Nash in the back, Allard steered his department-issued, new 1922 black Essex with white-walled tires up Main Street. He turned right on Portage Avenue and headed west, puttering along at twelve miles an hour. At Donald Street by Eaton's, he deftly manoeuvred around a stalled horse-driven milk wagon, avoided hitting a small group of pedestrians who were not paying attention to traffic, and then was compelled to slam on the brakes when the driver of a Model-T pulled away from the curb without bothering to check for oncoming autos.

"Someday people in this city will figure out how to drive," muttered Allard.

"Traffic signals are the answer. They're in use in the States already," said McCreary.

"I don't know. Won't that slow things down even worse?"

"Eyes on the road, Allard. You're going to run over someone."

In the backseat, Klein wasn't entirely certain why he was there. He had ushered Sarah back to the Kingston's chauffeur-driven car and assured her he'd be home by six o'clock for Shabbat dinner. Allard had then asked him to accompany him, McCreary, and Nash to Dickens's home. All three believed that Dickens could tie Reverend Vivian to the two attacks on the Sugarmans, despite some evidence to the contrary. He had hesitated. Klein always did his best work alone—apart from the recent and timely assistance offered to him by Alec Geller. And as much as he appreciated Allard's invitation to be part of the official police investigation, he knew that he had to proceed carefully. Being identified too closely with the likes of McCreary could backfire and taint his reputation as an independent operator.

But he had acquiesced. Though he still was not convinced that Dickens, or Reverend Vivian for that matter, had anything to do with the attempts on the Sugarmans, and even less with the murder of Max Roter, he was curious about what the police might learn. Plus there was Hannah Nash. Other than a memory of a fleeting kiss, there was nothing between them, nor would there be in the future—of that he was certain. He was in love with his wife. And yet, he still could not help himself. A half-smile from Hannah urging him to join the investigation and he couldn't say no.

"So you really think that this Dickens was the shooter?" Klein asked. "I was certain the shots came from the third floor of that house beside the synagogue."

"I had constables check it out," replied Allard. "The property belongs to a woman named Johnson. She wasn't there and the house was locked up tight. At the same time, my men found evidence that someone had been by the window facing the synagogue on the second floor of the library. The window was open sufficiently for a rifle to have been used. And one of librarians assured us that the window is always kept closed. So it seems to me that Dickens likely was the shooter and no doubt acting on Vivian's orders. The reverend was lying to us."

Klein nodded, but didn't say anything.

"Sam, you don't think Dickens or Vivian are involved?" asked Nash.

"I don't know. Something isn't right. I still want to speak to those two thugs who got away. They are the key to this."

"Or Saul Sugarman," offered McCreary. "He's a lot of things, but he's not a fool. I can assure you, he knows what's going on."

Allard accelerated the car as soon as he passed Spence Street.

"You're going to miss the turn onto Furby," warned McCreary.

"Never happen. But hold on."

As the car approached the corner of Portage and Furby, Allard turned the car sharply left, barely avoiding an oncoming eastbound streetcar. Nash, who was sitting behind McCreary, flew into Klein, who caught her. He held her for only a second. She fixed her hat and smoothed out her skirt and quickly moved back to her side of the car. As she did so, her left hand lingered on Klein's right hand before she pulled it away. He pretended not to notice.

"My word, Detective, perhaps you should slow down. I nearly pushed Sam out the door."

"Apologies, Mrs. Nash. I forget just how powerful these vehicles can be."

Allard pulled up in front of ninety-nine Furby Street, where George and Maggie Dickens lived. Another Essex with three constables and one of McCreary's MPP officers lurched to a stop directly behind them. McCreary ordered the men to search the back of the red brick two-and-a-half-storey house. A short, white picket fence surrounded the property. Klein noticed a young boy looking at them from an upstairs window.

"Must be the son, Charles," said Nash, noticing the boy as well.

"Charles Dickens? Really, that's his name?" scoffed McCreary.

"That's a lot to live up to. Maybe the parents are fond of the author," offered Nash with a shrug.

The front door of the house opened and a short, stout woman with a slim, long nose and over-sized ears emerged. Her hair was short and tangled and she was wearing a light red sweater, white blouse, and tan skirt, covered by a brown apron tied around her waist.

"Are you Maggie Dickens?" Allard inquired, introducing himself.

She nodded. "I am. What's this all about? Why are there constables in my backyard?"

"Is your husband George here, ma'am?" asked Allard.

"Why? Did he do something wrong?"

"Please answer the question."

"No. He's not here. Left this morning for work as usual."

"Where does he work?"

"Downtown at Standard Grain office, room 276 in the Grain Exchange building. Now, will you please tell me what this is all about?"

"It's an ongoing investigation, Mrs. Dickens. We believe your husband may have some information about a shooting that happened earlier today on Dagmar."

Maggie Dickens held her cheeks. "A shooting. Not George. He'd never be involved in something like that."

"Does your husband own a rifle?" McCreary asked, taking over the questioning. His tone was much harsher than Allard's.

"He does, yes. Likes to hunt outside the city, like lots of people."

"And what of his relationship with Reverend Vivian? Can you tell us something about that?"

"Reverend Vivian's a great man. He's trying to save this city. I'm very proud of George for taking up the cause against the bottle." The front door opened again and young Charles came out.

"Everything okay, Mom?"

"It is, dear, never mind. Go back inside."

"The boy not in school today?" asked McCreary.

"He wasn't feeling well. Now if there's nothing else, I'd like to tend to my son."

"Anyone have any other questions for Mrs. Dickens?" asked Allard.

"Yes, I have one," said Klein, stepping forward. "Mrs. Dickens, do you know if your husband has ever visited the town Vera near the US border?"

Maggie shuffled her feet and looked downward at the grass. "He has, yes. His company has an office there. Occasionally he travels to Vera to work with the elevator manager who lives there, Mr. Smythe."

"I see. Has he been there recently?"

"As a matter of fact, he took the train to Vera last week. Stayed for a few days."

"When did he return?"

"Early Monday morning. But I don't see how…"

"That's fine, ma'am. I have nothing more to ask," said Klein.

Nash looked at Klein, though remained silent.

"If you speak to your husband, Mrs. Dickens, please tell him to telephone me at A6568," said Allard. "Will you remember that? As I said earlier, it's very important we speak with him as soon as possible."

Maggie nodded and went back inside her house.

The three constables appeared and reported that they had found nothing suspicious in the backyard. Allard suggested that everyone return to the station. It was too late in the day to check for George Dickens at the Grain Exchange building and he doubted he would be there in any case. A visit to the Standard Grain office would have to wait until the morning.

Maggie Dickens peered around the curtained window and waited for the police to depart in their automobiles. When she was certain they were gone, she reached for the telephone and dialed a number.

"Hello, its Maggie. Yes, they're gone now. No, I didn't tell them anything. But we might have a serious problem."

11

As soon as Klein entered the General Hospital, he was hit by the pungent odour of carbolic disinfectant, a smell that numbed his nostrils. Since the influenza epidemic of 1918, which had taken the lives of more than 1,200 Winnipeggers, hospital officials were fanatical about keeping the facility clean and germ-free. Everyone from doctors and nurses to custodians were instructed to do their part to protect the hospital from infection. Above all, that meant the liberal use of carbolic disinfectant—each day, every day.

Klein made his way to the emergency clinic in search of his sister. Late on a Friday afternoon, the hospital was busy as usual. Groups of visitors, women and men, mingled about while several nurses outfitted in white—caps, ankle-length dresses, smocks, and shoes—manned a desk by the front of the room. Every so often, doctors in white coats with stethoscopes around their necks appeared, ushering patients in and out of hospital rooms. One man complained of a belly ache while another more elderly gentleman had a nasty cut on his hand. Drops of blood from the gash dripped onto the floor. A young physician rushed to assist him and quickly wrapped his hand in a bandage.

Two women sat off to the side coughing incessantly and everyone else kept their distance, including Klein. Tuberculosis was a common ailment in the city and it was said that when you entered the hospital with the disease you rarely came back out.

Once Klein had left the Dickens's home, he had asked Allard to detour down Sherbrooke to Bannatyne, so he could stop at the hospital to check in on Lou Sugarman.

During the ride over, another heated discussion ensued on the possible involvement of Reverend Vivian in everything that had gone on. Allard was fairly certain that Vivian and Dickens could be linked to the shootings at the CPR and the Shaarey Zedek, possibly even to what happened in Vera. Maggie Dickens admitted that her husband was visiting the town when Max Roter was killed, suggesting a possible connection. If Vivian was determined to put the Sugarmans out of business, Allard argued, perhaps he also intended to disrupt their cross-border bootlegging operation. Still, he agreed with the others that at this point, this was only conjecture. Klein decided to keep his thoughts to himself on any possible linkages between Max's murder and the shootings in Winnipeg.

Klein was only in the emergency clinic a few minutes when Rivka arrived.

"Shailek, I am so glad you're here," she said, hugging him.

"How is he?" asked Klein, lighting a cigarette.

"The doctor said that the bullet that hit his arm went right through. He should be fine, thank God. Come, they're bringing him back to his room soon."

Rivka led her brother up the stairs and down a long, sterile hallway to a room just past the nurse's desk. As Klein and everyone else in the city knew, money was a factor in obtaining decent healthcare. Doctors and hospitals charged the rich varying amounts depending on what they believed the patient could afford. It was the reason some physicians had annual incomes of $4,000 compared to hospital cleaning women who made less than $500 a year. If you were wealthy like Lou Sugarman, you could recover in a fairly comfortable private room.

Klein nodded at the two police constables stationed outside the room by the doorway who permitted him and Rivka to pass.

Rivka sat down at a chair by the window looking out at Olivia Street. "I'm glad they're here. What if the shooter comes looking for Lou here?"

"He won't," said Klein. "Too dangerous. He'd likely figure the police would be here. Isn't anyone else from Lou's family here?"

Rivka shook her head. "They're still at the cemetery, but Rae said she would come straight here. Saul, too, maybe. If he does come here, Shailek, you must promise me that there's to be no arguing or fighting. It'll only upset Lou. Will you promise? Please."

"You know the expression, *vos in der kort*?"

Rivka smiled. "A bad person is capable of doing anything bad."

"Exactly. That's Saul Sugarman. You can't trust him."

"That may be true. But you must move past this incident with Sarah, Shailek."

"It was more than an incident."

"Forget about it. I know you love her. And the children…"

Klein touched her arm. "Believe me, I'm trying."

"Sam, nice of you to visit," said Lou Sugarman as two nurses wheeled him into the room on an iron bed. "But as I keep telling the doctor, I'm ready to go home."

"Mr. Sugarman must remain here for a day or two at least," said one of the nurses. "He has a nasty bump on his head from falling on the ground and he's had surgery. He must rest."

"*Goyishe kop*" muttered Lou.

"I think it's your *kop* that has the problem," Rivka said, kissing his forehead. "Now, don't be so stubborn. Just listen and do as you're told."

He smiled. "Your sister is a real prize, Klein, do you know that?"

"Yes, I'm aware of that. A real prize."

"Enough, you two. Are you in pain, dear?"

"Not in the least," said Lou, grimacing.

"Mr. Sugarman, as I said earlier, must get some rest. A few more minutes and then I'm going to have to ask you both to leave," said the nurse.

Lou glowered at the nurse. "Can you please leave us, now? And shut the door."

"Don't be rude, Lou," said Rivka, turning to the two nurses. "I promise we will leave him shortly so that he can get proper rest."

Lou waited until the nurses left the room. "So what do you know, Sam?"

Klein hesitated. "You're sure you're up to talking about this now?"

"I'm fine. A bit of a headache and sore, but otherwise okay. So please go ahead."

"All right, Lou, have it your way. The police believe the shooter is one of Reverend Vivian's men, George Dickens. He was seen leaving the library across the street from the synagogue, possibly carrying a rifle."

"But you don't believe them, do you?"

"No. The reverend is determined to ruin you and anyone else involved in the liquor business. But murder? I just don't think so."

"So who the hell's trying to kill me?" Beads of sweat began dripping down Lou's face.

"That's a good question, Lou. What is it that you're not telling me?"

"Nothing, Sam ... I swear ... it..." More sweat formed on Lou's face which was now white. "Where am I? What am I doing here?" He grabbed Rivka's arm. "Tell Saul not to go through with it ... too dangerous."

"Not to go through with what, Lou?" asked Klein.

Lou tried to say something else, but his words were slurred. His eyes rolled back and he looked like he was about to pass out.

Rivka ran to the door. "Nurse, come quickly! There's something wrong." A few seconds went by but the nurses were nowhere to be seen. "Please, one of you, go get a doctor," she pleaded the constables.

One of them ran down the hall and less than a minute later returned with a doctor and the two nurses.

"Mr. Sugarman, can you hear me?" the doctor asked. There was no response. The doctor touched Lou's forehead and examined his eyes. "His pupils are dilated. He's out cold," said the doctor, looking at Rivka. "It's likely from the fall on the ground. He needs to rest, but I'm hopeful Mr. Sugarman should regain consciousness soon."

"When exactly will that be?" Rivka asked, her voice quivering.

"It's difficult to know," said the doctor.

"That doesn't sound reassuring. Could he … die from this?"

"As I said, Miss Klein, we need to wait and see."

"My God, Sam," cried Rivka, covering her face with her hands.

"Don't worry. Lou's strong. He'll recover," said Klein. "Come, let me take you to my place for dinner and then I'll bring you back."

"I can't leave him. What if he wakes up? He'll want to see me."

"Miss Klein. We'll watch him closely. And if there's any change, we can telephone you. Just leave us the number."

Rivka hesitated for a moment and then nodded at Klein. "What if Rae and the other members of the family come here? I should be here."

"If anyone comes, we will ensure they are duly informed of the situation and tell them to contact you," the nurse replied. "I assume the constables will continue to stand guard. Mr. Sugar-man's in good hands."

Rivka thanked the nurse for her kindness and reluctantly left the room holding onto Klein's arm. As he helped his sister down the hall, Klein wondered about what Lou had said: "Tell Saul not to go through with it … too dangerous." True, Lou was delirious, yet Klein sensed there was real meaning in what he said. What was he referring to? What was "too dangerous?"

From the moment Klein had accepted this assignment he had the gnawing feeling that there was a piece of the puzzle that Lou had omitted telling him. At once, Klein knew the solution to this dilemma, but he didn't like it. Either he could wait for Lou to recover—though there was no certainty of that—and ask him to explain further. Or, he could press the only other person who had the answers: Saul Sugarman. That could be problem-atic, if not impossible, he thought, since Saul clearly detested him as much as he detested Saul. He would definitely require McCreary's assistance and subterfuge if he was to unravel this latest twist.

By six o'clock, the sun had cooled slightly, though the high humidity made it muggier than usual for mid-June. Klein and Rivka paused for a moment as they exited from the hospital's main entrance when they saw Rae Roter and another woman coming towards them. Klein immediately recognized the red-headed woman he had seen at the funeral, Rae's friend from Vera. Behind Rae, Klein could see Saul Sugarman parking his Rolls-Royce.

Rae had the appearance of a woman who had been beaten down by the harsh reality of the past week. Her hair was slightly tousled and the lines on her face were accentuated. Beyond that, the lively spark that so endeared her to her many customers was nowhere to be seen.

Rae took one look at Rivka's worried face and knew immediately that something bad had happened. "What is it? How's Lou? Is he dead?" Instinctively, her left hand touched her heart and blood pulsated through her body.

"He's not dead, Rae."

"Thank God."

"It is serious, however. They had brought him back from surgery and he was fine. And then, as Sam can also tell you, he began sweating and talking without making sense and then he passed out. The doctor says it's probably from hitting his head after he was shot. But he is hopeful that with rest Lou will wake up soon. I'm trying to be strong."

"And you have been," said Klein, reaching for his sister's hand. She smiled warmly at him.

Once she fully processed the seriousness of Lou's situation, Rae's face turned pale and she teetered slightly. Her friend grabbed onto her.

"Joannie, I'm so glad you're here with her," Rivka said, turning to Klein. "Sam, this is Rae's friend from Vera. Joannie Smythe."

Joannie helped Rae to a nearby bench and sat her down. "You'll be fine, dear. Just rest a second."

"Jack Smythe's your husband?" Klein asked her.

"That's right. And you must be Sam Klein. Rae has told me

all about you. Even my husband has heard of you. I think your name's been in the newspaper a few times."

Klein offered her a half-smile. While he admittedly savoured the local fame that came with his work—the knowing looks he received on the street, the whispers he heard as he walked by, and the occasional complimentary beer and whisky at a Main Street bar—it could also be a liability when he wanted to be unseen.

Klein did find Mrs. Smythe appealing—with that figure it was difficult not to. He wondered if she might have some relevant information about Max's murder, something she failed to tell the provincial police because she thought it wasn't important. From Klein's perspective, it was in such seemingly insignificant details that cases were often solved.

"Might we speak at some point, Mrs. Smythe, about what happened in Vera?"

"Of course, though I don't know how much help I can be. Both Jack and I spoke to provincial police officers. However, I'll be staying for a few days at the Royal Alexandra Hotel. We can arrange to meet there if you wish in the next day or two."

"I'll contact you at the hotel, then," said Klein.

Saul Sugarman strode up to Rae. He ignored Klein, who did the same. Sam decided that it might be wiser just to watch Sugarman, rather than antagonize him. As much as it troubled him, seeing Sugarman's confident manner even as he stood in front of the hospital chatting with his sister, Klein could understand why many women, Sarah included, were captivated by him. Klein could not precisely put his finger on it, but Sugarman definitely had a natural magnetism, albeit of the unsavoury variety. Yet Klein knew all too well from his days at Melinda's that some women were easily ensnared by such men, only to regret it later.

"You're saying he might die," said Sugarman, his voice rising.

"Don't yell at me, Saul. I'm only telling you what Rivka has told me," said Rae.

"Mr. Sugarman, can't you see that you're upsetting her," said Joannie Smythe, grabbing Rae by the shoulders. "She's been through so much."

Sugarman turned to Rivka. "Could you please tell me what's happened."

With tears in her eyes, Rivka reviewed the details of Lou's surgery and the events of the past hour.

"I know he'll recover," said Sugarman. "He must."

Listening, Klein sensed Sugarman's genuine concern for his brother. Perhaps he did have one or two redeeming qualities.

"Did he say anything before he passed out?" Sugarman asked.

Rivka glanced at Klein for a moment. "As a matter of fact, he did. He whispered, 'Tell Saul not to go through with it … too dangerous.' Does that make any sense to you? The doctor said he was delirious."

Sugarman's eyes narrowed and his face became almost as pale as Lou's had been. "I … I have no idea what that could mean. Pure nonsense." He turned to Klein. "Can we speak for a moment?"

Klein nodded and he and Sugarman walked off to the side.

"What is it you want?"

"The police believe that Reverend Vivian is behind these

attacks and I agree with them. It must be him. I wouldn't be surprised if he engineered Max's murder as well. There can be no one else."

"Interesting," said Klein, rubbing his chin.

"While I respect McCreary's skills and those of the police, I want you to stop Vivian any way that you can. Do you understand what I'm saying?" His tone was almost desperate.

"Yes, I think I do. But I thought you wanted me off this case," Klein said coolly, trying not to seem like he was enjoying Sugarman's discomfort as much as he was.

"I've changed my mind. I'll pay you two thousand dollars. Do we have a deal?"

Klein's eyes widened. "That's a lot of money."

"It is, so what's your answer?"

"I'll find the shooter."

Sugarman beckoned Rae and Rivka to join him and the three of them headed for Lou's room. As Klein watched him walk away with the women, he was almost impressed with Saul's guile. As much as he hated him, he had to admit that Sugarman was no fool. Still, in Klein's view, Saul was too anxious, too certain that Vivian was the chief culprit. Klein did not believe what Lou had said was "pure nonsense" at all. On the contrary, seeing Sugarman's reaction, he was quite certain that Saul knew exactly what Lou had been talking about.

12

Klein was half a block from his house when he heard the excited shriek of his three children: "Daddy's home!" Freda, Bernice, and Mel bounded out the door and rushed into Klein's out-stretched arms. He hugged them all and then lifted up Bernice and Mel. Freda grabbed onto the back of his jacket as they made their way back to the front step where Sarah was sitting, waiting for them on the stoop.

Out of the corner of his eye, Klein noticed the round face of Mrs. Gertie Fester, their neighbour from across the street, pushed up against her front window. As was her custom, Mrs. Fester was keeping watch. Not much happened on Cathedral Avenue without Mrs. Fester knowing about it. Sarah often exchanged pleasantries with her. She had lost her husband Ralph, a tailor, a few years ago. She had no children and loved doting over the Klein kids. But Sam found her a nosy, if harmless, busybody. Recently, during his dispute with Sarah, Mrs. Fester had given him nothing but disapproving stares.

"Children, you're going to smother your father," said Sarah.

"We love Daddy," yelled Bernice.

Klein shrugged. "What can I say?"

"How's Lou?" asked Sarah.

"Not good, I'm afraid. But the doctor hopes he'll recover. We'll have to wait until tomorrow."

"I'm sorry to hear that, truly I am. But I have something that might cheer you up."

"I know, I can smell the roast chicken from here. It's my mother's recipe."

"No, not the food, though you'll like what I've made. Come in and you can see for yourself."

Klein followed Sarah into the house and there sitting on the living room couch was Alec Geller, somewhat banged up, and Shayna Kravetz by his side.

"Alec, what are you doing here? I thought you couldn't travel for a few more days," said Klein, warmly shaking Geller's hand.

"The doc let me go. Said I was fine as long as I promised to rest. So I took the next train and then Sarah suggested I surprise you."

"Well, it's a good surprise. And I'm glad you're back."

"Yeah, I've heard what's been going on from Shayna," Geller said, taking her hand and squeezing it lightly. "The shooter tried again at Roter's funeral for God's sake. It's a damn good thing he keeps on missing."

"Bad luck or bad aim, I'm not certain which. But Lou was hit in the arm and is in rough shape. Saul's been more fortunate," said Klein, glancing at Sarah. She immediately looked away.

"Mr. Sugarman was very upset after the shooting at the station. I can only imagine how angry he must be now," said Shayna.

"He's angry all right," said Klein.

His sarcastic tone was not lost on Sarah. "Please, Shailek, be good. We have company," she whispered in Klein's ear as she excused herself to tend to the children and the food in the kitchen. "Come, Shayna. If you can tear yourself away from Alec for a minute, you can help."

Shayna smiled and trailed after Sarah into the kitchen where, by the sound of it, an argument had erupted between Freda and Bernice.

Klein took a seat on the chair opposite Alec. "You think Shayna knows anything more about what Sugarman is up to?"

Geller shrugged. "I'm not interrogating her, Sam. All she told me is that since the incident at the station, Sugarman has made several long distance telephone calls to New York. And he's been having one tirade after the other around the office, as she said. I honestly don't think she knows what is going on, if anything. I can speak to her more about it, but in my own way."

"We need to know who he called. Rosen, I imagine, but I'd like to be certain."

"Did you ever receive a reply to your telegram to Rosen about what happened in Vera?"

Klein pulled out a piece of paper from his jacket pocket and handed it to Geller. "Read it for yourself. He's saying nothing."

Alec glanced at the telegram. "'No information about Vera.

Best to leave it alone. Rosen.' What the hell does that mean? If he has no information, why is it 'best to leave it alone?'"

"Good question. The police—who, I have to say, have been accommodating—as well as Saul Sugarman insist that the shootings in the city, maybe even in Vera, are connected to Reverend John Vivian. They're taking him at his word that he wants to put the Sugarmans out of the liquor business. One of his men, George Dickens, was seen leaving the library across from the Shaarey Zedek with what is thought to have been a shotgun. And this Dickens was in Vera when Roter was killed."

Geller sat up straight. "I know. I was told that as well ... and more."

"Go on," said Klein, lighting a cigarette.

"The woman whose house I stayed at and who nursed me back to health, Mrs. Tillsdale, knows just about everything going on in the town."

"Including who murdered Max Roter?"

"No, I'm afraid not. Like everyone else, and that goes for the officer I met from the provincial police, she thinks it was this bootlegger named Taylor, Frankie Taylor. According to Mrs. Tillsdale, he's real trouble. Nasty and dangerous. Ever since Roter and the Sugarmans started dealing with him about six months ago, he's been a problem. Got into a fight with another customer at a diner because he said the man, a fifty-year-old farmer, stared at him the wrong way. Taylor punched him twice in the face. The police questioned him about the incident but the farmer, for whatever reason, refused to press charges or cooperate."

"I imagine Taylor threatened him," said Klein.

"Probably. He shows up every week or so, usually late at night, to pick up a load of booze from Roter's warehouse. Then, he drives across the border into Hampton where the cases are loaded on trucks headed for Minneapolis, maybe as far as New York."

"For Rosen's operation, I presume?"

"That's what I heard, yes."

"So what about Dickens?" asked Klein, crushing out his cigarette in a glass ashtray.

"Dickens, as you're aware, works for the Standard Grain Company. In fact, I met him once briefly about six months ago when you had me trailing that grain broker Donald Lucas."

"Right, whose wife, Anna, was sure he had a second family hidden away."

Geller laughed. "That's the case. There was no second family. Lucas was just screwing around with a secretary. Dickens knew the secretary and Lucas so I asked him a few questions. He's a bit strange. Dickens has been reporting to Jack Smythe, the manager in Vera, on an expansion the company is planning. I don't have all the details. However, if Mrs. Tillsdale is to be believed, Smythe's the most popular man in the town. No one has a bad word to say about him. If anyone has a problem, Smythe is the first person they call. Dickens has been meeting with Smythe every few weeks."

"So what's so unusual about that?"

Geller lowered his voice. "Smythe's wife, Mrs. Joannie Smythe, is a real doll."

Klein nodded. "She's a doll, all right. Great legs. She's one of Rae Roter's close friends."

"That's right. Well, according to Mrs. Tillsdale, the Smythes have a lousy marriage. No matter how hard Mr. Smythe works, he can't seem to satisfy his wife's needs. She wants more of everything. And that includes in the bedroom. Apparently, Mrs. Smythe has an appetite that can't be satisfied. While Mr. Smythe is at the office in the evening, Dickens has been seen coming and going from their house—many times. It's hard to believe that Smythe doesn't know about it."

"I can't imagine Reverend Vivian would approve of that," said Klein. "Screwing another man's wife is almost as bad as being a drunk. And I've also met Dickens's wife. She's tough as nails. If Vivian doesn't kill him for this, his wife sure as hell will."

"Wait, there's more. A day or so before I arrived, none other than Sid Sharp showed up in town. I never saw him, but I know who he is. He was poking around, asking questions about Max Roter and Taylor. He might have also talked to the police."

"Sid Sharp, you sure?"

Geller nodded. "Yeah, he works for Saul Sugarman, doesn't he?"

Klein nodded. "He's Sugarman's errand boy."

"What else do you know about him?"

"He's got a nasty side to him. A few months back, there was a bartender at the McLaren Hotel. Last name was Ellice, as I recall. He was bad-mouthing the Sugarmans. Telling everyone who'd listen that the Sugarmans were crooks. That they were charging too much for their whisky, which was watered down.

The story goes that Saul sent Sharp to see Ellice who wound up with a few broken ribs. He left the city soon after. At the time, I asked Lou about it but he claimed to know nothing. Lou's a decent man, but he is a blind fool when it comes to his brother."

"So let me finish," said Geller, his voice rising. "Sharp has also been seen going in and out of the Smythe house—just a few days ago, in fact."

Klein lit another cigarette. "It's a great story, Alec, but I don't see what it has to do with Max's murder or what's been going on here. And we still don't know what's in those papers or who knocked you out. On the other hand, Mrs. Smythe might know something that could help unravel this. Hell, she might even have information about Frankie Taylor on the night of the robbery. Or she could know if anyone else had it out for Max. I suppose there's a good possibility that if she's in the city, Dickens will see her. If we could speak to Dickens, preferably before the police find him, we might be able to figure out if Vivian really is behind the shootings."

"What if that's true, Sam? Isn't it possible that Vivian could've ordered Dickens to kill Max? You know the murder has all but halted the Sugarmans' liquor trade in Vera and a few nearby towns."

"But for how long? The booze is still locked in the warehouse. Saul's no fool. He'll get those shipments started again. If Taylor has been scared off, then I can guarantee Rosen will send in another bootlegger. There's too much money at stake for him and the Sugarmans."

"So how do you want to handle it?" asked Geller, leaning forward.

"I want you to plant yourself in the lobby of the Royal Alex, where Mrs. Smythe is staying. With any luck, Dickens might show up real soon."

Their discussion was interrupted by Sarah's call from the kitchen that dinner was ready. Mel burst into the living room, grabbing Klein's hand. "Daddy come," he ordered.

The light from the setting sun, a mixture of red and yellow, burst into the kitchen illuminating everything it touched. Sarah beckoned Freda and Bernice, both wearing their best white cotton dresses with light blue flowery patterns embroidered at the hems, by her side. She struck a match and lit the two candles in the elegant silver candlestick holders that had once belonged to Klein's great-great-grandmother in Mezerich, the town in the Pale of Settlement in western Russia where the family once lived. Sarah instructed her daughters to embrace the flames, welcoming the Sabbath, and then to cover their eyes. Together, the three of them recited the Hebrew blessing for the Shabbat candles, proudly led by young Freda who had recently learned the blessings at the Peretz School.

Next, Klein poured each adult a glass of red wine and his children glasses of grape juice and he recited the Kiddush prayer as he did every Friday night. Lighting the candles and reciting the Sabbath prayers was the one religious custom both Sam and Sarah followed, mainly because they felt it was important for their children. Everyone then washed their hands in a bowl of water. Finally, Klein removed the napkin over the two challah loafs, lifted them, and, with his children's help, said the blessing on the bread. He ripped a piece off for everyone and passed the pieces around the table.

"Now, we can eat," Klein declared.

"Sarah, everything is delicious," said Geller. "I can tell you, I feel much better."

"Here, Alec, have another knish, and more chicken," said Shayna, piling up his plate with food.

Geller laughed. "She takes good care of me, that's for sure."

Sarah had outdone herself. There was cabbage borsht, stuffed roast chicken, carrot *tzimmes*, *kreplach*, potato knishes, and, of course, Klein's favourite: chicken *gribenes*—pieces of fried chicken fat. She liked to say that if you keep a man content in the kitchen and the bedroom, then you'll have a happy marriage. In that respect, Klein could hardly complain. Sarah may not have looked or acted like a typical North End matriarch, but she had mastered the art of cooking on par with Klein's late mother Freda, against whom she would forever be judged.

Alec finished his dinner and traded funny faces with Bernice and Mel across the table. Both children giggled.

"You'll make a wonderful father someday, Alec ... whenever that will be," Sarah teased him.

"Leave the man alone. He's been through enough," said Klein with a grin.

Alec laughed. "All in good time. And I promise you, Sarah, after Shayna, you'll be the first person I tell."

Shayna's face turned a deep red as Sarah and Klein chuckled.

When dinner was finished, Sarah served tea and honey cake for dessert. Klein broke off a piece of brown sugar from the small bowl on the table, wedged it between his back teeth, and sipped his tea.

"Mommy, I want to play outside," said Bernice.

"Me too," Mel chimed in.

Sarah considered the request for a moment. "Freda, will you watch them both?"

Freda nodded, proud to accept this responsibility.

"Bernice, Mel, you stay near the front of the house and listen to your sister," said Sarah.

Both children nodded. "Yes, Mommy," they said in unison.

As Alec helped Sarah clear the table of dishes—Alec's past experience in the orphanage made him handier in the kitchen than most men—Klein escorted Shayna into the living room.

"You and Alec are a good fit," said Klein.

Shayna flashed a large smile. "He means everything to me."

"Of course he does," said Klein, lowering his voice. "Shayna, I have a favour to ask of you. I'd like you to keep this strictly between us. I'd rather you not even speak to Alec about it."

Her smile vanished. "I ... I don't know. What is it you want?"

"You're aware of what is going on with the Sugarmans, with Max Roter's murder?"

She nodded. "How could I not be?"

"Exactly. And I know you are grateful that Saul Sugarman has offered you a job and that you wouldn't want to do anything to ruin that. But I have to tell you that not everything is ... how shall I put this … kosher with Saul. I believe that he is somehow responsible for what happened to Max and Lou."

"I thought Reverend Vivian's the one who planned these attacks. That's what I heard Mr. Sugarman say. And he was quite firm."

"You must believe me, Shayna, there's much more to it than that."

"So what do you want of me, Sam?"

"It's simple, really. I'd like you to keep your eyes and ears on Saul. You're close to him. He's arrogant enough not to pay attention to you. And I don't mean to insult you, but you'd agree he's like that."

"I do, yes."

"So over the next few days, maybe the next week, just watch and listen. If you see or hear anything that you regard as suspicious or out of the ordinary, I want you to contact me and me alone. Will you do this?"

Shayna glanced down at the floor. "I don't know, Sam. It seems dishonest to me. Can I think about it more?"

Klein was about to respond when he heard a shout from the front hallway. The door opened and Freda poked her head in. "Daddy, come here. Some men are talking to Bernice."

"Some men?"

Freda was about to cry. She pointed outside to the street.

Klein was stunned by what he saw. Parked in front of his house was the black McLaughlin Buick he had seen at the Shaarey Zedek with the two thugs. The taller man was behind the wheel. And the other gangster with the eyepatch was standing beside the car with Bernice in his arms. She was squirming to free herself. Mel stood farther back on the sidewalk.

Calmly, Klein approached the two men. When he reached Mel, he told Freda to come forward and take her brother back to the house. She did so. By the time, she reached the front stoop, Shayna, Alec, and Sarah were also outside.

"Shailek, what is going on?" Sarah cried. "Where's Bernice?" As Freda and Mel ran to her, she put her arms around them.

"Just stay there, all of you. I'm handling it," said Klein. Alec began to walk forward. "You, too, Alec, just stay put." Alec stopped moving but glowered at the man holding Bernice.

"Please put my daughter down," said Klein. His words were measured.

"Daddy, Daddy," cried Bernice.

Keeping an eye on the man in the car, whom he suspected was holding a gun, Klein moved towards Bernice, who had tears in her eyes.

"She's a cute kid," said the man with the eyepatch. He passed Bernice over to Klein.

Sarah ran forward and took her from him, hugging her closely. "Niecee, are you okay?"

The little girl nodded. "That man isn't nice. Not nice at all."

"Who are you and what you do want?" Klein asked the men.

"Yeah, we haven't introduced ourselves, have we?" said the man with the eyepatch. "You can call me Richie or One-eye Richie. And in the car behind me is Paulie the Plumber. He's packing so don't do anything stupid, Klein."

"I saw you arrive on the train from Minneapolis and then

there was that shooting. And again, today, you were at the synagogue. I'm pretty sure whoever was shooting was aiming at you as well."

"That's possible," said Richie. "Don't you think that's possible, Paulie?"

"I do," said Paulie, grinning. "Good thing he keeps missing."

"You still haven't said why you are now parked in front of my house and bothering my family."

"I'm getting to that, Klein," said Richie, moving closer. "Here's the thing. I know you've been poking your nose into the Sugarmans' business. Asking lots of questions about what happened in Vera and in the city."

"We've already talked about this."

"I guess we have."

"I was hired by Lou Sugarman. He's the one I answer to."

"Yes, yes, we know about that. Lou's not well, as you know. Might not even recover. And didn't Saul Sugarman fire you?"

"Not exactly."

"I don't know what that means, Klein, and really, I don't give a damn. We want you to stop your investigation into the shooting in Vera and anything else to do with the Sugarmans' business. Let the police do what they want. You go after Reverend Vivian."

"Is that who's been shooting at you? One of Vivian's men?"

"Difficult to say. In our line of work, we have as many enemies as friends."

"And what line of work are you in, exactly?" asked Klein.

"Protection."

"I see. Who are you protecting now?"

"We are here, Sam. We're here to protect you and your family. Neither of us would want to see any harm come to any of those delightful children of yours or that beautiful wife," said Richie, smiling. "We know all about her."

Klein clenched his fists and grabbed Richie's jacket collar.

Paulie immediately stuck a pistol out the window and pointed it at Klein's head.

"Everyone take it easy. Klein, we honestly don't want any trouble," said Richie, carefully pushing Klein's hands away. He glanced at Paulie, who lowered his weapon. "We're just here to give you a friendly warning, that's it. You're a smart man. You'll do the right thing."

One-eye Richie extended his hand towards Klein, but he would not shake it. "Suit yourself," he said with a shrug. Richie walked around the front of the car and got in the passenger seat. Paulie started the vehicle and a moment later, the Buick sped towards Salter Street.

Klein's palms were sweaty. He looked up and noticed Mrs. Fester's face in her front window. She looked white as a ghost.

Klein turned and walked back to his family, Alec, and Shayna. Bernice jumped into his arms. "Well, that was exciting, wasn't it, Niecee? I think it would be a good idea for you to not talk to strangers. Can you do that for me?"

Bernice nodded. "No more strangers. That man was scary."

"He was," said Klein.

"You okay?" asked Alec. "What did they want?"

"They want me to stop asking questions about the Sugarmans' booze business."

"You think Sugarman sent them?"

"Don't know. But he's involved with them one way or another."

"He would never hurt my children," said Sarah, her voice
trembling slightly. "I can't believe that."

Klein stared at her and shook his head. "Let's get the kids
inside." He put Bernice down and she ran to Sarah, who was
holding onto Mel's hand. Freda was right next to her. She and the
children went into the house followed by Alec. As Klein walked
forward, Shayna, who was standing behind him, grabbed his
arm.

"Okay, Sam. I'll do what you asked," she whispered. "Those
were your kids…"

Klein nodded, lightly grasped her hand, and they both
stepped into the house.

By ten o'clock that evening, Klein was exhausted. It had been as
busy and trying a day as he had had in a very long time. After the
children were in their beds and sleeping and Alec and Shayna
had left, Sarah returned to the kitchen to put away the dishes.
Deep in thought, Sam lay down to rest in his and Sarah's bed.

His mind was racing with a dozen different scenarios and
questions which he still did not have answers for. Sifting and re-
sifting through the many details of this case—Max Roter's murder in Vera, the possible involvement of the bootlegger Frankie
Tayler, the shootings at the CPR station and the Shaarey Zedek
Synagogue, and the two thugs, One-eye Richie and Paulie the

Plumber—he kept coming back to one focal point: Saul Sugarman. He knew that though he did not yet have all the facts, Sugarman, rather than Reverend John Vivian as the police seemed to believe, was the linchpin to understanding what had thus far transpired. Sarah, and perhaps even Alec and McCreary, who both knew of Sarah's relationship with Sugarman, would argue that he was inherently biased towards him, that he would never forgive Sugarman for what he had done. That may be so, he thought, but that was not governing his thinking in this case. He only had to uncover the evidence that would prove Sugarman's culpability.

Sarah walked into the bedroom and was pleasantly surprised to find Klein asleep. She stared at him for a moment, again berating herself for being so thoughtless and impulsive and for jeopardizing their marriage. "Shailek," she said softly.

Her voice roused Klein. "I must've dozed off," he mumbled.

She sat beside him on the bed. "Please tell me that the children are safe."

"They are, don't worry."

"I won't. I trust you."

"Anything else? Or can I go back to sleep?"

Sarah hesitated for a moment. "There is something I wanted to ask you about."

"I'm listening."

"That policewoman I met at the synagogue, what was her name?"

Klein's eyes widened a bit more. "Hannah Nash, why?"

"She seems very nice."

"Uh, huh."

"She's married?" Sarah asked, shifting her legs.

"Her husband died, some years ago."

"That's terrible."

"It is, but I think she's managed," said Klein, sitting up. "Why the sudden interest in Hannah?"

Sarah shrugged her shoulders.

"Out with it. What's really on your mind?"

"I … I think she likes you, Shailek, and I think you like her too," she blurted.

Klein stood up. "You're talking nonsense," he said.

"I don't think so," said Sarah, reaching for Klein's hand. "Why don't you get out of your clothes? You'll be more comfortable." Sarah undressed, slipping on a green lace nightgown.

Klein looked into Sarah's eyes and shook his head. He wasn't all that surprised by her questions about Hannah. She always had been perceptive. Whatever Sarah sensed, there was no point in discussing it further; his encounter with Hannah Nash three years ago was a pleasant memory and part of his past. His present and future were Sarah and the children.

He undid the buttons of his shirt and undressed. The June air outside was thick and sticky and the second floor of the house was particularly hot. Sarah got into bed and covered herself with a thin sheet. Klein slid back into bed and wrapped his arms around her. Within a moment, they kissed deeply and passionately.

13

The downtown safehouse was not a house at all, but a room located on the second floor of a dry goods warehouse close to the corner of McDermot Avenue and Princess Street. The property belonged to Adam Cole, a wholesale supplier of pots, pans, utensils, small hardware items, and assorted knick-knacks to shops and stores throughout the city as well as the country. He was also another of Reverend John Vivian's devoted disciples.

On Christmas Day, 1920, Cole, his wife, Hilda, and their four-year-old son, Luke, were travelling home in their automobile from a party in Stonewall, where Hilda's parents lived. Close to the city limits, a car, coming from the opposite direction and driven by Ted Thompson, twenty years old and drunk, crossed over to the wrong side of the road and crashed head-on into the Coles. Thompson broke his arm and was severely shaken. Similarly, Adam and Hilda were only slightly injured, but the impact threw young Luke from the vehicle. Ever since that tragedy, Cole had been one of Vivian's most avid supporters.

George Dickens's hands shook as he pried open the back door to Cole's warehouse. For the past few hours, he had been hiding out at a café in St. James where he knew everyone minded their own business. Still, after he had telephoned Hilda Cole, who had relayed the message from his wife Maggie that the police were searching for him, his anxiety level had increased dramatically. Every time a new customer had come into the café, Dickens nearly panicked.

Calming himself, he followed Vivian's protocol and made his way to Cole's warehouse.

The back room was dark and Dickens feared that he had misunderstood the plan.

"Anyone here?" he called out. He took a few steps forward and walked right into a pile of wooden crates. A few seconds later, a lantern flickered on from a room about twenty feet ahead.

"In here, George," said the distinctive voice.

Dickens's heart beat faster. It was Reverend Vivian. Following the light, he carefully plodded his way through the maze of crates filled with wool, bolts of cloth, and a high stack of brushes and brooms. He poked his head into a small room and there, sitting in a chair at a wooden table, was the reverend, his face and features illuminated by the lantern. He motioned for Dickens to sit in the stool opposite him.

"You've had a busy day, George," said Vivian.

"It was the craziest thing you've seen. I was in the library at the time we had planned. And I was about to fire a few shots, just to scare the Sugarmans as you had told me. But then…"

"There was someone else after them."

"Yes," said Dickens, wiping the sweat from his brow with his handkerchief.

"That's the price you pay for doing the devil's bidding. And Satan will follow the Sugarmans to their graves, for they are sinners beyond redemption."

"But now the police think that I was the shooter," said Dickens.

"Yes, George, I'm well aware of everything that has gone on. You must trust me. Can you do that?"

"Always. You know I have absolute faith in your judgment in anything to do with our battle."

"I know you do. So this is what I want you to do. Tomorrow morning at nine o'clock sharp you will meet my attorney, Graham Powers, at the main entrance to the Central Police Station. You'll bring your long sack with you…"

"My sack with my gun…"

Vivian held his hand up. "Please let me finish. In the other room, close to the exit, is a crate of shovels. Take one with you and place it in the sack. You'll tell the police, Detective Allard no doubt, that prior to visiting the library you had purchased the shovel from Cole's Wholesale. Here's the receipt dated today." He handed Dickens a slip of paper. "If asked, Cole will verify the purchase. You'll then tell the police that you merely wandered up to the second floor and opened the window because you weren't feeling well. It's as simple as that. Mr. Powers will handle any other questions or concerns. I expect everything will go smoothly and you'll no longer be a suspect in this incident."

"And then what am I to do?"

"Yes, we're not quite done with the Sugarmans yet."

From the other room, the sound of the back door could be heard creaking open. Dickens immediately stood up and grabbed a wooden pole leaning on the wall behind him.

"That's quite unnecessary, George. I know who it is. We're in here," Vivian called out into the darkness.

A moment later, Joannie Smythe walked into the room and Dickens relaxed.

"Mrs. Smythe, I'm so glad you can join us. You, too, have had an eventful day, I presume," said Vivian.

"I have indeed." Gone was her vivacious and alluring smile. Her hazel eyes were fixed on Vivian and her lips were pursed tightly together.

"You know Mr. Dickens, of course."

Joannie nodded. "Yes. It's good to see you again, George, even under these trying circumstances."

"So what's the news from the hospital?" asked Vivian.

"Lou Sugarman remains unconscious and the doctors and nurses are monitoring his progress. Have you any idea how this could've happened?"

"I've heard rumours, but I'd rather not speculate further at the moment. It only matters that these events at the railway station and the synagogue will serve our larger purpose. You must put aside your feelings for Mrs. Roter and think of what we are trying to accomplish."

"I am with you, Reverend … in everything."

Vivian stood up and lightly took Joannie's hand. "Always

remember that a bottle of whisky is responsible for the appalling abuse you've had to endure these many years."

"How can I serve you?"

"Mr. Dickens will speak to the police tomorrow morning so that he can be cleared as a suspect in today's shooting. He'll then meet you at your hotel. I assume you have Mr. Sharp under control?"

"I do, though it's been difficult."

"We all appreciate your sacrifice, Joannie. Your friendship with Sharp will prove useful, you know that?"

Joannie cringed slightly. "As I've said, I'm prepared to do my part."

"I know I can count on you. I want you to keep George safe and prepare him for the coming task. That should take place in a few days."

"The coming task?" asked Dickens.

"We have a golden opportunity, here, George. No matter what happens, this other party who has been causing so much havoc will be ultimately blamed. I'll ensure that. We're free to do not only what is necessary, but what is just."

Dickens, his eyes wide, stared at Vivian and Joannie.

"That's correct, George. You are going to send Saul Sugarman back to his Maker. For as it is written in Romans, chapter six, verse twenty-three: the wages of sin is death. Always remember that."

Saturday morning brought another day of warm and pleasant temperatures. By nine o'clock, the sun was already hot in the deep blue prairie sky and Winnipeg was alive with activity. The streetcars were full ferrying shoppers to Eaton's, FW Woolworth Company, Robinson's Clothes, and other downtown stores; the merchants and clerks who would faithfully serve them; factory workers; and lucky ones rushing to the CPR station to catch the early train to Winnipeg Beach for a day of sun at the lake and some fun on the town's boardwalk rides.

Winnipeg had long been a city divided between the "haves" and the "have-nots," as the bitter General Strike had made clear. But the lines, once fairly distinct, were shifting. A growing middle-class was challenging the rule of the traditional elite who ran city hall and even the children of immigrants were beginning to assert themselves in ways that made the White Anglo-Protestant majority increasingly nervous. Hence, among the Saturday shoppers were Ukrainian women from the North End who enjoyed venturing beyond Selkirk Avenue and a small contingent of middle-class Jewish women from River Heights who opted to skip synagogue services to get an early start.

Automobiles, too, increased the morning traffic, many chauffeuring refined ladies from their homes in Crescentwood, Wellington Crescent, and even as far as the city of Tuxedo. There was no class distinction when it came to these women. They were the wives of grain, banking, insurance, and business executives, planning to spend several hours shopping at Hollinsworth and Holt Renfrew, among other high-end stores they frequented. Then, close to one o'clock, their chauffeurs would drive them the short distance to the Royal Alexandra Hotel for a leisurely lunch at the Grand Café. Grilled Pacific halibut steak or hot-loaf of homemade fois gras with green peas were two lunch-time favourites.

Those fortunate enough to be on the guest list for the four o'clock wedding of Graham Powers's daughter Jean to Wilson Edmunds, the son of Graham's law partner Charles Sinclair, at the Holy Trinity Church would have to cut their shopping day short in order to prepare for the celebration later in the afternoon and early evening.

The wedding, which was only hours away, was the reason Graham Powers was pacing in front of the main entrance to the Central Police Station. When he informed his wife, Julia, that he had business to attend to for a few hours on the day of their daughter's wedding, she was not pleased. But Powers could not refuse Reverend Vivian's request to accompany George Dickens when he turned himself in to the police for questioning. Since he had left the crown's office and went into private practice with Charles Sinclair, the reverend was one of his most important clients and one who always paid his legal fees on time. Wedding or not, he could not jeopardize this relationship.

Powers was dressed in a grey suit, too hot for the weather yet he never would have conducted business wearing anything less formal. It just wasn't done. That was a rule he had learned from his late father, Alfred, one of the great lawyers in the annals of the Winnipeg legal establishment. Graham might not have agreed with his father on most issues—in truth, they bickered about everything from the time Graham was seventeen and especially once he became a lawyer—but proper business attire was not one of them.

Powers checked his watch; it was ten past nine. He looked in the direction of Main Street and there, walking towards him, was George Dickens.

"You're late, Dickens, and this is not a good day to be late," said Powers.

"My apologies, sir. I didn't sleep well last night and misjudged how long it would take to walk here."

Powers eyed Dickens up and down. "You don't look very well, Dickens. You look tired and your face is pale and white. In fact, if I was a detective, I would say that you were guilty of something. Are you?"

"Absolutely not," Dickens stammered. "It's just the heat. And I have lots on my mind."

"Well, clear your head, right now. You have to answer the questions you are asked in a way that will leave no doubt about your innocence. The reverend said you were capable of doing this. Is that true?"

Dickens nodded. "I've done nothing wrong. Please, let's get this over with."

Dickens followed Powers into the station. He was indeed as nervous as Powers had suggested. Reverend Vivian had insisted that he stay the night in Adam Cole's warehouse. There was a small, uncomfortable, metal-framed bed on the second floor of the building where he could sleep. Yet, following further discussion with the reverend and the charming Mrs. Smythe about the task ahead, sleep proved impossible. He knew he had nothing to hide regarding what had happened in the library, other than a white lie about his true intentions. That he could manage. What he feared were more probing questions about his views on the Sugarmans and his connection to the reverend that could make the police suspicious. If ever there was a time to be calm and collected, this was it.

Powers and Dickens found McCreary waiting for them at the top of the stairs.

"We'll talk in here," said McCreary, leading the two men into the same interrogation room where Reverend Vivian had been questioned a day earlier. There waiting for them were Detectives Allard, Nash, and Klein.

Powers was taken aback. "I thought this was to be a friendly chat. Mr. Dickens is happy to answer your questions. But I'd like to know why a private detective is involved in this." He glared at Klein.

"Graham, it's been a while," remarked Klein.

"Mr. Klein is consulting on this case with the approval of Chief Newton. Any objections?" asked Allard.

"I suppose not. Sure hope you know what you're doing. My experience with Mr. Klein is that when he's around, more problems arise."

"I couldn't agree with you more," said McCreary, lighting a cigar.

"Well, I take that as a compliment, Graham. I'm proud to say that your father felt much differently."

"Mr. Dickens, please sit here. Mr. Powers, you can take the chair next to him," said Allard.

For the next hour, Allard, taking the lead in the questioning, reviewed Dickens's movements on Friday and how he wound up at the library at the time of the shooting. With a coolness that even surprised him, Dickens explained how he had decided to play hooky from his job as a clerk at the Standard Grain Company and do some work around his house. He said he had purchased a shovel at Cole's warehouse and showed Allard the receipt. This was what he was carrying in the long sack at the library and which he presumed his neighbour Mary Turner had seen him with. On a whim, he had decided to visit the library, unfortunately at the time when the shooting took place across the street at the synagogue and when he ran into the bothersome Mrs. Turner.

"It's a good story, Mr. Dickens," said Allard.

"It's not a story; it's the truth," Dickens pleaded.

Powers leaned forward. "As I've told you, Mr. Dickens had nothing whatsoever to do with the shooting. Is he free to go now?"

"Not quite," said Allard. He looked back to Dickens. "Tell us, please: what is your relationship with Reverend Vivian?"

Dickens glanced at Powers for support. "Go ahead, George," the lawyer advised.

"The reverend is a great man. I serve him and the important cause he fights for: the abolition of the liquor trade."

"Isn't it true that Adam Cole, the owner of the wholesale company where you allegedly purchased the shovel, is also one of the reverend's avid supporters?"

"I believe that's true. So what of it? He's a good man and I only deal with men of high morality."

"I assume that Reverend Vivian, you, or Mr. Cole wouldn't

have been too upset if the shooter had, in fact, killed both Sugarmans?"

"I can't speak for the other two. I don't condone murder. But the Sugarmans have chosen the path of the devil. Their fate is sealed."

Klein shook his head. "May I ask a question, Detective?"

Allard looked at McCreary. "This is your vaudeville show, Allard, don't look at me," McCreary scoffed.

"Go on, Klein," said Allard. "But keep it short."

"Thank you. I want to ask you about your recent trip to Vera."

"I thought we were here to discuss the shooting yesterday. What does my client's out-of-town business have to do with anything?" asked Powers, his voice firm.

"Mr. Powers, it's not a problem. I can answer the question," said Dickens. "I was in Vera last weekend for business. My boss, Mr. Kingston, asked me to review the operations there with Jack Smythe, who runs the grain elevator in Vera. It's as simple as that."

"And you were there from Friday until Monday, is that right?"

Dickens nodded.

"You're aware that Max Roter, the husband of Rae Roter, a sister to the Sugarman brothers, was robbed and killed late last Saturday evening."

"Of course I know of it. Everyone in town was talking about it."

"It's a terrible thing, isn't it?" asked Klein.

"Again, as I understand it, Mr. Roter was also involved with the liquor trade. I'm afraid his fate was sealed as well."

"So you didn't have anything to do with his death?"

"That's it, Allard, McCreary. We're out of here," declared Powers, standing.

"No, I'll answer," said Dickens. "Mr. Klein, I have absolutely no knowledge of this crime. But as I said, it wouldn't surprise me if it had something to do with Mr. Roter's connection to the bootlegging business."

Powers looked at Allard. "Detective, unless you're planning to charge my client with a crime, we are now leaving."

"We're not charging him with anything, but we might like to question him again so I'd appreciate it if you could keep me informed if he is planning to leave the city again."

"I'll consider it," said Powers, grabbing Dickens by the arm and leading him out of the room. On the way out, they passed a constable who was out of breath, holding a telegram.

"Spit it out, Jenkins," Allard ordered.

"Yes, sir. I … I have a telegram for the commissioner," Constable Jenkins said, handing the piece of paper to McCreary.

McCreary read it quickly and gave it to Hannah Nash. "My word," she said.

"What is it? What's happened? Will one of you please tell me?" asked Allard.

McCreary took the telegram back from Nash and re-read it. "Early this morning, there were two other shootings, one in Crystal City, not far from Vera, and the other in Carnduff, Saskatchewan. Two men were killed, one in each town. The owner of a hardware store in Crystal City and a café operator in Carnduff."

"That's terrible, of course. But what has Mrs. Nash so upset?"

McCreary took a last drag of his cigar, blew the smoke in Klein's direction and butted it on the edge of the desk. "You know where these two towns are located, Allard?"

"Well, Crystal City I know is south of Winnipeg, close to the US border. Not sure of Carnduff."

"I've been through there," said Nash. "It's in southern Saskatchewan, about twenty miles from the border as well."

"That's right. And, as it turns out, both men were selling booze to bootleggers," said McCreary. He turned to Hannah. "Mrs. Nash, I think you and I are taking a train trip in the next few hours."

14

Klein left the police station trying to sort out what he had heard. He was not certain whether or not George Dickens was responsible for the shooting at the synagogue or the train station but he was sure of one thing: Dickens was hiding something from them. His calm manner did not fool Klein for a moment. Still, as he dodged the Saturday morning Main Street pedestrian traffic, the key question swirling in his head was the same as it had been for the past few days: could Reverend John Vivian have contrived all that had occurred? Moreover, in light of the recent killings in Crystal City and Carnduff, was the reverend's anti-liquor crusade so extensive that he had plotted murders outside the city, including in Vera? Could Vivian be that fanatical and ruthless? Klein's initial feeling was that, yes, he could.

Or was there another explanation, as he had thought from the beginning of this case: that everything that had gone on was somehow linked to Irv Rosen's bootleg operations and that quite possibly someone—Dominik Vitale or his sidekick, Vinny "the Pick" Piccolo, in Chicago seemed like the most logical suspects—was trying to drive Rosen from the lucrative business? That theory could explain the attempts on the Sugarmans. But Klein would have to learn more about the two recent killings. Who were the bootleggers these liquor traders were dealing with?

He had one other idea on how to figure this out. It was probably futile, yet he decided that he had little to lose. Sarah frequently pointed out that as a detective, Klein's unrelenting stubbornness was both a strength and a liability. There was always a fine line between being persistent as opposed to plain obstinate. Klein knew that bothering certain individuals, especially those with real or imagined power, could backfire. "No one likes a nuisance," Sarah repeatedly warned him. True enough, thought Klein, as he reached the Canadian Northern telegraph office, but sometimes being a *nudnik* produced results. He grabbed a pencil and wrote a message:

> To: Rosen c/o Ratner's, 102 Norfolk Street, New York, NY. Vera, Crystal City, Carnduff, Winnipeg. Need to speak with you soonest. Klein.

Klein considered asking about the two thugs, Paulie and Richie, who he believed were Rosen's men, or at least associated with him. Why were they still in the city and why were they so concerned about Klein's investigation that they showed up at his house? But, Klein knew, too, that Rosen had to be handled with great care; asking too many questions would merely anger him. Keep it simple, thought Klein, as he handed the clerk the telegram, and maybe Rosen would provide the answers he was seeking.

It was, of course, possible that Paulie and Richie's presence had nothing to do with the shootings, that the recent violence indeed had been masterminded by Reverend Vivian, and that there were other issues between Rosen and the Sugarmans that required the intervention of the gangsters. Either way, Klein wanted to find that out for himself. Another conversation with those two was needed, one in which his wife and children were not present and that Klein could control. Late last night, he had wisely sent a note to Melinda with a request to keep an eye out for Paulie and Richie and to notify him at once if they showed up at her house or any other brothel—which he was certain they would sooner or later. Not only did the ladies of Point Douglas possess many talents, but most of them were loyal and discreet. Paulie and Richie did not have a chance.

As the train meandered south of the city, Hannah was grateful for the short pause in the investigation. She eyed McCreary in the seat opposite her. He had his nose in the Saturday edition of the *Free Press* and, much to her surprise, had not said as much as a word to her since they boarded. He was a boor to be sure, but she had always respected his skills as a detective.

Hannah did have a few thoughts about what had transpired in Crystal City and Carnduff and how they might be connected to Max Roter's murder in Vera. And she was prepared to share them with McCreary whenever he asked. However, for the moment, she opened the book she had brought with her from Calgary and started reading.

"*The Beautiful and Damned.* What the hell kind of title is that?" asked McCreary.

Nash smiled. "It's by a young American writer, F. Scott Fitzgerald. His second novel."

"Never heard of him."

"Why doesn't that surprise me?"

"So, is it any good?"

Nash was slightly taken aback by the question. "You're really interested?"

"I wouldn't ask if I wasn't," said McCreary, lighting a cigar.

"Actually, you'd probably like it. There's plenty of drinking, smoking, and carousing."

"Sounds interesting," said McCreary. He drew heavily on his cigar and blew the smoke upward. He stared at Hannah for a moment as she continued reading her book. "So, what is it between you and Klein, Mrs. Nash?" His tone was calm as if he was asking her about the weather.

She quickly looked up at him. "There's nothing between me and Mr. Klein," snapped Nash, her face reddening. "That's rather forward of you."

"I meant no disrespect. I figure we're on the train. It's quiet and you might want to talk of it. I think it's on your mind."

"You do?" said Nash, her voice more easy. "Okay, McCreary. I do like Sam, I won't lie to you. And I suspect it's obvious."

"It is."

"But it's not what you're implying. He's a married man with a family. The fact is, I respect his abilities as an investigator. Though I'm sure you hate to admit it, Klein's instincts about a case are usually correct."

"He would have made a decent cop, I'll grant you that. But if he wasn't married…"

"And if I was the Queen of England, I wouldn't be sitting here having this conversation with you."

That comment brought a slight smile to McCreary's face. "Fine, let's talk business. What do you know about a Chicago gangster named Vinny Piccolo?"

"I've read reports about him. Dangerous and volatile. Parents were Italian immigrants and he was born in New Jersey. He's now twenty-five years old and has been involved in racketeering and prostitution since he was a teenager. A few years back, he got into a fight at a New York City saloon with a thug by the name of Tony Abruzzo. If memory serves me correctly, Piccolo came after Abruzzo with an ice pick, which is why he's fittingly called 'the Pick.' But Abruzzo didn't back down. He slashed Piccolo across the face with a knife. Left him with a nasty scar. Last year, Piccolo started working for Dominik Vitale in Chicago, overseeing his operations. Vitale and Piccolo were likely involved in the murder of 'Blue Eyes' Anthony Cellini, who tried to stop Vitale from bootlegging once Prohibition was in place. You think these two gangsters are somehow mixed up in what's happened?"

"You win the prize, Nash. That's it exactly. My best hunch is that we're caught up in a booze and gangster war between New

York and Chicago. Maybe between the Nate and Irv Mob, Nate Katz and Irv Rosen, on one side and Vitale and Piccolo on the other. We need to find out more about the two men killed in these towns. See who they were dealing with."

"Makes sense," said Nash. "Tell me, aren't the Sugarmans selling liquor to the Rosen group?"

"They are and I agree. It's quite possible that this feud is behind what's gone on in the city."

Thirty minutes later, the train pulled into Vera. Sergeant Sundell and two of his men were standing on the platform waiting for McCreary and Nash.

"Commissioner," barked Sundell. "Good to see you again, sir." The two provincial police officers beside him smartly saluted as well.

"At ease, gentlemen," said McCreary, awkwardly returning the salute. At that moment, he wondered how he had got himself into this position, policing the province when he would much rather have been back in more familiar territory in Winnipeg. "Sundell, I think you know Mrs. Nash from the Alberta Provincial Police. She's here to assist."

"Good to see you again, ma'am," said Sundell.

"Yes, Sergeant. I recall your recent visit to Calgary at the conference about American Prohibition."

"Bootleggers and booze. There's no end to this madness."

"Not madness, Sergeant, merely greed, insatiable greed."

Sundell nodded. "If you'll follow me, we can speak more freely at headquarters."

Late on a Saturday afternoon, Vera was busy—at least as busy as a town with less than 800 residents could be. A half-dozen horse-drawn wagons were parked in front of the hardware store and there were even a few Ford trucks crawling down Main Street leaving a cloud of dust as they passed.

"Just a normal Saturday here," said Sundell. "But folks are getting kind of anxious about the general store still being closed. They're tired of travelling to Emerson or Dominion City for groceries, me and my men included. Any idea when the store will be open again?"

"Can't say that I do. Up to the family, I suppose. But I'm sure something will be done very soon because there's a lot of booze in that warehouse. And right now, the bootleggers are finding their stock somewhere else," said McCreary.

"Which might explain what happened in Crystal City and Carnduff," Nash added.

Vera's provincial police office, if you could call it that, was a small room connected to the back of the post office. Inside there was a wide slab of wood propped up by two sawhorses, which served as a desk and a couple of wobbly old chairs. In the far corner of the room there was a cast-iron, wood-burning stove at least twenty years old.

"The government didn't give you much of a budget, McCreary?" asked Nash with a slight grin.

"You noticed. And this is nice compared to some of the other rural headquarters I've visited."

"I'd offer you both coffee, but with the heat, I didn't want to start up the stove. The café across the street serves a decent cup, however," said Sundell.

"Later. First give me your report. What have you learned about the two latest killings?" asked McCreary.

Sundell picked up some papers on the desk. "It's all in here, sir. The name of the individual shot and killed in Crystal City is Cornelius Jasper, who runs a hardware shop but was also selling liquor in small amounts to a bootlegger based in Munich, North Dakota. His wife found him by his liquor storehouse. So far, there are no witnesses. No one saw or heard anything according to Michaels who handled the investigation. It's the same story in Carnduff. I received a telephone call from a Constable Lipton. Angus Briggs was the café owner who was murdered. According to Lipton, his throat was slashed. Again, no one saw or heard anything. But like Mr. Jasper in Crystal City, Briggs was dealing booze with a bootlegger in Sherwood, North Dakota."

"Tell me, Sundell, is there anything in the report about who the bootleggers are connected to?"

"As a matter of fact, there is," said the sergeant, flipping the page. "The bootlegger from Munich is reputed to be Clive Molloy, a small-time hood and known to be an associate of Dominik Vitale, the Chicago gangster I'm sure you're familiar with."

"Interesting," said McCreary, looking at Hannah. "And the one in Carnduff?"

"Mr. Briggs was being supplied with liquor from the Sugarman brothers through a third party in Regina. We're not certain of the Sherwood bootlegger's identity yet. But the Saskatchewan police are fairly certain that he's mixed up with a ring of liquor traders operating out of Bismarck who send their liquor on to Rosen's men in Minneapolis."

"So, it seems you're correct, McCreary. There's a bootlegger war going on," said Nash.

"Seems so," said McCreary. He struck a match and lit a cigar. "What else, Sundell?"

"Only one other curious thing. Not sure if it means anything."

"Go on."

"The investigations in Crystal City and Carnduff turned up one fact. The same travelling salesman or drummer was visiting and staying overnight in each town on the very nights of the murders. Name is Henry Woodhead. Seems he travels by car as far west as Medicine Hat as representative for Cole's Wholesale Company in Winnipeg peddling small hardware items like shovels and garden utensils as well as pots and pans and the like."

"Cole's Wholesale. You sure about that?" asked McCreary.

Sundell glanced down at the report. "Yes, that's it. Cole's Wholesale on McDermot Avenue."

McCreary looked at Nash. "Didn't George Dickens say he purchased a shovel from Cole's Wholesale? And isn't Cole connected to Vivian? Maybe we have this wrong, Mrs. Nash. Maybe I was right the first time and the reverend is responsible. I'd like to speak to this Mr. Woodhead. Do you know where he is now, Sundell?"

"As a matter of fact, I do."

"You gonna tell me, Sundell, or keep it a secret."

"That's what I was about to tell you, sir. Mr. Woodhead drove into Vera about an hour before you. He's staying over at Mrs. Tillsdale's rooming house."

15

Sid Sharp, wearing the only suit he owned—dark grey but somewhat tattered—politely acknowledged the doorman in his impeccable red uniform with gold lace trim. Awkwardly holding a bouquet of red, pink, and yellow roses, he stepped into the imposing main entranceway of the Royal Alexandra Hotel. He immediately felt uncomfortable and for good reason. In class-conscious Winnipeg, the Royal Alex was part of a world in which Sharp, born on Flora Avenue in the North End to Russian Jewish immigrants, was definitely not a member.

Ever since the Canadian Pacific Railway opened the hotel in 1906 on the north-east corner of Higgins Avenue and Main Street, its majestic brick and granite exterior that personified Winnipeg's lofty aspirations symbolized wealth and opulence as well as the CPR's corporate power. There was no finer hotel in western Canada and for business travellers and tourists alike, the Royal Alex was the first choice of where to stay while visiting the city.

Sharp scanned the magnificent and spacious Grand Rotunda, a fine example of classical Edwardian architecture, which echoed the similar design of the CPR station directly across the street. The high ceiling in the rotunda was distinguished by gold-bordered, octagonal compartments, while the key feature of the lobby was its thick, white columns with finely engraved gold etchings at the top, resembling the laurel wreaths worn by Roman emperors. Rows of soft, brown leather couches and an assortment of chairs, wood tables, Persian rugs, and green foliage accentuated the rotunda's splendour.

Naturally, late on a Saturday afternoon, the hotel was busy. A long line of recently arrived travellers were checking in at the front desk. Other guests made their way to the Grand Café for cake and coffee. In the Tea Room, small groups of women—several meticulously outfitted in pink and yellow, flowered and plain organdie dresses and others in darker, silk-embroidered charmeuse dresses—enjoyed a late afternoon music performance by the hotel's pianist, violin, and cello players.

Nearby, their husbands, business executives in the city for work and social engagements, relaxed on the leather couches and chairs, smoking cigars and discussing politics and grain and stock prices. Various opinions echoed through the rotunda on the number one topic of the day: how the Panama Canal, one of the true wonders of the modern world, would impact Winnipeg's status as a railway, grain trade, and wholesale centre.

The canal had been completed in 1914, but the war had prevented it from being fully used. More than one businessman pointed out that owing to the canal, during the past two years Vancouver's port had been busier than ever. One rather loud gentleman asserted that Vancouver, whose population was increasing at a steady rate, would overtake Winnipeg as the country's third largest city.

"That would be a damn shame," the gentleman declared to the half-dozen executives surrounding him and hanging onto his every word. "The railways and grain trade put this city on the map, but it will be a canal built in mosquito-infested Panama that's about to change that. And, as usual, blame the bloody Americans. Teddy Roosevelt is the one who engineered the $350 million project in the first place."

In search of the elevators, Sharp first approached the hotel's main staircase. With its marble and bronze railings, the staircase was wide enough for a visiting royal couple to feel right at home. He moved passed a bride and groom posing for a photograph and then changed direction when he saw the row of elevators to his left.

He asked the smartly uniformed attendant to take him to the fourth floor. In his rush and excitement, Sharp, who was usually more astute, failed to notice Alec Geller, not so conspicuously watching his every move from the vantage point of the news stand.

"Beautiful day outside, isn't it?" remarked the elevator operator.

"Yeah, it is," muttered Sharp.

"I'm sure your wife will like those," the operator said, motioning to the bouquet of roses.

Sharp ignored the comment. The elevator stopped at the

fourth floor and he started walking to his left. He was looking for room 412, which was halfway down the hall. Taking a deep breath, he knocked twice. The door opened and there stood Joannie Smythe, resplendent in a flowing, baby blue, lace-trimmed chiffon negligee.

"Sid, you're a darling," she said as he handed her the roses. "I do hope you were discreet."

"I was. It's busy downstairs. I'm quite certain no one paid any attention to me."

"Good. Come in, please," she said, taking his arm and leading him into the room.

"You ... you look beautiful," he said with a gulp. "You're the most beautiful woman I've ever seen, in fact."

Joannie blushed. "That's very sweet of you to say." She moved closer to him and kissed him lightly on the mouth.

Sharp could barely control himself. He grabbed her with his large hands, drew her to him, and kissed her again with all the passion he could muster. She undid the top button of his shirt, took his hand, and led him to the bed.

Reading a newspaper, or at least pretending to do so, Geller positioned himself on a comfortable chair from which he had clear view of the elevators. An hour passed and still no sign of Sharp or Joannie Smythe. As he sat there, he tried to fathom how a lout like Sharp could wind up in the room of a beauty like the married Mrs. Smythe. Discounting Sharp's sexual prowess, which he sincerely doubted, Geller figured that there had to be another reason for Mrs. Smythe to risk her marriage on someone of Sharp's ilk. Geller just didn't know what it was. And as Klein had told him more than once: of all the mysteries of the world, the most difficult one to solve is why two people might be attracted to each other.

At long last, one of the elevator doors opened and out stepped Sharp with a stupid grin on his face. Behind him was Joannie Smythe. He briefly looked at her. She seemed to not acknowledge Sharp though Geller was certain that he detected a slight farewell nod. Sharp turned and walked briskly to hotel's main doors and into the street.

Mrs. Smythe paused to fix her black cloche hat. Not that Geller was an expert on women—far from it, as Shayna frequently reminded him—but as soon as Sharp was gone, he noticed that Mrs. Smythe's expression became sombre, even anguished. A minute or so later, a man approached her. Geller instantly recognized him; it was George Dickens. He moved close enough to the two of them so that he could eavesdrop on their conversation without being seen, as both Dickens and Smythe might recognize him.

"Mr. Dickens, good, you're on time," said Joannie.

"Everything okay, Mrs. Smythe? You look upset," said Dickens.

She waved her hand. "It's nothing I can't handle."

"What are my instructions?"

She took out a piece of paper from her purse. "You're to go to this address, a house on Arlington Street. There's an elderly woman I know who lives there. Her name's Mrs. Waters. She'll provide you with a bed and food until it's time. George, it's important that you not be seen. I know that will be difficult, but it's crucial. Do you understand?"

"I do. I won't disappoint you or the reverend."

"I know you won't. Here's some money. There are Bucknam & Walmsley taxis across at the station. Take one to Mrs. Waters's house. Now go. And George," she said, touching his arm, "God speed."

"You're certain of this, Alec? Joannie Smythe told George Dickens to hide out in a house on Arlington?" asked Klein.

"I know, it sounds crazy, but she's working with Vivian and Dickens. At least, that's what I gathered," said Geller. "However, I'm quite sure that Sharp paid her a visit in her room before she met with Dickens."

The two men were sitting on the steps of Klein's home, while the children played on the grass in front of them.

"Mel, leave Niecee alone. Right now," ordered Klein. Little Mel sheepishly did what his father told him. "If you're a good boy, I'll let you listen to the radio in a little while. You'll be able to hear someone very good playing the piano." That definitely got Mel's attention as well as Bernice's.

"Yes, Niecee, you can listen too. Just behave, both of you."

Klein lit a cigarette and pondered the full meaning of what Geller had told him. "This is yet another example proving that some people have layers that must be peeled back before you can arrive at the truth of the matter." Klein flicked the wooden match onto the grass. "The beautiful Mrs. Smythe clearly is more complicated than we both thought. As I see it, there are two questions that we need to answer. The first is what's Vivian up to with Dickens? And why is it so important that he stay out of sight? The only answer I can think of is that there may indeed be a plan to go after the Sugarmans. And if that's the case, then my second question about what the hell Mrs. Smythe is doing with Sharp, one of Saul Sugarman's *shtarkers*, is also answered."

"She's using him to get at Sugarman," offered Geller.

"That would be my guess. I believe, Alec, what we have going on here are two separate plots against the Sugarmans, one taking advantage of the other."

"I'm not following you, Sam."

"Let's assume that despite what the police believe, Vivian was not in fact responsible for the shootings at the station or the synagogue, nor was he involved in Max Roter's murder. These events are instead connected to a bootleggers' war going on between Rosen and one of his competitors, likely in Chicago. And the Sugarmans have been caught up in the middle of it. This could explain Max's murder as well as why those two thugs have been in the city and threatening me. Rosen likes to do things his own way and our new friends, Paulie and Richie, are here to make sure of that. I'd imagine that they are trying to find the mystery shooter before he finds them."

"And the reverend? What's he got to do with this?"

"He's very clever, I'll grant him that. If my hunch is correct, then Vivian has figured out what's going on and is merely making the most of the opportunity presented here."

Geller popped up from the step. "Get Dickens to finish off

the Sugarmans and wait for the police to blame it all on the bootleggers."

"It's as perfect a situation as you can ask for."

"So what's next?"

Klein dropped his cigarette butt on the sidewalk and stamped it out. "I have asked Melinda and her ladies to watch out for Paulie and Richie. Sooner or later, they'll spot them. I will speak to Joannie Smythe and find out more about why she's joined Vivian. And I want you to search out where Dickens is hiding."

"I've checked Henderson's already. There's no person or family named Waters listed on Arlington Street. The house must belong to someone else, maybe someone connected to the reverend. That would make the most sense. I will get on it, Sam. Now, if you don't mind, I have to get back to Shayna. We're catching the vaudeville bill at the Pantages, a comedy burlesque from New York."

"Yeah, Sarah and I used to do that before we had those troublemakers," he said, motioning to his children. "Freda, Bernice, Mel, in the house. Now."

"Can we listen to the radio, Daddy?" asked Bernice.

"We'll see."

"Hooray," they cheered. They knew that when Klein said "we'll see," he really meant, "yes." The trio halted what they were doing and marched in a row up the steps, saluting their smiling father as they passed.

"Alec, can you wait a minute? I need you to do something for me on your way downtown. I want to send a telegram to Hannah Nash in Vera."

"Well, McCreary, I don't know about you," said Nash, leaving Mrs. Tillsdale's rooming house, "but I'm fairly certain that Henry Woodhead's not guilty of any murders in Manitoba, Saskatchewan, or anywhere else for that matter."

"I agree. That was a bloody waste of time," said McCreary, lighting a cigar. "And I never want to hear one more word about drummers, jobbers, agents, or the struggles of life as a travelling salesman."

Hannah grinned. Their conversation with Woodhead, a short, balding, and anxious man, was pleasant enough. He had indeed educated them both on the intricacies of stocking a prairie general store and the art of drumming up business. After repeated questioning, Woodhead had confirmed that he had known Max Roter and had recently conducted business with him as well as the two men killed in Crystal City and Carnduff. But he also insisted that he knew nothing of the shocking violence that had occurred and was as stunned as everyone else in each town when news of the murders were publicized. More to the point, he asserted over and over again that he was not in any way connected to Reverend John Vivian and knew nothing about his employer, Adam Cole, associating with the reverend. Hannah believed him as did McCreary eventually.

"I think it'll be difficult to tie Vivian to Roter's murder and to the murders in the other towns, McCreary. My feeling is your first thought was correct: that the shootings are related to an internal battle between the bootleggers. It's the only thing that can explain these deaths," Nash said.

McCreary took a deep drag on his cigar. "Appears to be the

case. But that means it'll also be a lot harder to stop." He checked his watch. "There's a train in about two and a half hours back to the city. Last one tonight. I say we head back and let my men follow up. Sundell's a good man."

"That's kind of you for saying so, sir," said Sergeant Sundell, walking up behind them.

"What is it, Sundell?" asked McCreary.

"I have a telegram for Mrs. Nash. Arrived about twenty minutes ago." The sergeant handed Nash the slip of paper.

She read it quickly and looked up. "Sergeant, where might we find Dr. Lewis?"

"Doc Lewis, he lives in a house over on the edge of town, just past the grain elevator."

"Why do we need to speak to the doctor?" asked McCreary. "We could be having dinner."

"A favour for Sam. He needs some information. Says it's related to what's been going on in the city and it might prevent another shooting."

McCreary raised his eyebrows. "Well, if Sam Klein 'says so,' then by all means…"

Dr. Zachariah Lewis lived in a large, white house with a picket fence. There were two tall oak trees in the front and a bountiful vegetable garden in the back. The home served as both his medical office and residence. He shared it with his wife, Penelope, who was confined to a wheelchair. More than a decade ago, she had been trampled by a runaway horse. Penelope had been born on a nearby farm and though Lewis would have preferred to live

221

in the city, he consented to practicing medicine in Vera to make his wife happy.

"So let me get this straight," said McCreary, rolling his eyes. "Klein wants us to ask the doctor about Joannie Smythe's medical history. Because he says she's mixed up in some scheme being hatched by Reverend Vivian, who we just decided did not have anything to do with the murders here or in the other towns. Does that sound right?"

"That's the problem with you, McCreary. You're one of the best detectives I've worked with, but sometimes a case is like a Chinese puzzle box: there are many layers to it and it is not always clear immediately how each layer fits together."

"As long as we're on the ten forty-five train, be my guest."

Hannah walked up the steps to the porch and knocked on the door. A moment later, it opened.

"This better be an emergency. It's been a long day," said Dr. Lewis.

"Hello, Doctor. We're not here for any treatment," said Nash. She introduced herself and McCreary. "We won't keep you long. We just have a few questions for you. It has to do with the shootings here and elsewhere, including in Winnipeg, that you may have heard about."

"I was about to tend to my wife. She's resting in the other room, but if it's only a few questions, please have a seat on the porch and we can talk here," said Lewis, showing them two chairs. "Now, what can I do for you, Detective and Commissioner?"

"You know Mrs. Joannie Smythe?" asked Nash.

"I do, of course," replied Lewis.

"She's a patient of yours?"

"I can't say. But since I'm the only physician in the town, I'll let you both draw your own conclusions. Let me ask you: why do you want to know about Mrs. Smythe? Has she been hurt? Is she in trouble?"

"Not yet, but we believe she's in danger or may put someone else in danger. That's why we need you to answer these questions. Has Mrs. Smythe ever been attacked or hurt by her husband?"

The doctor's eyes widened. "Again, I am not at liberty to say anything about this. It would be against the oath I've taken as a physician. Doctor and patient confidentiality is sacred, as I'm quite sure you both know."

"Yes, I do," said Nash, glancing at McCreary. He pointed to his watch. She was quiet for a moment and then turned back to the doctor. "Why do men abuse their wives?"

The doctor mulled over the question for a moment. "To assert their power, I suppose. Women now might have the vote, but they give up everything, their legal rights in particular, as soon as they marry. Some men who feel inferior need to make that clear from time to time. Do you know in Canada, under provincial law, that even if a husband deserts his wife, the law will compel him to give her financial support only if she's pure and virtuous in the eyes of the state? That means that she can never be seen in public or private with another man. Absurd, would you not agree?"

"I would, yes." Hannah, herself, had gone through several legal battles to assert her own property rights after her husband had died.

223

"The other main problem, and the reason for the spate of shootings, are related entirely to liquor. However, too often, liquor is used as an excuse for domestic violence—a rather convenient excuse, I'd add. The fact is, some men are brutes and use whisky as a crutch. It's quite pathetic, really. I've seen enough heartache to last me a lifetime."

"One last question, Doctor, on which I'd like to hear your view. Why would a women stay with man who abuses her? Why not just divorce him?"

"A difficult question, but an easy answer, I'm afraid," said Lewis. "It's not only that divorce is frowned upon. In a small town like Vera, seeking a divorce is perceived as an attack on God and the church. Most women I know cannot handle the humiliation. And the fear of what would happen to them is genuine. Thus, they unfortunately conclude that it's wiser to remain in an unhappy, even volatile marriage than face the wrath of the community gossipmongers and an unknown future. But I have to add that from what I understand, the situation is changing. More women are opting for divorce. Now, if you'll excuse me…"

"Doctor, one final question, please," said Nash.

Dr. Lewis nodded. "Go on."

"Would you agree that an abused woman who finds the courage to fight back is capable of just about anything?" asked Nash.

"Are we speaking generally or specifically about Mrs. Smythe?"

"I don't know, you tell me."

Dr. Lewis was silent for a moment and then gazed into Hannah's eyes. "Yes, I believe she'd be capable of being very unpredictable, possibly dangerous. This would particularly be the case if this woman was being guided by a third party, someone who offered her the security and salvation she was seeking. Do you understand, Detective?"

Nash nodded her head. "Thank you, Doctor," she said, turning to McCreary. "I believe we have a train to catch."

16

The sun was setting by the time Klein arrived Sunday evening at Lou Sugarman's home on Scotia Street near Luxton Avenue. The impressive two-storey brick house was set back from the street and faced the Red River. Built in 1900, Sugarman had owned the property for eight years. The front lawn was shaded by an assortment of maple, elm, and fir trees. And there was a large, navy blue davenport on the porch where Lou and Rivka enjoyed spending a quiet evening—providing the mosquitoes did not harass them too badly. The home had four bedrooms and the only thing missing, Lou liked to joke, was the sound of children. Lou hardly needed such a big house, but as he told Klein, he had to do something with his money and investing $12,000 in a scenic Scotia Street property seemed like a smart idea.

Klein was eagerly greeted by a group of men assembled in front of the house who had come to pay their respects to Max Roter and his family. He recognized most of them: Arkady

Kessler who ran the steam bath on Dufferin and McGregor where Klein liked to unwind; Manny Morroznik, a genial pharmacist and talented piano player; Hymie Plotzer who owned a dry goods shop on Selkirk Avenue and often supplied Jewish general store merchants with supplies; Norman Lunger, a kosher butcher; and garment factory owner Moses Asner, the definite *macher* of the bunch. Anti-union and a staunch believer in market forces, Asner got rich off the work of his underpaid tailors and seamstresses, mainly Jewish immigrants or the children of immigrants. During the strike of 1919, he had sided, vocally at least, with the Committee of One Thousand and refused to hire back those employees whom he deemed "Bolshevik hooligans." A wealthy bachelor, Asner lived in a swanky room at the Royal Alexandra Hotel.

"Make way, gentlemen, Mr. Sam Klein has arrived," announced Kessler. "You haven't been in for a *shvitz* lately, Shailek. I'm sure you could use one."

"No time, Arkady."

"I don't doubt it. Shootings and murders. What the hell's going on? This isn't Russia, for God's sake. I just hope that Lou makes it. Rae says that his eyes opened briefly this morning, but then he went back to sleep."

"He'll make it. Lou's as tough as they come."

"Maybe so," said Asner, "but anyone who makes all of their money selling whisky is only asking for trouble. You think Max was killed for any other reason?"

Several of the other men sighed. "Asner, not here," said

Kessler. "His widow's in the house. This is a shiva; have some decency."

Asner waved the back of his hand. "I don't need any steam bath operator telling me what to do."

"You think that Saul's in danger, Sam?" asked Morroznik.

Klein shrugged. "Can't say, Manny."

"Can't say or won't say," said Asner.

"Gentlemen, always a pleasure, but I'm going to say hello to Mrs. Roter," said Klein.

In fact, after being briefed by Hannah Nash earlier in the day about her cryptic yet revealing conversation with Dr. Lewis in Vera, he was more certain than ever that the Sugarmans were in grave danger from two separate assailants. The first, as he initially suspected, was related to a bootlegging war that they were caught up in; the second was being orchestrated by the admittedly clever Reverend Vivian and almost certainly involved George Dickens. The two thugs, once he found them, could provide the answers to the former problem, and Joannie Smythe, who he assumed would be at the shiva, was the key to figuring out what Vivian and Dickens were planning. How Max Roter's murder fit into either of these, if at all, remained to be determined, but Klein had a theory.

Leaving the men, Klein entered the house. He saw that according to Jewish custom, the hallway mirror had been covered with a black cloth; during mourning, those who had lost a loved one were not to be concerned with their appearances. About twenty people, mainly women, were sitting in the parlour chatting loudly. In the adjacent dining room, the mahogany table had plates of honey cake, cinnamon rugelach, and strudel. There was also a half-empty bottle of Canadian Club whisky, Max's favourite, and a row of shot glasses. Klein approached Rae Roter who was sitting on a low chair, minus the cushion, surrounded by several women, one of whom he was pleased to see was Joannie Smythe.

"Mr. Klein, it's nice of you to come by," said Rae.

Klein nodded at her and at Joannie. "My condolences again. As Lou has asked of me, I'm doing my best to find the person who was responsible."

"I know you are," said Rae, patting Klein's hand. "You remember my friend from Vera, Mrs. Smythe?"

"Yes. It was nice of you to stay in the city, Mrs. Smythe. I'm sure Mrs. Roter appreciates your support." Klein studied her face for a trace of fear, doubt, or insincerity, yet she revealed nothing of what she was thinking or feeling. She merely glanced at him and offered a polite smile.

"I hear that Lou awoke for a moment."

Rae shrugged. "The doctors don't know what it means. He was very groggy and then went unconscious again. Clearly, he isn't out of the woods yet and I'm worried."

"I completely understand. Are the police still there?"

"Yes, as far as I know. Why? Do you think he's still in danger?"

"I don't know. Possibly," said Klein, looking at Joannie for a reaction. But, again, there was nothing. "I don't see Saul here."

The question annoyed Rae. "I have no idea where he is or when he might be here. As I'm sure I don't have to tell you, Mr. Klein, my brother Saul's a difficult man."

Klein politely smiled. "True enough. Mrs. Roter, may we speak somewhere privately?"

"Rabbi Samuel will be here shortly to lead the prayer service."

"I'll be brief … I promise you."

Rae stood up and led Klein up the stairs into Lou's office. She shut the door and looked into Klein's eyes. "What would you like to know?"

"Was your husband having any problems or involved in a dispute of some sort with someone other than possibly Frankie Taylor?"

"The police already asked me this and as I told them, Max was a friend to everyone in Vera. Whatever happened must be connected to the liquor business, don't you think?"

"That would seem the most likely answer, yes."

"But you don't believe that, do you, Mr. Klein?"

"Honestly, I don't know. Though, I'll admit, it makes the most sense given what's happened in the city. Your husband may well have been an unfortunate casualty of a bootlegging war. If the police could find Taylor and I could hear what he has to say, then we might get the information we need to unravel this. Or…"

"Or what?"

"Or the robbery and shooting at your store were related to something else entirely. Let me ask you: did you ever see your husband with a bundle of papers tied with a string?"

"Max was always busy with business reports and correspondence. What papers are you referring to exactly?"

"Last week, my associate Alec Geller visited Vera and your store. Jack Smythe gave him the keys. He found a small pack of papers hidden in the compartment of a desk drawer in your husband's office. But before he could examine them, he was attacked. He's fine and is back in the city. I've been wondering what was in those documents that someone did not want him to see."

Rae's face flushed slightly. "I … I've no idea. I can assure you, though, Max was not doing anything illegal or corrupt, if that's what you're implying."

"I never thought that." He paused for a moment. "What was Mr. Roter's relationship with the Smythes?"

Rae stared awkwardly at him. "That's a strange question. Joannie's my friend, but Max liked her. He tolerated Mr. Smythe. I wouldn't call them friends."

"What can you tell me about their marriage?"

Rae shifted in her chair. "I don't feel especially comfortable speaking about this."

"It may be important. Please, go ahead."

"Their marriage is like that of everyone else. It has its good moments as well as its bad. Joannie wanted to have children, but could not. I think that has strained things between them. And then there is…"

"Mr. Smythe's drinking."

Rae nodded. "Yes. Joannie's a very private person, yet I know for a fact that he has hurt her, and more than once. I've seen the bruises on her arms and I know she has been punched in the stomach at least once. I've tried to speak with her about it many times, but she refuses to talk about it. She only says that she is handling it. I asked what she meant by that, but she wouldn't say.

I'd add that she's seemed more at peace with herself recently. I can only assume that the situation with Jack has improved."

"Would she ever leave him?"

Rae shook her head. "Never. Joannie's much too proud and divorce is just out of the question, especially in a town like Vera. I think the shame would be worse, in her view. That's obviously not true, yet I believe that's how she sees it."

"I assume Mr. Roter knew of this?"

"He did, yes. We spoke of it. Max heard the gossip. But his view, most of the time, at least—Max could change his mind on things—was that what happened between a husband and wife was their own private business. I don't know, I think he had a soft spot for Joannie. He always doted on her in the store and ensured that she found everything she was looking for. I teased him about it once and he denied it."

"Rae, the rabbi is here. He is about to lead the prayers," someone shouted from downstairs.

"Mrs. Roter, one last question. Have you ever heard Mrs. Smythe mention Reverend John Vivian?"

"I heard Max talk and yell about him plenty. He has a real *goyishe kop* and is *meshuggina* about the liquor business. Max said he was trying to ruin the family. But Joannie talk of him? No, never."

In the dining room, Klein joined Rabbi Samuel and the other men who had crowded around the table for the afternoon and evening prayer services. The davening was mostly silent reading along with the usual loud mumbling as the men recited the prayers to themselves as quickly as their lips could move. About the only aberration was the rabbi's invitation to Rae to stand beside him for the recitation of the Mourner's *Kaddish*. There was immediately an uncomfortable murmur from several of the men, including Hymie Plotzer and Norman Lunger, traditionalists who believed strongly that men and women should pray separately.

Klein hardly paid attention to this brief and ancient dispute. As he stared at the Hebrew words in the siddur, his mind could only focus on recent events. He reviewed his conversation with Rae and decided that it was imperative for him to also speak with Joannie Smythe. He would offer to escort her back to her hotel. As the last words of the *Kaddish* were being said, Klein looked for Joannie among the women in the parlour. Then he checked the kitchen. But she was gone.

With Paulie the Plumber at the wheel, the Buick sped north down Main Street. At the corner of Sutherland Avenue, Paulie turned sharply to the right, drove a few more blocks, and then steered left onto Annabella Street. As he did so, a young boy darted out from behind a wagon.

"Watch out for the damn kid," shouted Richie.

Paulie slammed the brake and the car jerked to a stop inches from the startled boy. "Kid, you tryin' to get killed?" Paulie screamed. "For Christ's sake, watch where you're going."

The stunned boy ran back to his house and was greeted by his distraught mother. She eyed Paulie and Richie, but had the good sense not to say anything to them.

"Move," ordered Richie. "Number 118, down the street on the left."

He easily found the address and parked the car a short distance from their destination. Madam Melinda's brothel, a red, two-storey, wood-frame house, was in a state of disrepair. The front gate was broken and one of the second floor windows was smashed.

Paulie looked at Richie. "You sure this is the place? It's awfully quiet." Richie took out a piece of paper from this pocket. "118 Annabella. This is it."

Two decades earlier, during the heyday of the semi-legal Point Douglas brothels, the horse-drawn wagons and taxis were lined up and down Annabella Street (called Rachel Street until 1913) and nearby MacFarlane Street. Men from all walks of life, respectable and otherwise, found their way to Madam Melinda's and about twenty other busy brothels in the neighbourhood, which were open for business all day, every day.

That was in the past, however. Eventually, the nightly carousing, half-clad harlots parading throughout the neighbourhood, and crime forced the police to heed the moralists and close the establishments down—or at least try to. Some of the madams sold their homes for rock-bottom prices and relocated to out-of-the-way streets in St. Boniface and Transcona.

Melinda was one of the few exceptions. She made a side deal with the police—$200 a month that she paid to McCreary until recently—that kept them happy. And she ensured that the women who worked for her did not cause her neighbours any undue problems. They kept her many clients happy and contented and life in Melinda's self-contained world went on without a hitch.

Standing near the car, Paulie and Richie, as was their habit, scoured the area. Not seeing anything unusual or anyone suspicious, they proceeded up the short walkway and knocked on the door. A young woman with short blonde hair wearing a flimsy red satin negligee answered.

"Gentlemen, welcome," she said with a broad smile. "I'm Martha. Come in, please."

She led Paulie and Richie into the parlour. The windows were covered with gaudy tapestries, the same ones that had hung there for years. In the dimly lit room, the two men were greeted cheerfully by two other women, also dressed in negligees, lounging and smoking on the turquoise sofas. They were in their early- to mid-twenties and were attractive, though both, like Martha, had ruby red lips, heavy eye shadow, black mascara, and abundant rouge on their cheeks. One of the women had shorter hair and a flapper appeal. Richie judged her to be Creole, or possibly Spanish. The other woman was lily white with long, dark hair. She had a slightly rougher look and had a more fulsome figure.

"Don't just stand there, Martha. Get these gents some whisky," said the woman with the dark hair.

"Of course, Miss Nell."

"My name is Nell. And that's Lulu. She doesn't speak much English, but then, she doesn't have to, does she? Tell me, how can we serve you today? The Lord's Day, no less," she said, chuckling.

"By the look of your fine suits and fancy fedoras, I'd say you two aren't from around here, are you?"

"We're just visiting," said Paulie.

"Thought so," said Nell.

"Madam Melinda here?" asked Richie.

"You know her?"

"No. Just heard of her like everyone else in the city."

"She's working in her office in the back of the kitchen. I can fetch her if you like."

"How about in about two hours?"

Martha returned with a bottle of whisky and two glasses. She poured two shots and handed one each to the men.

"So what's your pleasure?" asked Nell. "No, let me guess." She sized up Paulie. "You're a handsome one. I'd say that Martha here would be right for you."

Paulie smiled and nodded.

"And you, sir," Nell said, glancing at Richie, "you have a more discerning taste. And since you've walked in, you haven't taken your eye, the one without the patch, off of Lulu."

Richie laughed as he swigged down the whisky. He put the glass on the table near the sofa and grabbed Lulu's hand. He motioned to her. She stood up, drew her finger over his face, and led him down the hallway. Martha took Paulie's hand and led him up the stairs.

"Come on, honey pie, my room's up here."

As soon as the women and their clients had vanished, Madam Melinda appeared.

She was wearing her usual evening attire: a black lace and

chiffon dress that was cut low in the front, revealing her ample cleavage. Her dark hair was shorter and greyer than it once was, yet at 51, Melinda remained a beautiful and lively woman. She was also business-savvy. She had prospered and survived as the most celebrated madam in Winnipeg for more than two decades by being both fair and tough. She didn't tolerate excessive drinking or the heavy use of opium or Indian hemp, easily available from nefarious dealers in Chinatown and several Main Street saloons. A girl who couldn't handle her liquor or her clients did not last long in Melinda's employ. For those who excelled, there was room, board, and 40 percent of the money they earned.

"Did I hear some happy customers?" asked Melinda.

"You did, Melinda," replied Nell, sitting up. "Two out-of-towners, I think."

"That so? They tell you that or you just guessing?"

"They said they were visiting. But from the look of their fine suits and hats, they got some cash to spend. One's with Martha; the other's with Lulu. That one is a little scarier-looking."

"Scarier? In what way?"

"Has a black patch covering his right eye. Kind of fellow you wouldn't want to meet in a dark alley late at night."

Melinda's eyes widened. Klein had asked her to be on the lookout for a gangster with a black eyepatch who had a partner.

"I have to make a call. Nell, don't let those two men leave before I speak with them."

"I wouldn't worry about it. They'll be busy for a little while."

Outside on the street, a black Model-T slowly passed Paulie and Richie's Buick. The driver made a mental note of the address. He also glanced at the shotgun lying on the passenger seat.

He could not quite believe that he had missed his mark on two occasions. To say that his boss was unhappy was an understatement. He could not afford to screw this up again or he'd be a dead man. That was a certainty. So he had to get this right. He knew he could eliminate one problem immediately. But he had his plan set and decided to stick with it. Wait, he told himself and be patient. Soon, Paulie the Plumber, One-eye Richie, and the damn Sugarmans would be ancient history.

17

Early Monday morning, the Royal Alexandra Hotel's stylish café, illuminated in a sea of sunshine from the skylights, was still quiet. Klein requested a table in the corner where he could keep an eye on the entrance, but not be immediately noticed. At this hour, only a handful of businessmen were dispersed throughout the room. Most were having breakfast served on elegant white tablecloths. Some chatted quietly about pending meetings; others were immersed in the morning newspaper reading about the ongoing conflict in Ireland between the Republicans and the pro-British forces as well as the sports news that on Saturday the New York Yankees had lost to the lowly Detroit Tigers by a score of nine to two. No one bothered to look at Klein as he sat down, which suited him just fine. He ordered coffee and toast and then lit a cigarette.

He still regretted not being home when Melinda had telephoned him. By the time he had returned the call, Paulie and Richie had left her house. She had introduced herself to them, trying to elicit as much information as possible. Paulie began to chat with her about travelling to the city from Minneapolis, but Richie immediately cut him off. Melinda had told Klein that they were both satisfied customers and that she was certain that they would return in the near future. As Melinda pointed out, once a man like Richie has a sensuous woman such as Lulu, he will always come back for more. Klein said that he would be there around eight o'clock in case they showed up.

He sipped his coffee and had to admit that it tasted a lot better than the black swill served at Dolly's. Not having a lot of money never really bothered Klein. Ever since he was young, he had hustled to eke out a living, yet he was more or less content with what he had. At the same time, on those rare occasions when he dined at the hotel or visited a mansion on Wellington Crescent or Roslyn Road, he could understand the attraction of wealth and the privileges it bestowed. Who didn't want their every whim met?

As he contemplated a life with a palatial house, servants, high-priced automobiles, and a stable of horses, the hotel waiter brought his toast with a side of the café's strawberry jelly. He was about to sample it when he saw Joannie Smythe enter. He stood up and approached her.

"Mrs. Smythe, if you're here alone, please join me."

"Mr. Klein, I'm surprised to see you here."

"Ma'am, would you like to sit at the gentleman's table?" asked the café maître d'.

She hesitated for a moment. "Very well."

Once they were seated, Joannie ordered a poached egg with

toast and tea. "Now what is it you want from me, Mr. Klein?" Her tone was friendly, but firm.

"It was good of you to travel to the city to be with Mrs. Roter."

"Yes, I think you told me that last night. As I said, she's a friend, and so was Max. It's a terrible tragedy. But that's not why you've chosen to have breakfast at the hotel in the hope of speaking with me, is it, Mr. Klein? From everything I know about you, you're much too clever for that."

Klein took a sip of his coffee and lit another cigarette. "What can you tell me about a man named George Dickens?"

"Mr. Dickens works with my husband at the Standard Grain Company. He visits Vera from time to time and we've had him to dinner. I don't know him very well."

Klein watched for any sign of hesitation, but saw none. "When was the last time you spoke to him?"

"As a matter of fact, he was in Vera about a week ago, when Max was killed," she said, noticing Klein's raised eyebrows. "You don't think that George…"

"Had anything to do with Mr. Roter's murder?"

"That's preposterous. You can speak to my husband. We were at the Roter's store that night. We left and came home and then Jack and Mr. Dickens spoke privately. Jack will vouch for him."

"I'm sure he will."

"Your sarcastic tone troubles me, Mr. Klein. I'm not certain what you're implying."

Klein shook his head. "My apologies. I wasn't implying anything, only that perhaps your husband or Dickens may have seen something."

"The police have questioned Jack and he told them everything he knows. I have no idea what, if anything, Mr. Dickens saw."

"Do you know that Dickens is a loyal follower of Reverend John Vivian?"

Smythe shifted in her chair. "I … I know nothing about Mr. Dickens's interests outside of work. As I said, we chatted over dinner some time ago. He spoke of his wife."

"You are familiar with the reverend?"

"Only what I've read in the newspaper. He's the leader of a crusade against liquor, against what your clients, the Sugarmans, are involved in."

"That's right. And you support this crusade, as you call it?"

"Liquor has ruined many a family, Mr. Klein. But I'm certain you know that. If the reverend can help make a positive difference in peoples' lives, if he can protect wives and children from the abuse the bottle causes, then I'm in favour of that," said Smythe. She was about to continue, but then caught herself. "I talk too much. Now, Mr. Klein, I really must be going."

"Just one more question. You're entitled to your opinions about liquor and Reverend Vivian, but would you agree that his methods and the fact that he and his followers have resorted to violence are open to question?"

"Sometimes the ends justify the means. Or that's how he'd put it, I suppose. As I said, I only know about him from what I've read."

"Interesting you should say that."

"You had another question?"

Klein nodded. "With the strong feelings you have against liquor, I find it rather curious that you should be so close to the Roters. You're aware, of course, that Max, the man you admired so much, was selling the Sugarmans' liquor to US bootleggers? And he probably got killed for it."

Smythe stared at Klein for a long moment without saying anything. "You don't live in a small town like Vera without knowing everything that's going on with your neighbours. There are some secrets, but not many. So, yes, I knew about Max's liquor warehouse and his relations with bootleggers like Frankie Taylor. It was common knowledge. Yet Max was as kind a person as is Rae. And in some circumstances, kindness must take precedence over any other failings."

Klein was impressed by her intelligence and composure. As she rose from the table, he decided he would try one last ploy to unhinge her.

"Mrs. Smythe, allowing George Dickens to kill Lou or Saul Sugarman, or both, will not solve anything and certainly won't cure your husband's nasty temper."

The colour drained from Smythe's face. "Mr. Klein, I have no idea what you are talking about. Your suggestion that I am hiding some terrible facts from you about Mr. Dickens and my husband is foolish in the extreme. And here I thought all that hype I'd heard about you, that you are a gifted detective, was true. Now I know that it's definitely not. Please excuse me."

She abruptly turned and marched out of the café, leaving Klein to mull over their conversation.

Outside on the street, Alec Geller was waiting. He had orders from Klein to follow her everywhere she went. Sooner or later, Klein had told him, she'd lead them right to Dickens.

"We are going back there tonight, aren't we, Richie?" asked Paulie, grinning like a schoolboy. "That Martha's a babe. I really gotta see her again soon and I saw how you were looking at that Lulu."

Richie laughed. "Keep it in your pants, Paulie. We'll stop by for another visit later. But the boss is getting antsy. He's not happy with what's gone on here and wants it over. There's a lot of cash at stake and he can't have the Sugarmans bumped off. We got to stop whoever is trying to do this, and now."

"You got an idea who's been taking pot shots at us and them?"

"I do and it's not that goofy preacher. I don't know what the hell he's been up to, but I aim to find that out real soon. Look, there she is. Let's go say hello."

Paulie and Richie were stopped on Portage Avenue in front of the Electric Pastry Shop. Paulie turned left onto Kennedy and parked the car. Sarah had just opened up her shop when they walked through the door. The three of them were the only ones in the store.

She immediately recognized the two men from the disruptive visit they had paid to her family on Cathedral Avenue.

"What is it you want now?" asked Sarah. Her tone was matter-of-fact but her hands were slightly trembling. When she had asked Sam about these two men, he had ignored her questions, telling her not to worry anymore about it. Sarah, however, was no fool. She had met and dealt with many rough men in her past life and her experience told her that they were dangerous.

"We came to look at dresses," said Richie.

"Yeah. We want to buy something real nice for my mother," said Paulie, smiling.

"Well, I don't want your business, so please leave or…"

"Or you'll do what?" asked Richie. He moved closer to her. "I want to speak to your husband. You know where he is?"

"I don't. He left early this morning."

"Yeah, well, I'm a bit impatient. Maybe you can phone him for me."

"I told you, I wouldn't know where to call him. There's usually a constable who comes walking by this time of the morning."

Richie removed his fedora and moved even closer to Sarah. The foul smell of coffee and tobacco on his breath permeated her nostrils. "We don't worry about the police much. Ain't that right, Paulie?"

"That so, Richie."

Sarah tried backing up, but she was up against a hat display. Richie grabbed her right arm and squeezed it tight.

"Let go of me," she shouted, striking Richie in the face with her other hand.

"You bitch," he said, raising his hand.

"Stop! Now!" Saul Sugarman was standing in the shop entrance. "Get the fuck out of here, both of you."

Richie let his arm drop and released Sarah. "Tell your husband I want to talk to him today." He motioned to Paulie to follow him.

Sugarman glared at both of them, though said nothing more.

"We wouldn't have hurt her, you know," Richie said to Sugarman.

As soon as they were out the door, Sarah began to shake. "Thank you, Saul. If you hadn't come in…"

Sugarman half-smiled. "Well, I told you that I'd always be around to watch you."

"Those thugs listened to you pretty quickly. Not even an argument. Do you know them?" asked Sarah more calmly.

"I don't," said Sugarman, looking away from her.

Sarah did not believe that for a moment. "Can I get you a cup of coffee? And I am sorry about the other day."

He gazed back at her, his eyes roving up and down. "That was my fault entirely. I know when the time's right, you'll see things my way."

Sarah ignored his lurid glances. "Saul. I'm grateful to you for helping me. But you must stop thinking this way. What you are suggesting will never happen."

His body stiffened. "I think I'll pass on that coffee. I have a matter to attend to."

"I wanted to ask you about Lou," said Sarah.

But Sugarman didn't hear a word she said. He turned and walked quickly out of the store.

Saul Sugarman marched into the reception area of his office. "Shayna, they in there?" he gruffly asked.

Miss Kravetz jumped up. "Yes, sir. I tried to tell them to wait here, but they just barged right in like they owned the place. I don't know..."

"Stop, Shayna. It's fine. I'll deal with it. Hold my calls until they've left."

Sugarman pushed open the door and saw Richie lounging in his chair with his dirty shoes planted on the desk. "Will you get the hell out of there," he yelled, slamming the door behind him.

"Sure, Mr. Sugarman. I was just having some fun," said Richie.

"Yeah, we did like you asked," said Paulie. "We put the fear of God into that bitch."

Sugarman smiled. "You did, I'll give you that. But you know she's going to tell her husband about this."

"We're not afraid of Klein. He's not so tough," said Paulie.

"Well, I'd still be careful. And what's this I hear about you going to that brothel on Annabella? You do know that Klein used to work there? And that big-mouth Melinda, who owns the place, has told him you've been there. You shouldn't go near the place. If you want to pay for women, there's another house in St. Boniface. I'll give you the address."

"Don't you worry about us, Mr. Sugarman," said Richie. "We're here to make sure nothing happens to you and that's what we've done."

"You're kidding, right, Richie? Since you've arrived, I've been shot at twice and my poor brother is lying in a hospital bed unconscious. Have you told Rosen about that yet?" asked Sugarman. He could barely contain his anger.

Richie stepped back. "The boss knows everything that's been

going on. He says we have to stay here until the problems have been fixed. He doesn't want another incident like in Vera."

Sugarman shook his head. "Vera? Even the great Irv Rosen doesn't know who killed Max, does he?"

Richie did not reply.

"Didn't think so. Now both of you get out of here. I got a business to run. You tell Mr. Rosen that everything is proceeding just as we planned and no one, certainly not Klein, the police, or Reverend John Vivian is going to stop us."

"I don't think that's who he's worried about," said Richie.

"Then I suggest you two boys do your job and find the son of a bitch who's trying to stop us."

As Richie and Paulie left, Sugarman called out to Shayna. "I need to make a telephone call. Come in here, please."

18

All through the day, Sarah had been busier than usual at the shop. There was a steady stream of customers, mainly young women and their mothers browsing for dresses and hats for the June wedding season and outdoor garden parties. Money was not an object and sales, for a change, were plentiful for afternoon dresses of blue silk, white viole, and flower prints, along with trimmed white satin and white ribbon hats. It was so busy at the noon hour that when Betty Kingston stopped by to chat, she insisted on staying to help Sarah deal with the rush.

Betty's lively personality and presence kept Sarah's mind off her earlier and unsettling encounter with the two men as well as Saul Sugarman's curious intervention. The more she thought about how Saul happened to save the day, the more suspicious she became. It was the men's reaction to Saul that troubled her the most. There was no objection or backtalk from them, only compliance. Perhaps they thought Saul had called the police, but that didn't seem likely either. The one disturbing thought that she could not shake was that the men knew Saul and maybe even were in his employ. Had Saul actually orchestrated their visit and rough treatment of her so that he could save the day? So, that somehow his rescue would make her see him differently? It seemed crazy to her that he could do such a thing, but as she knew all too well, nothing was beneath Saul Sugarman.

Sarah had called Sam's office several times during the day, but neither he nor Alec was there to answer the phone. She wasn't especially worried about the thugs searching for Sam; she knew he could handle himself. Still, she wished she could speak to him about what had transpired.

The front door of the shop swung open and in ran Bernice in her yellow sailor dress. "Mama, I'm here," she announced, side-stepping several customers to find Sarah.

"I can see that, Niecee. This is a surprise. Where's Molly?"

Bernice pointed to the teenage schoolgirl trailing behind her. "Molly, what are you doing here? I told you I'd be home just after six," said Sarah, her tone sharp.

"I know. I'm sorry. Please let me explain. This morning when I was out with Bernice for a walk, I bumped into David Neumann and he asked me out on a date to a showing of *My Old Kentucky Home* at the Capitol. The movie starts at six o'clock, so I thought…"

"You thought you could drop off Bernice to go on your date."

"Yes," said Molly, staring down at the floor. "Freda's with her friend Naomi down the street and Mel's playing next door at Mrs. Resnick's. So it was just Bernice."

"Very well, Molly. But before you leave, I have one more

thing for you to do. There's a hat at Eaton's that Betty says I must see today. I'm going to close the store for about twenty minutes. You watch Bernice for me and then you can go on your date."

"That's fine, Sarah. Thank you so much."

Sarah bent down to her daughter's level. "Niecee, you stay with Molly while Mama goes out for a minute."

"No. I want to come," said Bernice with tears in her eyes.

"Now don't start crying."

Bernice held out her arms. "Mama," she wailed.

The three or four customers in the store looked disdainfully at the crying child.

"Very well, Niecee. Come on, Molly. You can watch her outside of Eaton's while I run in."

Molly took Bernice's hand and the three of them made their way the few blocks to Eaton's through the late afternoon rush.

Crossing Donald Street, Sarah told Molly to wait in front of one of the large display windows that Bernice always enjoyed looking at.

"No more crying, Niecee," said Sarah, kissing her daughter's cheek. "Be a good girl. Mama will be right back."

Bernice nodded.

"Don't let go of her hand, Molly. You know she likes to wander."

"Of course," replied Molly, squeezing Bernice's hand a bit tighter.

As Sarah entered Eaton's, Molly pointed to the display of all-wool bathing suits in the window. "I like that red one with the black stripes and less than three dollars," Molly said to Bernice. "Which one would you like to wear, Niecee?"

Before Bernice could reply, Molly was tapped gently on the shoulder. She looked behind her and came face-to-face with David Neumann—and her heart started racing. He looked dapper in a light grey suit with a double-breasted jacket, a white shirt with a rounded collar, and shiny black boots. And with his hair parted on the side and combed back, his penetrating, deep brown eyes, and his Mediterranean appeal, David was the spitting image of Rudolph Valentino, one of her favourite movie stars—or so she imagined him.

"What are you doing here?" Molly gushed.

"I was going to look in the store for a new tie before we were to meet in the theatre," replied David.

"I'd be happy to offer you a woman's opinion if you'd like. But I have to watch Bernice for a few more minutes. Mrs. Klein should be back soon."

Molly and David chatted aimlessly about the warm weather, the film they were about to see, and the fact that the bathing suits Molly had been admiring were barely knee-length.

"It seems old-fashioned to me. I've read that women bathing by the sea in France or Italy wear bathing suits more than six inches above the knee. I think that would be much more comfortable and attractive," said Molly.

"I completely agree with you," said David. "And I'd be happy to accompany you to the beach if you wore such attire."

"Oh, David, I think you're teasing me."

Molly was so enthralled in the conversation that she did not notice that Bernice was pulling her in the opposite direction. Determined to see another display window, Bernice slipped her hand free from Molly's grasp.

Another five minutes passed before Sarah emerged from Eaton's carrying a hat box. She saw Molly and David practically kissing on the sidewalk.

"Molly, where's Bernice?" she said loudly.

Molly's face went white. "She … she was just here … she was looking at the window…"

"Bernice, Niecee," Sarah called out.

Molly and David fanned out among the carriages and mothers congregated along the front of the store. Sarah was sweating. She looked right, then left, then right again. But Bernice was nowhere to be seen.

Sarah approached two women attending to their children. "Have either of you seen a young girl?" Sarah asked, barely able to get the words out. "She's wearing a yellow outfit."

"I'm sorry, we haven't," one of them responded.

"What about you?" Sarah said, turning to another woman holding her infant and standing close by.

The woman shook her head.

"Niecee, Niecee, where are you?" Sarah shouted.

Seeing her panic, a young mother carrying her son approached. "Excuse me, ma'am, are you looking for a little girl wearing a sailor dress with a bow tie, a yellow dress?" the woman asked Sarah.

"That's right. She's my daughter. Do you know where she went?"

"A man took her by the hand and led her into a car that was stopped over on the street there," she said, pointing to Portage Avenue. "She wasn't crying or anything so I thought it must've been her father."

Sarah dropped to her knees on the sidewalk. "Oh my God, oh my God. Niecee," she cried.

A fleet of police automobiles were parked in front of the Klein home. Groups of neighbours stood outside as rumours swirled about what was going on.

"Little Mel was hit by a car," one woman said.

"No, it was Freda and it was a horse, not a car," said another.

"You're both wrong," said one of the women's husbands. "I heard from a constable that Sam's been arrested. They say he robbed a bank!"

Across the street, Mrs. Gertie Fester's wide nose was naturally pushed up against her front window as she watched the scene unfold with tremendous interest.

An hour earlier, two constables had tracked down Klein on Selkirk Avenue and brought him to his house. Sarah had rushed to him, crying inconsolably. It took fifteen minutes before he could grasp the full story, or as much as she was able to tell him through her tears. Detectives Allard, Nash, and McCreary showed up shortly after. They briefed him further on the series of events that had led to Bernice's possible kidnapping. He was beside himself.

Allard had questioned Molly and David at the Central Police Station and constables had spoken to several witnesses

254

including the young mother who told Sarah about the man who drove away with Bernice in his car. Yet the woman and the other Eaton's shoppers who were questioned did not agree on much. The mother said the car was a green auto, perhaps a Buick. Another witness insisted it was a black Model-T and that the man was tall with dark skin. Yet a third witness said the man was white, short, and stout and driving a red Cadillac. In short, the police did not have much to go on. There was a chance, Allard had reassured Klein, that if she was kidnapped the perpetrator would contact the family soon for a ransom payment. But after hearing Sarah's story of the day's events, he was skeptical.

"Shailek, where is she? What if they hurt her?" Sarah cried.

For some reason that she could not entirely understand, she had not told Sam or the police about Saul Sugarman's involvement in rescuing her. Or her suspicions that he may have known the two men. Her first thought was that, given Klein's hostility towards Sugarman, if she did tell him, he might do something rash and she could not risk that. She decided, even in the state of mind she was in, that it would be best if she made a personal plea to Sugarman. If he truly knew something about Bernice's abduction or knew where the two men were hiding out, then the chances were much better that he'd tell her. An altercation with Klein or the police would surely be much worse.

"I'll find her. I swear to you, I'll find her," Klein said, trying to comfort her. But he, too, feared the worst.

"Those two thugs have her," Klein told Allard. "I told you they were here the other day. They warned me about investigating

Roter's murder and the shootings and now they've acted. It's the only answer."

"Why take your little girl?" asked Nash. "What does it get them? I'm sorry, Sam, but it doesn't make much sense to me."

"Me neither. If this is about money and booze then why snatch your kid?" said McCreary. "There's something we're missing here."

"Anyone think Vivian has something to do with this?" asked Allard.

McCreary shook his head. "Vivian's after Sugarman, so he gains nothing from going after Klein."

"I agree. The reverend may be linked to the shootings, but I doubt very much he'd stoop to kidnapping a child," said Nash.

Klein knew that there were other possibilities, but he could not discuss them in front of Sarah. They were too terrible to contemplate.

Seventy miles away in Vera, a black Ford drove slowly down Railway Avenue and pulled up in front of Grace Tillsdale's rooming house. The driver wiped his sweaty palms and in the darkness glanced at his sleeping cargo in the back seat. At eleven o'clock, the town was silent. Still, he ensured as best as he could that there was no one in sight. He then exited the auto, opened the back door, and carefully picked up the little girl. Fortunately for him, the chloroform that had knocked her out in Winnipeg had yet to wear off. Reaching the front door, he kicked it gently. A second later, Grace Tillsdale opened it.

"Come in, come in," she said. "And who do we have here?"

"This is the little girl I told you about, Mrs. Tillsdale. She needs a place to sleep for about three days. But it's very important that she not go outside at all. She must stay in the house at all times. Do you understand?"

"Of course, I understood the first time you told me. I haven't lost my memory yet, you know."

"I know that. I was just making certain," said Jack Smythe. "And please don't tell anyone about this. It shall be our secret. There's no one else staying here, is that right?"

"No one. And with all of the money you gave me earlier, you've bought all the rooms for a few days. So she'll have the place to herself."

"That's good," said Smythe, panting slightly. "The girl's parents asked me to help them out. They had to leave the city for a few days. But they left these firm instructions that I would like to honour." He wiped his brow.

"That seems rather odd. Why didn't she just stay with you and Joannie? And to stay inside, especially with the beautiful weather we've been having, seems foolish."

"Please, Mrs. Tillsdale, no more questions. Can you do what I am asking?"

"Now don't go getting testy, Jack. If that's what you'd like, then yes, I can do what you wish. Now, I see that she's sleeping. You can carry her into the bedroom at the top of the stairs on the right. One more thing, Jack. What's her name?"

"Bernice. Her name's Bernice."

19

Melinda was shocked by the phone call she received from Klein. His dear little daughter, Bernice, was missing. And she may have been abducted by those two gangsters, Paulie and Richie, who had been at her house. It seemed impossible but, of course, in her line of work, Melinda had seen all sorts of disturbing tragedies: husbands and wives murdering their respective spouses, fathers abusing their daughters, and parents treating their children like animals. But while not much surprised her, she could not bear to think about poor little Bernice suffering alone and scared, or the heartache this was causing Sam and Sarah. Pouring herself a full glass of whisky, she swigged it down in one long gulp.

She left her back room office and spoke quietly to Devlin, a hulking, twenty-five-year-old, Irish immigrant from Cork, whom she had hired a few months ago to keep an eye on things. He was a bit rough around the edges and wasn't quite as adept as Klein had been when he had minded the brothel a decade ago.

But Melinda had noted that the resourceful young man possessed useful skills. Last weekend, when three drunken clients got into a loud and physical argument over which one of them was going to visit Nell's bedroom first, Devlin stepped in and quickly resolved the dispute. Not that the rowdies had much of a choice: he pushed all three of them up against the wall and threatened to break every bone in their bodies if they did not stop fighting and resolve their argument over Nell. They did so by taking turns rolling a die; the one who rolled the higher number went first, and that was that.

Devlin had not been working the other night when Paulie and Richie had first visited, but Melinda had filled him in and given him an order: if anyone fitting their descriptions—and Richie with his eyepatch was impossible to miss—asked for Martha and Lulu, he was to notify her at once.

It was a typical Monday evening. A few farmers, regulars, who were in the city to purchase supplies, stopped by as they usually did. As Melinda liked to put it, "They were in and out quickly, so to speak." Their pockets were full of cash and they were always polite to the ladies. They paid for all the whisky they drank, bought a round for everyone in the parlour, and generously tipped Tom, her aging black piano player, who entertained at the brothel three times a week.

Also visiting was one of Lulu's standing customers, a middle-aged accountant who liked to be spanked, and a virginal young man from River Heights named Leon, whose friends had purchased him a night at Melinda's as a birthday present. After spending time with Martha and Gracie, he left with as wide a grin as Melinda had ever seen on a satisfied customer.

Close to eleven o'clock, Devlin was having a cigarette and speaking with Lulu when the door swung opened and in sauntered Paulie and Richie. They were chuckling and appeared relaxed and happy to be there. As soon as Richie saw Lulu, he nodded to her.

"I'm back for seconds," he said.

"You can have as much as you like," said Lulu, "as long as you're paying."

"And where would Martha be?" Paulie demanded.

As soon as Devlin saw them, he knew these were the two Melinda had told him about.

"If you two gentlemen would step this way for a moment, the madam would like a word," said Devlin.

"Is this really necessary?" asked Richie. He let go of Lulu's arm. "You go keep the bed warm. I'll join you shortly."

Richie and Paulie followed Devlin into the kitchen, where Melinda was sitting smoking a cigarette and nursing another glass of whisky.

"So why'd you do it?" she asked. Her voice was barely audible, though she enunciated the syllables of each word with a determined deliberation. Her eyes were piercing and narrowly focused.

Richie and Paulie looked at each other. "What the hell are you talking about?"

"Why did you take Klein's daughter?"

"Take Klein's daughter? I think you've had too much of that hooch, lady."

Melinda stood up. "You don't have the little girl? You didn't kidnap her?"

"As I said, I don't know what you're talking about. I came here to go the limit. And that's what I'm going to do. Come on, Paulie."

Melinda was dumbfounded. Klein had been so certain that they were involved in the kidnapping, but seeing their genuine incredulity, she now didn't think that was the case. She judged Richie unpredictable, even dangerous, yet she was certain he really had no idea what she was talking about. But if they were not involved in taking Bernice, then who was?

Outside on Annabella Street, the same black Model-T that had passed the house last night pulled up and stopped. The driver fixed his fedora and reached for his shotgun. This would have to be done fast, but with precision, he thought. He wasn't about to disappoint the boss again.

He walked casually to the front door and knocked. When Devlin opened it, he hit the young bouncer hard on the side of his head with the butt of the gun. Devlin's knees buckled and he fell to the floor, momentarily stunned.

Ahead of him, the intruder could see Paulie and Richie in the parlour; both had women on their arms. He moved closer and before either of them could react, he raised his gun and shot, first Richie and then Paulie. The shells hit them in the middle of their chests. It happened so quickly, the few people in the room

261

ALLAN LEVINE

were in shock. Both men fell over, blood pouring from the holes in their torsos.

Martha screamed as if she had been awoken from a terrible nightmare, while Lulu, whose face was splattered with Richie's blood, stumbled backward. The shots and curdling screams brought Melinda to the parlour, but it was too late. The gunman was already back in his car and roaring down the street.

Sarah, exhausted from crying, finally fell asleep sitting in a chair by the front window at about eleven thirty. She said she'd stay there until Bernice was found. But Klein was still wide awake. He got up, checked on Freda and Mel who were also fast asleep, and went downstairs for a cigarette. Earlier, Freda had kept asking him why so many police constables were in the house and why Bernice was not there. Klein had done his best to reassure her that Bernice would be home soon. Yet his eight-year-old daughter was no fool. She had heard her mother sobbing and from the anguished look on her own face, he knew that she was as worried as they were.

The entire evening had passed in a haze of commotion. By ten o'clock there still had been no call or message about who had Bernice and what they wanted. Reporters from the *Free Press* and *Tribune* had tried entering the house asking to speak with Klein. He refused to talk with them. Instead, Allard gave the journalists a statement about Bernice's possible kidnapping and a request that anyone with information about the girl's whereabouts should contact the police at once.

A friendly police constable at the hospital had driven Rivka to the house. She was distraught and in disbelief. Klein had tried to reassure her as well that Bernice would be found, though she was not entirely convinced. Sarah's friend Betty Kingston had rushed over and said that in the event a ransom was demanded, she and her husband, Nicholas, would provide the Kleins with as much money as they needed. Sarah was grateful, while Sam wasn't certain how to react. He made it a habit of never taking a gift of money from anyone, though in this case, if it came down to Bernice's safe return, he knew he would make an exception.

Alec Geller was there, too. He told Klein that he would do whatever he wanted. Klein had insisted that he tell him what had transpired with Joannie Smythe. Geller reported that she had spent the day wandering up and down Portage Avenue. She had had no contact with Vivian and as a result, Geller still had no idea where Dickens might be hiding. The only possible lead Geller had was Sid Sharp, whom he suggested they question.

"Sharp was in her room so he might know what she's been up to," Alec had said.

Klein told Geller to resume his investigation of Mrs. Smythe tomorrow. And despite Alec's protestations that he should be searching for Bernice instead, he reluctantly agreed.

Klein butted out the cigarette he was smoking and immediately lit another one. He poured himself a shot of whisky and downed it. Why, he wondered, would a woman like Joannie Smythe have anything to do with a mule like Sid Sharp, who worked for Saul Sugarman, the enemy of Reverend Vivian? Unless Mrs. Smythe's relationship was part of Vivian's scheme to target the Sugarmans. Who knew what the hell was going on? And at that moment, he had to admit he didn't care. All he wanted was his little girl back. How frightened she must be. The image tore at his heart.

A few minutes before midnight, the phone rang and he jumped up. So did Sarah, who bolted from the chair and ran towards the phone. Klein was there first and picked up the receiver.

"Sam, it's Melinda. You need to get to my place right away. The police will be here in a minute."

"What's happened, Melinda?"

"Those two men you told me to watch out for, Paulie and Richie…"

"Yeah, what about them?" asked Klein, his heart racing. "Do they know anything about Bernice?"

"They've been shot. Sam, they're dead."

20

Klein waited for Rivka to arrive back at the house so that Sarah and the children would not be by themselves. Sarah had asked him who had called and he had told her. Yet when she pressed him for details, all he said was that there had been a shooting at Melinda's and that he didn't know if it had anything to do with Bernice's disappearance or not—which was more or less true. This hardly placated his distraught wife.

"Shailek, do you think I'm a fool," said Sarah through her tears. "Bernice is missing and I'm sure it has something to do with those two men who were at the house and this case you're involved in. Is that it? Do they have Niecee? Were they involved in the shooting?" She was speaking rapidly.

Klein couldn't lie to her. "I don't know if they took her or not. But..." he said, reaching for her hand. "They were the ones who were shot. They're both dead."

Sarah held her hands up to her mouth. "Oh my God, I don't understand. If they took Niecee, how will we find her? How will we find her, Shailek?" Her knees buckled and Klein grabbed her and hugged her.

By this time, Freda and Mel, who had awoken from the commotion, were standing at the top of the stairs, both crying as well.

Rivka looked at Klein. "I'll look after her and them," she said, taking Sarah into her arms. "Now, go do what you have to do to bring Bernice back safe."

Usually the two mile walk from his house to Melinda's took Klein about forty minutes. But with his adrenalin surging, he made it in under twenty-five, taking a shortcut down Burrows Avenue and then onto Rover Avenue. As he turned from Rover to Annabella, he could see several police automobiles parked in front of Melinda's. His heart sank. Sarah might have been right: if Paulie and Richie had Bernice and now they were dead, they might never find her.

He started walking up the path to the front door when a rookie constable, who didn't recognize him, told him to stop.

"I'm Sam Klein, let me through."

"I don't care if you're Prime Minister Mackenzie King, I have orders not to permit anyone but police or the ambulance attendants from the hospital in. Understand?"

Klein looked at the young constable. He wasn't an especially big man, though Klein did not doubt that he could take care of himself. At the same time, Klein's anger was boiling over and he knew he wasn't thinking rationally. Before the constable knew what had happened, Klein had grabbed his arm forward and threw him to the ground.

"Now, as I said, I'm going into the house."

On his back, the constable reached for his revolver.

"Put that away, Parsons, you fool. Didn't I tell you to let Sam Klein through?" bellowed Allard.

"I'm sorry, sir. I guess I didn't hear you," said the constable, dusting off his uniform trousers.

"Thanks, Allard," said Klein. "You think he would've shot me?"

"He just might've. Come on, McCreary and Nash are already here. They're speaking with Melinda. You still haven't heard anything about your kid?"

Klein shook his head. He could barely breathe.

The house was upside down. There was blood everywhere. The parlour rug tapestries and sofas were covered in red splotches. The bodies of Paulie and Richie were still lying in the middle of the floor with white sheets stained in red covering them. Dr. Jake McDonald, who had assisted the police for more than two decades, was standing over the corpses, searching the room for anything that might aid the investigation.

Allard led Klein through the kitchen. Lulu and Martha were huddled together by the table. Martha was shaking and whimpering like a puppy. Lulu was smoking a cigarette and gazing into the distance. Though both women knew Klein, neither acknowledged him. They moved into the back office and Klein locked eyes with Melinda. Standing beside her were McCreary and Nash.

"Sam, I'm glad you're here," said Melinda, hugging him. "How's Sarah? I've been sick about what happened. I know Niecee will turn up soon." Melinda was never one to be emotional, yet the kidnapping and the shooting left her drained. Tears streamed down her cheeks.

Klein gently eased her back. "Tell me what happened."

"She doesn't think they had anything to do with taking your kid," said McCreary.

"Is that true, Melinda?"

She nodded. "Honestly, Sam, when I spoke to them about it, they truly had no idea what I was talking about. I swear to you, they didn't take her or know who did."

Klein's heart sank. If Melinda was correct, then where did that leave him? His mind raced. Who had Bernice? And why?

"Then who shot Paulie and Richie?" asked Klein.

Hannah stepped forward and related what Melinda had told her. "We've spoken to the women they were with."

"Lulu and Martha in the kitchen?" asked Klein.

"Yes. Martha is too shaken up to talk but Lulu provided us with a good description of the shooter. We all think it's likely that this must be the shooter from the railway station and the synagogue. Except this time, he didn't miss."

"So did Lulu help identify him?" asked Klein.

"She did. McCreary thought her description of the culprit sounded familiar. He had a constable drive back to the station to get a mug shot. We showed it to Lulu and she positively identified him as the shooter," said Nash.

"So who is it?"

McCreary reached into his jacket pocket and handed Klein a sheet of paper. Klein looked at it and his jaw dropped. "Frankie Taylor. He's the shooter."

"Amazing, ain't it," said McCreary.

"But that's impossible. Why would Taylor, who works for Rosen, like Paulie and Richie did, kill them? And why would he go after the Sugarmans? It doesn't make much sense unless, I suppose, Taylor's now working for someone else."

"My thought exactly," said McCreary. "This might also explain the death of the storekeeper in Vera."

"Taylor double-crossed Max Roter," said Klein.

"He must've. We need to find that son of a bitch right now before he leaves the city."

The next morning, Sarah roused herself from the chair in front of the window. The house was still quiet. Rivka was asleep upstairs in Freda's room. Around two o'clock in the morning, she had lain down beside her niece to comfort her and eventually fallen asleep. Walking into the kitchen, Sarah found Klein sleeping at the table. The ashtray next to him was full of cigarette butts. She thought of waking him, but she knew that he'd be furious with her for what she was about to do. She knew that Rivka would stay to help Klein with the children. She decided to let Freda sleep as late as she wanted to and miss school that day.

The sense of panic that had overwhelmed her had curiously vanished. She had awoken with a renewed sense of purpose and cautious optimism; she felt in her heart that Bernice would be returned unharmed. She had to be.

Sarah slipped quietly out of the house, leaving a note for Klein and Rivka on the telephone table that she would return in a few hours. When she reached Main Street, she hopped on a downtown streetcar and forty minutes later was at the Boyd Building. She took the elevator up to the fifth floor and walked towards Saul Sugarman's office. Shayna had not yet arrived for the day. There was a flickering light behind the door where Saul worked. She steadied herself, took a deep breath, and walked in.

Sugarman was studying several pages of a document. He glanced at Sarah when she entered, but did not acknowledge her. Then he resumed his work. She stood before him in silence for a full minute, before she lost her patience.

"Saul, do you know why those two men who were in my shop the other day took my daughter? Where is she?"

Sugarman glanced at her. "I'm sorry about your daughter, Sarah. Truly I am, but I have no idea who has her or where she is."

"But those two men ... you knew them didn't you, Saul? That's why they listened to you the other day when you told them to leave me alone. It had to have been them..."

"I know who they are, yes. They're connected to someone in the States that I'm doing a business deal with. But, Sarah, you haven't heard yet, have you? Didn't that husband of yours tell you yet?"

"He told me. I know all about it. They were shot and killed at Melinda's last night. Who are they, Saul?"

"Their names are Paul Backhouse and Richard Tazman."

"Do the police know who killed them?"

"I've heard rumours."

"'That's all you have to say?" said Sarah, her voice breaking up. "My God, what if those two men took Bernice. Now they're dead and she could be trapped, alone somewhere."

Sugarman reached for Sarah's hand, but she pulled it away. "It doesn't seem likely," he said. "A constable I spoke to who was at the brothel told me that before the shooting these men had spoken to Melinda and denied they had anything to do with the kidnapping."

"If that's so, then where is my Bernice and why hasn't the person who took her contacted us for a ransom? Unless they're not interested in money. It's too terrible to think about." She buried her face in her hands.

"Sarah, don't cry. Trust me, this'll turn out okay. Let me look into it further. I know lots of people, some not so pleasant, who might have information. I might be able to find out something."

With tears in her eyes, she looked warily at Sugarman. She knew he was untrustworthy, but what choice did she have? "If you can find her and bring her back to me, Saul, I'd be forever in your debt."

Sugarman didn't say anything, but his eyes glistened in the morning sun shining through the window.

"Daddy, breakfast!" Mel cried out. But he got no reaction from his father.

"Here, let me try," said Freda, pushing her young brother aside. "Daddy, wake up." She tugged at Klein's arm.

He immediately lifted his head and awoke in a fright as if he was having a nightmare. "What is it? What's going on?" he muttered. Wiping his eyes, he could see Freda and Mel standing in front of them. Mel was smiling, but Freda was glum. He smiled at both of them. "Don't worry, honey, we'll find her. Now where's your mother?"

"She's not here," said Rivka, walking into the kitchen holding Sarah's note.

Klein took it from her, read it, and looked back at his sister. "Where could she have gone at seven in the morning, especially with everything that is going on? I need to get downtown."

Rivka put her hands on his shoulders. "I'll give the kids breakfast and stay with them. I'm sure whatever she's doing, she must think it will help to find Bernice."

Klein said nothing. He was less optimistic than his sister and filled with a sense of dread about Bernice and now Sarah.

Despite scouring the city, the police had been unable to locate Frankie Taylor. Allard had men posted at the CPR station and the Union Station on Main and Broadway, but still there was no sign of him. After sleeping on it, Klein felt even more strongly than he had last night that Taylor might be the key— the key to explaining Max Roter's murder and the shooting attempts on the Sugarmans. This was assuming Klein's working theory was correct: Reverend Vivian and George Dickens, now with the likely assistance of Joannie Smythe, had not yet acted on their plot to eliminate the brothers. They, too, would be stopped in due course before they could carry out their improbable scheme. Most critically, and regardless of a lack of evidence, Klein's instincts told him that Taylor also knew something about

Bernice's disappearance. Or, at least, that's what he needed to believe.

Freda and Mel were finishing the porridge Rivka had made for them and Klein was having a cup of coffee and a cigarette when there was a loud knock on the front door.

"Maybe it's Niecee. She's come home," said Freda, clapping her hands.

"Both of you stay right there," Klein ordered.

"I'll keep an eye on them, Shailek," said Rivka.

Klein very much doubted that it was Bernice, but it could be the contact from the kidnapper he had been waiting for. His stomach churned. He felt like he was drowning, struggling with all of his might to keep his head above the water, yet ultimately unable to. He grabbed the handle of the door and yanked it open. A messenger boy about fifteen was standing on the stoop.

"You Mr. Sam Klein?"

"I am," said Klein. This was it, he thought, information about Bernice.

"I have a telegram for you—please sign here," said the boy.

Klein scribbled his initials and the messenger gave him the telegram. His hands were shaking. He tore open the envelope and read it.

Look for Taylor at 247 King Street. Rosen

His heart sank. Nothing about Bernice, though apprehending Taylor was almost as important. He knew he had to go to the police station immediately.

Frankie Taylor paced back and forth in the small, dingy room. He felt like a caged animal at a zoo; he was trapped with nowhere to go. The boss had ordered him to ditch his Model-T in a back alley off Pacific Avenue and he had done so reluctantly. He was then told to proceed to an address on King Street, a Chinese laundry.

When he got there, the owner, a friendly-enough China-man named Lee, escorted him to the room in the back where he was to remain until the morning. The place made Taylor very uncomfortable. He had heard the stories of such laundries being infested by vermin, though, poking around, he could plainly see that Lee's establishment was clean. Nonetheless, the sooner he was able to leave the better, he thought.

He was to have been picked up at six and driven out of the city. But six o'clock came and went and the driver and car had not shown up. He was angry as well as anxious, yet he had been instructed not to phone anyone, the boss in particular. Taylor figured the police would be watching for him at the train sta-tions. So he was stuck in this room full of noxious smells—soap, sweat, and other strange odours he had no clue about—until he could figure out another escape plan. Worse, he was forced to listen to the three male workers manning Lee's vats of boil-ing water and ironing boards. They spoke rapidly in Taishanese which to Taylor merely sounded like annoying gibberish. Lee, whose English was barely understandable, had offered him tea, but he found the strong, sweetly floral smell of the drink unappealing. The same went for the tangy pork—at least that's what he thought it was—and fried noodles—"worms," he and his friends derisively referred to them—he was given. How he yearned for black coffee and eggs and bacon.

Had he not been so careless and clumsy, he would have been out of Winnipeg long ago. Instead, he had had to improvise. Paulie and Richie had finally got what they deserved. One of the Sugarmans was in the hospital and possibly dead already, and the other one would meet his maker soon enough. The boss had said there were to be no loose ends and Taylor had no doubt that that would be the case.

He knew that he was playing a very dangerous game. Double-crossing Rosen and Katz was more than risky; most of his associates would have told him it was a death sentence. Maybe so, but this was war and to his mind he had picked the winning side—and not coincidentally, the side that had offered him the most money. He had his own plans and running booze from towns in Manitoba to North Dakota for the next decade was not in the cards.

He sat down on the rickety bed, picked up his shotgun, and held it tight. Where the hell was his driver? Was he the one now being double-crossed? His problems, he knew, started that night in Vera ten days ago when Roter was killed. He had explained to the boss what had happened, though he got the feeling that his side of the story was not entirely believed. And then when he failed to carry out his assignment as efficiently as he should have, there was another long distance, profanity-filled reprimand.

Staring at the four dusty walls, he realized that he could not stay in this fleabag laundry much longer. Sooner or later the cops were going to find him. There was only one other person in the city who could assist him. The boss had warned him never to contact him, but what choice did he have? He walked out of the room and saw Lee in a cloud of steam surrounded by huge sacks of clothing, bed sheets, and tablecloths.

"I need a telephone," said Taylor.

The laundry owner looked at him but clearly did not understand what he was being asked.

"A telephone. To make a phone call," Taylor said slowly.

"Telephone, yes, yes," Lee finally said. "At front of store."

He led Taylor past a row of shelves on which the clean, folded laundry was wrapped in brown paper. And next to the shelves, there was an older-style wall telephone. He lifted the receiver and cranked the black handle on the side.

"Hello, may I help you?" said the female operator.

"Connect me with A6592."

There was a pause, a few clicks, and then Taylor heard a voice. "Hello."

"Reverend Vivian, this is Taylor."

21

Taylor heard nothing. "Reverend, did you hear me? It's Taylor," he repeated.

Another few seconds passed, and then he heard the sound of the distinctive deep voice.

"Operator, are you still on the line?" asked Vivian. There was no reply.

"I don't think she's there," said Taylor, his tone impatient.

"Taylor, have you lost your mind? What are you still doing in the city? And why would you call me?"

"I'm in trouble. I don't know if the boss double-crossed me or not. But whoever was supposed to pick me up this morning didn't show. You heard about the shooting at the brothel last night?"

"Yeah, I heard. Congratulations, you finally hit your target. What do you want from me? Do you realize what would happen if anyone found out we were speaking? You've put the whole plan in jeopardy by your stupidity."

"I told you, there's no one else I can turn to. Reverend, I'm desperate. I need you to arrange transportation for me to get out of the city. I'm in a Chinese laundry at 247 King Street. Can you help?"

There was another long pause. Vivian was furious. He had purposely and cautiously managed this operation with the utmost of care. There was much at stake, not the least of which was a payoff that he could never have imagined. Keeping Joannie Smythe and George Dickens focussed and committed was paramount. Their devotion and faith in him and the cause could not be questioned. He wanted nothing to do with Taylor, but he wanted the boss to find out what was going on even less. That would only lead to further questions he would rather avoid. And he had no desire to become embroiled in gangster politics. If Taylor was in hot water, then there wasn't much he could do for him. At the same time, the thought of Taylor captured by the police and interrogated was inconceivable. He did not trust him and in his view, the risk of Taylor squealing like a stuck pig was too great. In short, he had no other choice but to assist him.

"Give me thirty minutes and a black Oldsmobile will be in front of the laundry. Until then, stay where you are and for God's sake, don't make any more telephone calls."

Vivian hung up the receiver and for the first time in a long time he was stricken by a sense of panic. He knew he had to be the one to drive Taylor; entrusting this task to anyone else was far too risky. He would have to move up the timetable. He picked up the receiver again and dialled the number to the Royal Alexandra Hotel. Mrs. Smythe required new instructions.

Alec Geller was back in the lobby of the Royal Alex and he wasn't happy about it. He had wanted to be out on the streets searching for Bernice. The idea of her as a captive made him sick to his stomach. And he knew, as Klein must have, that the longer there was no contact from the kidnappers, the less likely it was that she would be found alive. That was too terrible to contemplate. Yet Klein had insisted that he resume his stakeout of Joannie Smythe at the hotel. He had promised to notify Alec if there was any news about Bernice. So Geller sat in a corner of the Grand Rotunda pretending to read the newspaper and waiting impatiently for Mrs. Smythe to make her next move.

He didn't have to wait long. Glancing up, there she was, her red hair flowing onto an olive-and-white-checked summer dress with a wide, white collar. One look at the tension in her face and he knew that something had happened. She moved gracefully across the lobby and nearly every man in the hotel noticed her.

Geller stood up and was about to follow her when Sid Sharp appeared. Alec inched closer to them and positioned himself behind one of the columns, close enough so that he could hear their conversation.

"I'm sorry, Sid, I have to go out," said Smythe.

"What do you mean, you have to go out?" said Sharp.

"Just what I said. We'll have to do this another time. I promise I'll call you as soon as I get back."

"That's not good enough, Joannie."

"It'll have to be, Sid. Now, I have to go."

She turned and as she did so, he grabbed her arm.

"You're hurting me. Let go of my arm or I'll scream, so help me God."

Sharp noticed that they had attracted the attention of other guests and the bellman, who looked like he was about to approach them.

"I didn't mean to hurt you, Joannie," said Sharp, releasing his grip. "You know I'm not like that. Not like that son-of-a-bitch husband of yours."

"I know you're not Sid, but don't ever do that again. Or it will be the last time I'll ever have anything to do with you. Do you understand?"

He nodded dutifully and she patted his cheek softly. Her power over him was total. It still surprised her, despite her many charms and sexual prowess. Here was Saul Sugarman's tough fixer, the man he called upon to solve sticky problems in any way necessary, and she had him behaving like a newly trained puppy. Men might rule the world, she thought, but never under-estimate the ability of a skilled woman to compel any man to do her bidding.

"There's one more thing, Sid. I want you to tell Mr. Sugarman I have to get back to Vera on Friday morning. We can finalize our arrangement for managing the warehouse at a later date."

Smythe waited until Sharp was out of the hotel and out of sight before she also exited. Geller followed behind her, though kept his distance. She walked briskly to Main Street and boarded a streetcar. Geller sprinted and caught it in time. Breathing heavily, he took a seat at the back. Smythe was sitting slightly ahead of him. When the streetcar reached Portage Avenue, she darted out and began walking west. Geller trailed her, fearing that he was about to waste another day watching her shop.

At Smith Street, the number of pedestrians swelled and he lost sight of her. He turned and looked in every direction, but still could not see her in the crowd. He crossed Smith, kept walking, and then saw her half a block ahead, heading towards Donald Street. She was coming out of Andrew's Jewellery beside the Capitol Theatre. She walked to a westbound Portage Avenue streetcar that was boarding and he trailed her onto the car.

Twenty minutes later, she disembarked at Arlington Avenue and began walking north towards St. Matthews. Geller followed her off the streetcar, paused for a few moments, but kept his eye on her. She had to be going to see George Dickens, he figured. A few houses from the end of the block, she turned right into the walkway of a small bungalow. The awning over the living room window was broken and the house's dull, blue paint was peeling badly in spots. A black Labrador was snoozing in the morning sun on the porch. Smythe stepped over the dog, which paid no attention to her, and entered the house without knocking. Geller stopped and made a mental note of the address: 387 Arlington Street.

Though he was excited by his success and wanted to share the news of his discovery with Klein, he thought it might be best to watch the house for a while to see if Smythe or Dickens left. Surveying the quiet, working-class neighbourhood, he decided that his best vantage point was closer to St. Matthews.

He walked nonchalantly past the house, trying his best to not draw any undue attention from the elderly woman across the street tending to her flowers, when he felt the sharp point of a revolver in his back.

"Stop moving," said the person holding the gun. "Now walk slowly into the house, and no sudden movements if you know what's good for you."

Geller did as he was instructed. "Just take it easy. No need to do anything foolish, George," he said.

"Good guess, kid. Now move," said Dickens.

As soon as Geller reached the front steps, the door opened and standing before him was Joannie Smythe.

"Won't you come in, Mr. Geller," she said.

"It would be my pleasure. Not that I have a choice in the matter. When did you figure out I was following you?"

Smythe smiled. "Almost as soon as I left the hotel. Then when I was walking on Portage Avenue, I was certain. I'm afraid you weren't as inconspicuous as you thought. And you were concentrating so hard on me when I got off the streetcar on Arlington, you failed to notice George, who was watching out for me at safe distance, of course. He caught sight of you trailing me immediately. We always take such precautions, you understand."

Geller nodded and followed Smythe into the house. "Now what?"

She closed the door and turned to George. "Put that gun away. There's no need to frighten Mr. Geller any more than you already have."

Dickens did what she asked. "Sorry, kid. I just didn't want you to run."

"What the hell's going on?" asked Geller.

"Please, sit down for a moment. We just want to talk to you and then you're free to go. You might be interested in what we have to say."

"Like how you're plotting to murder Saul Sugarman."

Smythe dropped her head. "We were, that's true, but not anymore. The reverend has deceived us."

"Okay, you have my attention," said Geller, sitting down on a chair.

"And there's something else, too," said Smythe, glancing at Dickens.

"What?" asked Geller.

She cleared her throat. "I think I know where Sam Klein's little girl is."

Acting on the information provided by Klein, Detective Allard assembled six constables to accompany him to the King Street address, along with McCreary and Nash. McCreary had objected to Nash being included, since it was not general policy for the handful of female constables on the Winnipeg force, who rarely, if ever, left the station without a male escort, to participate in anything as dangerous as apprehending a suspect. But Allard, who was in charge of the operation, had insisted—as had Nash. As for Klein, Allard had told him he could come with them as long as he stayed back near the vehicles while Taylor was being arrested. McCreary didn't like that decision either.

The final member of the team was a diminutive, middle-aged Chinese man with short, black hair named Charlie Kwang who frequently acted as an interpreter for the Winnipeg police in any matters dealing with the 900 or so members of the city's Chinese community. Many of them—and the vast majority were men—regarded Kwang as a pariah for helping the white authorities crack down on gambling and opium use. Neither vice, as morality inspector "Big Ed" Franks was forced to concede recently, was that much of a problem. Yet that did not stop the police from pursuing Chinese men engaged in either practice as much as possible.

In any event, Kwang may been a small man, but when challenged, he knew how to handle himself in a fight, as a gang of toughs had learned a few weeks ago when they had come after him following a raid by the police on their regular mah-jong game. Klein had once seen Kwang defend himself in a bar brawl on Main Street and was amazed at his quickness and the strange yet graceful manner he moved almost every part of his body. At times like that, it was as if his abilities transformed him into a human weapon, in Klein's view.

Everyone had gathered inside the main entrance to the station. The constables were checking their revolvers.

"We want to take Taylor alive if at all possible," said Allard. "The suspect is hiding out in a Chinatown laundry at 247 King Street that belongs to a proprietor named Lee. That means there'll be workers who likely won't speak English, but Mr. Kwang is here to help us with that. I want this done quickly, quietly, and efficiently. We have the element of surprise. Taylor is armed and dangerous so let's be careful. Any questions?"

"And if we accidentally shoot a Chinaman, who's going to notice? One less 'chink' in the city," whispered Constable Michaelson.

"Damn right. Why are they in this country? There's talk that the government might ban any more of them from trying to get in, even if they can afford the $500 head tax," said Constable James.

"Michaelson, James, you got something constructive to add?" asked Allard.

"No, sir, we were just chatting about things," said Michaelson.

"Yeah, well, no one gives a damn about what you think. Is that clear?"

"Yes, sir," both of them said in unison.

"Wonderful. Now let's go arrest this bastard. If you'll pardon my language, Mrs. Nash," said Allard.

"No problem. I'm just thankful the commissioner didn't offer his opinion on immigration. We'd be here all day."

"Enjoy your fun all you want at my expense," said McCreary, lighting a cigar. "But I honestly care about the future of this country."

"We know you do," said Klein, rolling his eyes.

Allard, McCreary, Kwang, and four constables pulled up in two cars close to the King Street laundry. Two other police vehicles with Nash, Klein, and Constables Michaelson and James stopped in the alley behind the shop. The agreed-upon plan was for both groups to proceed inside at precisely eleven o'clock.

Allard checked his pocket watch and then pulled out his revolver. "Everyone clear. It's the store with the red and white sign board. Now, I've been in these laundries before. The door will have a chain of small bells on it so once we go inside, we can't hesitate. The odds are, Taylor will be in the back room. So even if he hears us, we can flush him out towards the back door where the other men and Mrs. Nash are."

As soon as Allard's team stepped out of their cars with their guns drawn, they were noticed by pedestrians on King Street, who stopped to watch. Other laundry, grocery, and shop owners in the vicinity opened their doors so that they and their curious customers could peer out. Everyone in Chinatown knew what a raid looked like.

Allard and McCreary led the way. Kwang and the constables were right behind them. The front window of Lee's laundry was covered in newspapers, preventing them from seeing inside. At exactly eleven o'clock, Allard charged in first and, sure enough ,the bells on the door began to ring. Lee was behind the front counter and immediately held up his hands.

"Where's the white man called Taylor?" Kwang asked him in Taishanese.

Shaking, Lee pointed to the back room.

"Get down and stay down," Kwang ordered. Lee did as he was told.

Entering the back part of the laundry, Allard and his group were hit by a cloud of billowing steam. Two of Lee's workers were standing by vats of boiling water, while one man was ironing clothes. Kwang held his finger to his lips and told them to lie down on the floor. They did as they were instructed.

"Taylor, this is Detective Allard. We have the shop surrounded. No one has to get hurt. Come out slowly with your hands in the air."

There was only silence.

"Taylor, there's nowhere for you to go."

Again, there was no reply.

Allard motioned for McCreary, Kwang, and two constables to stay put while he and two of the men moved forward. They slowly entered the room where Taylor had been hiding, but he was nowhere to be seen. Using the back door of the shop, Constables Michaelson and James appeared with their guns at the ready.

"Lower your weapons. He's not here. Check the rest of the area," Allard ordered.

Outside in the alley, Klein and Nash waited in an uneasy silence.

"How are you holding up, Sam?"

"I try not to think of the worst, but it's difficult not to."

"I can't even begin to imagine. I pray she'll be returned safely."

"Thanks, I appreciate that. I've never been a big believer in the power of God and all that, but since Bernice has disappeared, I've been praying a lot, myself."

Their conversation was interrupted by the distinct sound of a boot cracking a twig. They both turned in the direction of the noise but it was too late. Frankie Taylor had grabbed Nash from behind and was holding a knife to her throat.

"Take one more step and I'll slice her," said Taylor.

"Take it easy. Don't do anything stupid. You know there're police inside the laundry. They're not going to let you go," said Klein, inching forward.

"Not another movement."

Nash looked at Klein for support and a glimpse of a smile crossed her mouth. Then, in a deft move that caught Taylor and Klein by surprise, she threw her left elbow into Taylor's midsection as hard as she could. He grimaced slightly and the knife dropped from his hand. Klein quickly grabbed it. Nash turned so that she was facing Taylor and before he could react, she kicked him hard in the groin area. He dropped to his knees in agony.

Allard, McCreary, Kwang, and the constables stormed out of the shop into the alley. With their guns at the ready, they surrounded Taylor, who was still on the ground wincing in pain.

"I don't think he'll be any trouble, now," said Klein, smiling at Nash.

"What happened?" asked Allard.

"Nothing. I just hit him where it hurts," said Nash.

"Most impressive, Mrs. Nash," said Kwang.

"Yeah, I've always said that she knows how to handle men," McCreary joked.

"Get that hood on his feet and bring him to the station. Take the Chinaman too," Allard ordered his constables.

Wheezing, Taylor was hoisted to his feet. "I'll tell you

anything you want to know. I'll confess, but you have to protect me."

"Protect you from who?" asked Allard.

"Rosen. Irv Rosen. He's going to send someone to bump me off. I guarantee it."

Half a block away, Reverend John Vivian sat in his black Oldsmobile dumbfounded. The spectacle of Taylor in handcuffs being led away by the police was disconcerting to say the least. In his view, Taylor was weak and not to be trusted. Vivian knew that Taylor would do anything to save himself, including implicate him in this mess. A report to the boss was required and it wasn't a chore he particularly relished. Vivian had to hand it to Taylor, he had accomplished the near impossible: he was now the enemy of two of the most powerful and feared gangsters in the world: Irv Rosen and Vinny Piccolo.

22

Once Taylor's mugshot was snapped by the police photographer, his height and the size of his ears and nose measured, and his fingerprints taken, he was handcuffed and escorted to the second floor interrogation room. The constable shoved him into a chair. Allard, McCreary, and Nash were already in the room. Klein was standing to the side but growing increasingly impatient. He had no idea whether or not Taylor had been involved in Bernice's kidnapping. At that moment, glaring at this nefarious bootlegger who had murdered two men and probably also killed Max Roter, he didn't care. Nor was he thinking clearly.

"Where's my daughter, you son of a bitch? What have you done with her?" Klein blurted out. It took every ounce of strength he had not to lunge across the room and wring Taylor's neck.

"Klein, I'm doing the talking here," said Allard.

"Then do it … please."

"I'm going to ask you this question only once, Taylor, so

you'd better answer truthfully. Do you know anything about the kidnapping of Klein's daughter, Bernice? She was abducted the other day in front of Eaton's."

"No, I don't," said Taylor. His tone was gruff and belligerent. "I might be guilty of a lot of bad things, but I don't kidnap children. Never. So I have no idea where she is or what you're talking about." He looked over at Klein. "I don't have your daughter, mister, and I don't know who does. You gotta believe me."

Klein slumped against the wall. That was not the answer he wanted to hear, but it was the one he expected. Taylor was a bootlegger and murderer, yet his gut told him that he was probably telling the truth; he didn't have anything to do with Bernice's disappearance.

"Detective, you said you were going to protect me," Taylor said to Allard.

"All right. Why is it that we need to protect you from Irv Rosen?" Allard asked.

"'Cause I double-crossed him for money. Lots of money."

"Is that why you also killed his two men, Paulie and Richie, at the brothel?"

"If I answer that, are you going to make me a deal?"

"Yeah, a deal that the hangman'll treat you nice when you're on the gallows," said McCreary.

"I don't know, Taylor," Allard cut in. "Depends on how honest you are. I don't speak for the Crown lawyers. So why don't you pretend that I'm your priest and make a full confession. And then we'll see what we can do for you."

"Can I have a butt?" asked Taylor.

Klein took out a cigarette, gave one to Taylor, and offered him a light.

"Okay, you have your butt. Now talk," said Allard.

"Had I not been so careless with my shooting, this whole operation would've been over that day at the train station. And then I missed again at Roter's funeral. Just bad luck, I suppose."

"So you went to the brothel to get rid of Paulie and Richie?"

Taylor nodded. "Yeah, I bopped them. They deserved it."

"So why go after the Sugarman brothers, then? Is it because they supply Rosen with booze?"

Taylor smiled. "That's part of it, yeah. I wasn't trying to hit both Hebes. Just the one who's the boss."

"You mean Saul Sugarman?"

"Yeah, he's the one. How's the other brother, who got shot? He going to make it?"

"We don't know yet. But why did you want to kill Saul?"

Taylor took a deep drag on his cigarette. "It's quite a story."

"Yeah, I'm sure. We all want to hear it."

"A few months ago, I learned about a secret meeting that took place in New York called by Rosen and Katz. Sugarman was also there.

"Who told you about it?" asked Allard

"It's not important. I have my sources," said Taylor.

Allard eyed Taylor. He wanted to know everything the bootlegger did. But he also did not want to become embroiled in an argument about what was probably a minor point. He decided to let it go. "All right, Taylor, continue."

Taylor leaned forward. "I found out that Rosen had this

plan, a goofy plan if you ask me, to take over all bootlegging operations from New York to Minneapolis. And that included all the liquor coming into Chicago. He had amassed more than $250,000 dollars. Sugarman was supposed to come up with another $200,000 and become the chief supplier. He told Rosen he'd expand his warehouses and set up new ones in every border town he could."

"A bootlegging monopoly, in other words," said Allard.

"That's right."

"Did Rosen tell you about it later?" asked Allard.

Taylor nodded. "Not in so many words. But he did tell me to be ready for something big that was happening which would shake up the businessness permanently. I didn't ask him too many more questions."

"I guess Piccolo wouldn't be happy about that?"

"No. He wasn't supposed to find out until everything was in place, but someone, and I'm not sure who, told him. In the first week of May, one of his men contacted me. I confirmed what he knew and he offered me a lot of dough, a hundred grand. How could I turn that down? The only condition was that I had to switch sides and get here to bop Sugarman. Paulie and Richie weren't supposed to be in the city. When the boss found out, he told me to bop them, too. I just didn't count on Rosen figuring out what I was up to so soon. Stupid, I guess."

"I guess. What about Max Roter? The night you picked up booze from him, you were already on Piccolo's payroll? You took the liquor and then you came back to kill him and take the money you had given him?"

"No, that's not what happened. I didn't kill Roter. Piccolo wanted me to, that's true. I talked him out of it. Believe it or not, I liked Max. We had a profitable arrangement. I picked up the booze from Roter's warehouse like usual and gave him the cash. Then I drove off and took the cases to Hampton. I thought Rosen was getting suspicious and I wasn't ready to let him know that I had gone over to Piccolo. Besides, it wasn't a huge shipment. When I heard what happened to Roter, I was as surprised as anyone. I even went back to Vera a few days later to nose around, though I couldn't find out anything. I don't know who killed him or why."

"Is there anything else you're not telling us?"

"Isn't that enough?"

"Is there anyone else in the city on Piccolo's payroll? Anyone else gunning for Saul Sugarman?"

Taylor looked down at the floor for a moment. "No, there's no one else. It was just me. Listen, if you don't protect me, then I'm a dead man, done for. No one speaks about Piccolo to the police or goes against Rosen and lives to talk about it. No one."

"What do you make of that, Klein?" asked Allard, turning his automobile right onto Main Street. "Never heard anything like it before. But if anyone could pull off such an improbable scheme, I guess it would be Rosen."

"I have a confession of sorts, too. It was Rosen who told me where we could find Taylor. Sent me a telegram," said Klein.

"I figured you might've been in contact with him. You must

admit that it's out of character for him to do that. Why tell us about it? Why not just finish off Taylor himself?"

Klein shrugged. "Only Rosen knows the answer to that. It may be part of his larger scheme. Who the hell knows what he's thinking. However, if he wants to eliminate Taylor, trust me, he'll find a way."

"I suppose. Even if he goes to prison, he won't last a day unless he's placed in solitary."

"I wouldn't count on him being safe in solitary either. Dangle a bit of cash in front of a low-paid prison guard and that would be that. I am a bit surprised however."

"About what?"

"Rosen's smart, I'll give him that, but his scheme has some holes in it. It would've taken a lot of muscle and money to make it work. From what I know, there are hundreds of gangs in Chicago making big money out of bootlegging—not only Piccolo and Merv Callaghan's North Side Gang, but many, many others. He would've had to pay them all off or get rid of them. If you ask me, Piccolo finding out what was going on may have prevented an all-out gang war. Now it's just Rosen and Piccolo trying to kill each other. A few more dead bodies will show up, but sooner or later they'll sit down and negotiate a treaty."

"No choice, I suppose. Damn Prohibition. Haven't those American politicians figured out yet that they've dug themselves into a deep hole from which there's no escape?"

"As I like to say, sometimes smart people do stupid things. Speaking of which, you going to speak with Sugarman about this?"

"I am. He must've known all along what was going on. He merely chose not to tell us."

"No matter what Taylor says, Piccolo might still be after him."

"Agreed."

"And what about Roter? If Taylor didn't kill him—and I don't think he did—then who the hell did? McCreary says that his men have come up empty. No one in that town is talking."

Klein stared out the window of the car as they passed Selkirk Avenue.

"Hey Klein, you listening to me?"

"Sorry, I was thinking about Bernice. If I don't hear something soon … I don't know what I'm going to do."

"I can't begin to understand," said Allard.

He turned the car left onto Cathedral Avenue, crossed Salter, and pulled up in front of Klein's house. Standing on his porch were Alec Geller and Joannie Smythe, and they both looked frantic.

23

Klein jumped from Allard's vehicle, his head spinning. "Alec, what is it? Did you find something about Bernice? Tell me."

"Easy, Sam. We might have some information about where she is."

Sam looked at Joannie. "What do you know about this, Mrs. Smythe? Please, say something. Why are you here?"

She looked at Klein and Allard. "I ... I think your daughter's in Vera, or at least she was. She may be in the city by now. Oh dear, I'm not certain."

"In Vera? With who?" asked Klein.

"Maybe we should go inside," said Allard.

Klein opened the front door and led everyone into his parlour.

"Now, please Mrs. Smythe, from the beginning. Why do you think Bernice was in Vera?" asked Klein as calmly as he could.

"Last night I received a telephone call from a friend of mine, Grace Tillsdale. She runs a rooming house in Vera. She told me that someone brought a little girl named Bernice matching your daughter's description to her house. She was given instructions to keep the girl inside and paid for her services. Mrs. Tillsdale had heard about the kidnapping and she realized who exactly she had. She was going to call the provincial police…"

"Allard, we have to tell McCreary. He can contact his men…" said Klein.

"Wait, please Mr. Klein, there's more. She's not there anymore. That's what I'm trying to tell you. Early this morning, Mrs. Tillsdale telephoned me again and told me that Bernice was gone. That someone had picked her up and may be driving her back to the city. The little girl's unharmed, I do know that."

"That's twice you used the word 'someone,' Mrs. Smythe," said Allard. "Who exactly are you referring? I believe you know."

Joannie stared downward. "I do, yes. It was my husband, Jack. He's the one who took Bernice to Mrs. Tillsdale's and he's the one who drove her back to the city."

"Your husband? Why would he have done that? Why would he have kidnapped my daughter?" asked Klein.

"It has to do with money, I'm afraid. Jack owes a lot of money. And if he was offered a fee in exchange for taking your little girl, then he might have done it. He's desperate and trying to stay out of jail, but that's probably impossible now."

"Do you know who he's working for?" asked Allard.

"I don't, but whoever it is, they must be paying Jack a lot. Since he started drinking … It hasn't been good between us for a while."

"Did your husband murder Max Roter or have anything to do with it?"

"Jack kill Max? That's impossible. They were friends."

"Did you ever think your husband could be involved in the kidnapping of a five-year-old child?" Allard asked pointedly.

"No, of course not, but commit murder for money … I can't conceive of such a thing."

"Tell us the whole story, Mrs. Smythe. We need to know."

"This is not a story with a happy ending like the fairy tales you read to your children, Mr. Klein. I don't know the exact details of what Jack did. But from what I have gathered, he lied to his employer, Mr. Kingston, about a land purchase. He then used the company's money to speculate in the grain market and lost all of it. I believe it's about $25,000, perhaps more. He's been trying to figure out a way to repay it. The last time we spoke about this, Mr. Kingston was starting to ask many questions, which made Jack drink more and…" She covered her eyes with her hands.

"He hit you, didn't he?" asked Klein.

"Sam, that's an indecent question," said Alec.

Tears were streaming down Joannie's face. "Yes, yes. I should've left him, but the humiliation is too much to bear."

"Instead you found Reverend John Vivian. Isn't that so?" asked Klein.

"When I first met the reverend he offered me the peace of mind I was searching for. So strong and devoted. I can only describe it as intoxicating, being in his presence. He convinced me that the evil of drink must be destroyed at all costs. And I believed him. I still believe him."

"What did he ask you and George Dickens to do?"

Looking at Allard, she hesitated for a moment. "The reverend wanted to take advantage of the attacks on the Sugarmans. He knew that we could strike and it would be blamed on someone else. Or so I believed at the time. Mr. Dickens was to kill Saul Sugarman. That was the plan."

"And why tell us this now?'

"Because … because the reverend's a liar. He deceived me, Mr. Dickens, and all of his followers. The other day I learned from Mr. Cole that Reverend Vivian had taken money from a gangster in Chicago, a man who supports the bootlegging business, and that he is doing this man's bidding. In other words, he sold his soul for thirty pieces of silver as Judas did to our Lord Jesus Christ."

"Piccolo? Vivian's working for Piccolo?" said Klein, looking at Allard.

"Mrs. Smythe, what happened to Dickens?" Allard asked.

"He's gone. Maybe back to his wife, I'm not certain. When Mr. Geller tracked me to the house on Arlington where George was hiding, we both decided to put a halt to this insanity. Especially when I learned about Mr. Klein's daughter."

"If what you say is true—that Vivian's been paid by Piccolo to murder Saul Sugarman—then won't he go through with it?"

"I believe he will, yes."

Sarah had absolutely no desire to open her store. She was beside herself with worry and had no interest or patience in dealing with the mundane questions posed to her by her customers. Did it really matter if the trimmed summer hats came with a ribbon colour other than white or that the embroidery on the silk dresses were too elaborate? At the best of times, these petty shopping queries annoyed Sarah. Today, with nothing but Bernice on her mind, she couldn't bear them.

But Betty Kingston had convinced her that it might be a good distraction from the constant worry and she offered to help her and keep her company. She and Betty had only got to know each other well recently. Yet Sarah had decided that her new friend truly was the "unflappable" flapper, as she had dubbed her. Sarah had never met someone so optimistic. Then again, Betty did not have a care in the world. Her doting husband ensured that she had everything her heart desired. From her earliest days in Winnipeg, Sarah had always believed that a hefty bank account was an integral element of perpetual happiness. Betty's joy and gregarious lifestyle certainly reinforced that view.

"Never mind those dumbdoras," whispered Betty, rolling her eyes in the direction of two "misses" who had been in the store for more than a half hour trying on dresses and middies. "They're not going to buy anything."

"So you'd like that pongee middie? Only two dollars," Sarah said to them.

The young women, probably nineteen and stenographers in nearby offices, giggled like schoolgirls. "Too much, I'm afraid, on our pay cheque," said one of them. "We have got to get back to the office or we'll be fired."

"Dumbdoras. Told you so," said Betty.

Sarah gave Betty a hug. "I don't know what I would've done without you today."

"Well no one likes being Edisoned for eight hours a day by tomatoes or face stretchers."

That comment brought a smile to Sarah's face. "I honestly have no idea what you say half the time, but it does make me laugh. And I need that right now. Being Edisoned? You mean being asked lots of stupid questions?"

Betty nodded.

"But what's a face stretcher?"

"You know who Irene McRae is?"

"Of course, she comes into the store often."

"And how does she dress, in your opinion?"

"A bit too much rouge and powder and she prefers the latest fashions for younger women."

"Exactly. She's thirty-five, not married, and tries to look twenty-two. That, my dear, is a face stretcher."

"Betty, you are terrible. You slay me, as I think you'd put it."

The door of the shop opened and Sarah turned around abruptly to see who it was. Her shoulders drooped when a female customer walked in.

Betty lightly grasped her hand. "You're waiting for that bad egg Saul Sugarman, aren't you? You're hoping that he might help you find Bernice? I'm afraid I wouldn't put any faith in him or that happening."

"I know, you're right. I'm desperate," said Sarah, choking back tears.

On cue, as if he was an actor in a stage play, Saul Sugarman strutted into the shop. He ignored Betty Kingston and stepped close to Sarah. He did not look like a man with good news to share.

"You have nothing to tell me, have you?" Sarah asked, dejected.

"I don't. I spent a few hours calling around to people who might know something. But no one could tell me anything of value," said Sugarman.

"I was praying..." said Sarah, looking down.

"I know you were. The world's an ugly place, Sarah. Who knows why anyone does anything. Greed, corruption, envy, it's all out there. Sometimes people are merely bad because they don't know any other way."

Betty glared at Sugarman, her jaw clenched. But she said nothing. She was not certain if he was telling the truth or not. But she knew that antagonizing him with further questions would only make matters worse and upset Sarah even more.

Sarah moved closer to Sugarman. "If you learn anything else, please contact me at once. I don't think I can stay here much longer. I have to get back to my family."

"Of course, I understand." He turned, looked dismissively at Betty, and strutted out of the shop exactly as he had entered it.

"I'm sure that slimy devil is trying to help you, Sarah," said Betty. "But honestly, and I know this is a terrible thing to say, if whoever's trying to put a bullet in that man succeeds, you won't find me crying about it."

By eight o'clock that evening, Klein had heard twice from Allard, though he had nothing positive to report. Neither Jack Smythe, who possibly had Bernice, nor Reverend Vivian had been located despite a city-wide police search. Allard had assured him his constables would not stop until his daughter was found.

To make matters worse, Sarah had yet to arrive home. Klein had telephoned Sarah's shop at about three, but there was no answer. Sarah must have closed the shop early. Klein had fed Freda and Mel—thankfully his friendly neighbours had brought over cheese, bread, and herring—and got them ready for bed. Still Sarah was absent and Klein was starting to worry.

He was upstairs with Freda when he heard the front door open.

"Sarah, where have you been?" asked Klein, embracing her.

"I'm sorry, Shailek. I decided to walk home from downtown and I must've lost track of time. I sat by the river for a time. I don't know, I guess I was hoping to see Bernice."

"This morning you went to ask Sugarman for help, didn't you?"

"What can I say? He says he tried, but he knows nothing."

Klein raised his eyebrows. "Someday you'll understand that he's been toying with you. And now he's using our missing daughter to play with your emotions."

"I'm no fool. I know what he's doing. I had to try. I don't think

I can stand another minute of this. We're never going to see her again," she said, collapsing into a chair beside her.

Klein took both her hands in his. "Don't say that. The police have a new lead. We found out that she was taken to Vera."

"What? Is she there now?" asked Sarah, quickly standing up.

"No. She's gone but she might be in the city. The police are looking for a suspect. She was alive and well this morning. We know that."

"In Vera. Then, as I've feared, this all has to do with the case you're working on. With Max Roter's murder."

"I'm afraid it might. I don't have all of the facts yet. But I can't tell you how terrible I feel ... If I'm responsible for any harm that comes to Bernice..."

Sarah put her arms around his shoulders and drew him close. "It's not your fault, Shailek. It's not your fault..."

With his car parked on Powers Street close to Cathedral Avenue, Jack Smythe squinted in the darkness at five-year-old Bernice Klein asleep in the back seat. He grabbed the half-empty whisky bottle lying next to him, opened it, and took a gulp. It had been a very long day. He had kept the kid on a farm in Kildonan where the owner didn't ask any questions for much of the afternoon. The farmer's wife had fed her and she seemed content to play with their mutt and watch the cows and horses.

Nevertheless, he felt sick. How had he made such a colossal mess of things? A party to a kidnapping, hitting Joannie, and worse. All because of his stupidity and greed. And for what? He was about to be exposed. In the past week, Nicholas Kingston had been asking too many questions about expenses he had marked in the accounts book. Kingston was smart, Smythe knew that. It was only a matter of time before he figured out Jack had taken $20,000 from the company to cover a margin call.

Six months ago, he had listened to some bad advice from a grain trader. He had assured Smythe that the price of wheat was going to drop below sixty cents a bushel. So, using a fake client name, he and his partner went "short," selling wheat futures on the Exchange floor, wheat that they did not own. Smythe had anticipated pocketing about $15,000. Instead, when the price started to rise instead, above eighty cents, he had had to come up with the $20,000 to cover his losses. Desperate, he borrowed the funds from his company's bank account, telling himself that he would be able to repay it over time. That was wishful thinking at best. He had started drinking more and taken out his troubles on Joannie more than once.

His so-called saviour had doled out enough money for Smythe to keep on doing what he was ordered. But not anymore. It stops now, he mumbled under his breath.

"Kid, wake up," Smythe said, slightly raising his voice. When Bernice still did not open her eyes, he shook her gently.

"I want my mommy," Bernice said, yawning.

"No more crying. You're going to see your mommy in a moment."

"I am!"

"Yeah, it's Christmas in June. So are you listening to me?"
Bernice nodded.

"I'm going to open the door and you're going to run down to

your house. Look out the window. Can you see it there? It's the third house."

"That's where I live."

"That's right, kid. Now get out of here."

Bernice did as she was instructed and ran into the night. She climbed up the front steps and looked up at the door. "Mama, Daddy. Open up."

Klein and Sarah were in the kitchen, sitting at the table in silence, exhausted from worry.

"Shailek, did you hear that?" said Sarah, standing up. "I swear it sounds like Bernice."

"What? It was nothing. Probably a stray cat."

Again, the cry from outside. "Mama, Mama."

Klein heard it this time, too.

"Oh my God! Shailek, it's her, it's her."

Klein jumped up and ran to the front door. Sarah was right behind him. He pulled it open and there was Bernice, looking a little dishevelled, but otherwise unharmed. In tears, Sarah picked her up and tightly embraced her. Klein was speechless as he, too, hugged his daughter and wife.

"You're back, Niecee. You're back."

On top of the stairs, wiping the sleep away from their eyes, stood Freda and Mel. Both were smiling from ear to ear.

24

Wednesday morning, Shayna Kravetz walked down Portage Avenue on her way to work with a distinct spring in her step. Alec had called her early with the fantastic news: Bernice Klein had arrived back home safe and sound. Shayna was so happy that she had bawled for twenty minutes.

The story spread through the North End like an out-of-control wild fire. Everyone on the streetcar was talking about it, with, of course, the usual speculation of why she had been returned. One middle-aged woman suggested that the kidnapping had been a hoax concocted by the Jews to gain sympathy while another whispered about a gang of Chinese men she had heard of who sold white girls into slavery. "They did unspeakable things to her and then decided they didn't want her," the woman said. Fools, thought Shayna as she disembarked. Nothing, particularly such absurd yammering, was about to ruin her delightful mood.

As she entered the Boyd Building, she noticed a sign in Sarah

Klein's dress shop that indicated the store would be closed for the day. Given everything that happened, that wasn't surprising. Reaching the fifth floor, she jaunted off the elevator and into the office.

"Mr. Sugarman, have you heard the wonderful news?" Shayna cried out.

But the door to Sugarman's private office was closed and all Shayna could hear was the sound of objects and paper being strewn about. He was on another rampage about something, thought Shayna. Yet another Sugarman temper tantrum.

A moment passed and then Sugarman, huffing and wheezing, stomped out. "Good, you're here. I need to be out of the city for most of the day."

"You're going out of town?" asked Shayna.

"It's none of your business. Just clean up my damn office, it's a mess," said Sugarman, walking out.

He had decided to take the train to Vera. The matter of the warehouse needed his attention and he could not wait for Lou to recover and deal with it. The liquor had to be moved.

Shayna watched the door slam as he left. Why did she continue to work for him? He was usually miserable and angry and no matter what she did or how efficient she was, he was never satisfied. It, unfortunately, came down to money. Her weekly pay cheque was higher than that of any other secretary she knew in the city. How could she possibly walk away from such a job and salary? Perhaps someday soon, when Alec finally asked her to marry him, she might be able to quit. Until then, she was stuck with Saul Sugarman. It hardly surprised her that he had never married; what woman in her right mind would want to cater to him the rest of her life?

She laughed at the thought as she bent down and began collecting correspondence and notations that he had thrown about the room. Picking up several pieces of paper, a few words jotted on the piece at the top of the pile caught her attention. She scanned it and her eyes widened. Reading it a second time more slowly, she began to tremble. Her hand instinctively covered her mouth. It took her only a few seconds to realize the full extent of what she had read. She went to her desk and picked up the telephone.

"Alec, it's me," she said softly into the receiver, her voice shaking.

"What is it, Shayna? What's happened?"

"I'm coming to your apartment right now. We need to see Sam immediately."

About forty miles outside of Winnipeg, the train to Vera stopped for no apparent reason. The conductor walked through the cars informing the passengers that he did not know the reason for the delay. He asked everyone to be patient. A handful of passengers grumbled, but the majority resigned themselves to this unintended inconvenience—except, that is, Saul Sugarman.

Sugarman never accepted that his power was limited, that he could not control each and every situation he found himself in. It was the reason why, even now, with incontrovertible evidence supplied by his police sources that Frankie Taylor had sold out Rosen for Piccolo and had been trying to kill him, he refused to accept that Rosen's scheme—and his own potential for huge profits—had failed. Whatever obstacles Piccolo had put in their way, he would sweep aside. In his mind, the Rosen-Sugarman bootlegging takeover was still intact.

He regarded this trait, what he perceived as determination and the will to win, as his key strength, unaware that everyone else who entered his orbit thought exactly the opposite. In Winnipeg and beyond, Sugarman's penchant for absolute control merely made him a contemptible bully. And so, as was his style, he berated the poor conductor for more than an hour until the train started moving again.

At the back of same train car, Reverend John Vivian, with a hat pulled low, watched this pathetic one-sided confrontation unfold. The anger he felt towards Sugarman was intense, he could not deny it. The money Piccolo had paid him was almost an afterthought—or so he had convinced himself. Ridding the world of a corrupt sinner such as Sugarman was surely doing God's work. He was tempted to pull out his revolver and do the deed right there and then, saving the conductor and the other passengers from this thoroughly despicable human being. But he knew that if he wanted Sugarman's demise to have meaning, he would have to stick to his plan.

The train pulled into the Vera station almost two hours late. As soon as the conductor opened the door, Sugarman pushed his way through and disembarked. Vivian did the same and followed him down Main Street, though he guessed where Sugarman was headed. When he reached Roter's shuttered store, he turned left and took the path that led to the warehouse. As he expected, the locks on the door were open and he entered.

In the dim light, he felt a sense of relief and pride. The shelves, from floor to ceiling, were stocked with liquor cases containing thousands of bottles of booze, just as they had been the fateful night Max had been murdered. With that traitor Taylor in police custody, Rosen had arranged for another bootlegger, one he and Katz completely trusted, a hood known only as "Philadelphia Ray," to bring in a convoy of three trucks and six men that night after midnight so that liquor shipments from Vera could resume. In their brief telephone conversation late last night, Rosen had not told Sugarman what he was going to do about Piccolo's interference, only that it would be taken care of real soon. Sugarman was to continue making his plans as though nothing had happened.

He could have entrusted Smythe with the task of ensuring that Ray's trucks were loaded, instead of travelling all the way to Vera, yet Smythe could no longer be trusted. He had, in fact, become a liability.

"Smythe, its Sugarman. Where the hell are you?"

For a full minute, Sugarman stood waiting for a reply. Then a response.

"Back here," said the familiar voice.

Annoyed, Sugarman made his way down a narrow corridor between two high rows of shelves and followed the flicking light of a lantern. He walked as far as he could and arrived at an alcove with a small desk, where Max had kept his inventory records. He saw Jack Smythe sitting on the chair behind the desk with a gun in his hand. There was an open bottle of whisky in front of him. Then Sugarman looked to his right and was startled to find Klein, Alec Geller, and Joannie Smythe standing there. Klein glared at him, but said nothing.

"What's this?" Sugarman demanded to know, taking a step back.

"Stay where you are. No sudden movements," Jack Smythe implored him. His voice was raspy and strained.

"Okay, Jack. I'll stand here. But would you like to tell me what you're doing? And what are they doing here?"

"I'm setting things right, that's what I'm doing, Saul. I decided that I'm no longer your errand boy. That no amount of money is worth what you've put me through. I only regret that I found this out so late." He pointed the gun at Sugarman.

"Jack, stop, don't do this, please. We can figure it out. We'll hire you a lawyer," Joannie pleaded.

Smythe smiled. "I love you, dear, and I'm sorry, deeply sorry for having raised a hand to you. Blame the damn booze—it makes a man do crazy things." He picked up the bottle in his other hand and took a swig. "No lawyer's going to get me out of this mess. I'll hang for sure. So let me first tell you my story."

"You don't want to do this," said Sugarman.

"Yeah, I think I do. As you all likely know, I made some bad decisions. I took money from the company's bank accounts that I stupidly squandered speculating in the grain market. I was desperate to repay the funds—so desperate that I asked Max for help. He and I worked out an agreement but because of the amount involved, he was forced to consult with you, Saul. By the way, kid," he said, looking at Geller, "that's what you found that night you were searching Max's store. I knew Max had a copy of it and I had been trying to locate it. It was one of the documents tucked into that bundle of papers. I didn't think you'd still be there and I had no choice but to stop you from finding it. You'll have to believe me, I didn't want to hurt you, but I'm glad, truly glad, that you recovered."

"I'll live," said Geller.

"What about Max? Did you kill him?" asked Klein.

"I did. My God, I did. By then, I was drinking too much and Sugarman was dangling all of this cash in front of me. I wasn't thinking straight."

"Jack, how could you? Max was our friend," cried Joannie.

"I know he was. And I'll never forgive myself. That night I waited until that bootlegger Taylor left and then I put a shotgun through the window and fired. I took the money Max had and just kept it."

"But why did you do it? What had Max done?" asked Klein.

"Don't answer that," said Sugarman.

Smythe laughed. "Too late, Saul. I did it because if I didn't, Sugarman was going to expose me. There was a lot of money on the table. I couldn't say no. And why did Max have to die, you ask? Because he had done the unthinkable: he disobeyed the great Saul Sugarman. When Max learned that Sugarman had agreed to be partners with Rosen in this outlandish, outsized bootlegging plan, he argued with him incessantly that it was bad for business. That it would only lead to a gangster war, which they would be caught in the middle of. And that, by the way, is exactly what happened. Max did something he shouldn't have and told Frankie Taylor of the scheme."

Klein shook his head. Now he understood who had told Taylor about the plan. It had been Roter.

"He hoped Taylor might be able to talk Rosen out of it," continued Smythe. "Instead, as I understand it, Taylor went to Piccolo, was bought off, and, well, you know the rest. Sugarman was angry when he found out what Max had done and believed that he could no longer trust him. He berated and blackmailed me until I agreed to get rid of Max. I'm so sorry, Joannie. I don't know how I could've done it."

Tears welled in Joannie's eyes. "Jack, put the gun down, please."

"No, I can't do that yet. Because there's more to this sad story."

"Sugarman next made you kidnap my daughter, didn't he?" said Klein.

"I don't know what you're talking about Klein. You're as crazy as Smythe is," said Sugarman. A thick bead of perspiration formed on his forehead.

Klein held up a piece of paper. "You know what this is, Sugarman? It's a page that was found in your office and given to me by Shayna. From what Joannie learned from Mrs. Tillsdale, I already knew that Smythe was involved in the kidnapping, though not why he had done it. Then I read this and understood that you were pulling the strings. Shayna said you were coming to Vera, so the three of us drove out here in a police car as quickly we could. I'm only glad that your train was delayed."

"I don't know what that bitch gave you."

"It's a list of instructions: where my wife's store is located, what my daughter Bernice looks like, and where she should be taken. If you're going to kidnap a five-year-old, you should be a lot more careful where you leave such incriminating evidence. I'd like to wring your neck. How could you do such a thing?" Klein shouted.

"I don't know what…" Sugarman stammered.

"Don't even bother to deny it, Saul," said Smythe. "It's true. I took her, Klein, when your wife was at Eaton's. This is no excuse, but I did it partly because if I had not done so, he would've hired someone else to do it. And God knows what would have happened to your little girl. I knew I could keep her safe. But when I heard what was going on in the city and how much pain this was causing you and your family, I had to end it. So I brought her back to you. He wanted to keep her for at least another week and then who knows? I'm fairly certain that this was all about punishing your wife for spurning him."

Klein was stunned. "You did this because Sarah wouldn't leave me to be with you? You wanted to teach her a lesson? Is that it? Can you be that callous a human being?"

"Sarah deserves better than you. Always has. But when I could see that she would never be mine, I had to make her suffer. It was the only way."

"You're mad, you know that?" said Klein.

"He may well be, yet it is me who's guilty here," said Smythe, lifting his gun. "I'm a coward at heart. I can't face a trial and a hanging. I love you, Joannie."

"Jack, put the gun down, please," Joannie pleaded. "Don't do…"

It was too late. Smythe shoved the gun against his temple and pulled the trigger. His head exploded in blood and he slumped forward on to the desk. Joannie screamed and fell to the floor. As Klein and Geller went to help her, Sugarman turned and began walking down the corridor. He had not taken more than ten steps when Reverend John Vivian appeared. He pointed a gun directly in Sugarman's face.

"Stop right where you are," ordered Vivian.

"Reverend, what are you doing here?" Joannie Smythe cried.

"I'm here to send this sinner back to where he belongs. You and George abandoned me and the cause…"

"That's a bald-faced lie. I believed in you," she yelled. "But everything you told me and George was a lie. This isn't about morality and ridding the world of liquor. It's about money. You're no better than he is," Joannie stammered, looking at Sugarman. She had to catch her breath.

"What do you mean?" asked Sugarman.

"Not another word," said Vivian.

"He's in cahoots with Piccolo to stop your grand scheme," she said, trying to gather herself. "He's been paid off. Reverend John Vivian is a charlatan, a fraud, an imposter."

"So I took the money. But don't you see the irony in all of this, my dear Joannie? We take the profits of evil for our own worthy work and, in exchange, we eliminate one of the very perpetrators of this malevolence."

"That's a convenient justification for your actions."

As Vivian and Joannie spoke to each other, Klein and Geller backed up against the shelving. Slowly Klein reached behind him and, with Geller helping him, pulled a crate of liquor forward. Klein looked at Geller and with one tug they brought the crate and the bottles inside crashing to the floor. The sudden noise of glass breaking was enough for Sugarman to push the gun away from his chest and from Vivian's hand. It fell to the ground. Seeing his opportunity, he lunged at Vivian, sending him reeling backward. Geller meanwhile grabbed Sugarman and dragged him across the floor to where Joannie was cowering behind Jack Smythe's limp body. With all his strength, Vivian stretched his arm forward, reaching for the gun. His fingers touched the barrel when a boot stomped on it and then kicked the gun away.

Klein stood up as Saergeant Sundell took hold of Reverend Vivian and handcuffed him.

"Sundell, what took you so long?" asked Klein.

"McCreary told me to give you some time to piece everything together."

"He did? That's awfully nice of him. I'll have to thank him!" He looked behind him at Geller who was tightly holding onto Sugarman. "You can take him too. He's responsible for the murder of Max Roter and for the kidnapping of my daughter."

Sundell handed Vivian, who was still dazed, to one of his men and he took Sugarman from Geller. He tossed another pair of handcuffs to Klein. "Be my guest."

"With pleasure." Klein twisted Sugarman's arms and slapped the handcuffs on him.

"You think you've won, Klein. You've won nothing. I have lawyers. You have no case."

"I guess we'll find out soon enough. But I can tell you one thing: Irv Rosen might want to find himself a new partner."

25

S aul Sugarman was right. His high-priced team of lawyers led by Graham Powers were skilled enough to convince a jury that Sugarman should not be hanged. For his direct involvement in the murder of Max Roter and the kidnapping of Bernice Klein, he was sentenced to twenty-five years at a federal penitentiary with the possibility of parole to be determined at a later date.

Curiously, Klein was ambivalent about Sugarman escaping the noose. The thought of him rotting away in a tiny cell for the next two decades was, in Klein's view, just punishment for the turmoil and pain he had inflicted. Sarah, so thankful to have Bernice back, never uttered Saul Sugarman's name again.

But she did spend many days and evenings reflecting on what had transpired and how she had allowed herself to be ensnared by someone so deceitful as Sugarman. It had led to the kidnapping of her precious daughter. She shuddered at the thought of what might have been. And it had almost cost her marriage and a life with the only man she ever loved. She was deeply troubled by her actions and promised herself that she would be stronger in the future. She owed that and more to Sam and her children.

Three weeks after the events in Vera, Lou Sugarman finally woke up and soon fully recovered. He admitted to Klein that he had known what Saul and Rosen had been scheming, yet had absolutely no idea that his brother was behind Max's death. It was too shocking for him and Rae to contemplate that Saul had also manipulated Jack Smythe into kidnapping Bernice. Lou speculated that Saul had encouraged him to hire Klein in the first place to investigate Max's murder so that Klein would be busy and distracted. Still, his obsession with Sarah was difficult to comprehend.

Lou did make one significant decision. With the sole power, now, to run the Sugarmans' operation, he sold the family's liquor interests for a sizable amount to a Toronto distillery. And almost overnight, the Sugarmans were no longer supplying bootleg liquor to the likes of Irv Rosen and Vinny Piccolo. Instead, Rae decided to reopen the general store and run it on her own.

Lou soon heard that the two gangsters had negotiated a peace agreement and the booze war and killings stopped, at least for a time. After everything that had transpired in Winnipeg and Vera, Rosen changed his mind. He had come to the conclusion that enforcing a bootleg monopoly was next to impossible and could only lead to more unnecessary violence and bloodshed. Everyone knew that prohibition in the United States contributed to police and political corruption and encouraged thousands, if not millions, of Americans to break the law. From Rosen's distorted perspective, selling bootleg booze was the most lucrative business opportunity he could have ever imagined.

That's why Reverend John Vivian had been fighting such a losing battle. Yes, before he, too, was corrupted by Piccolo, he had echoed the sincere sentiments of generations of "drys"—moral reformers who saw in liquor only exploitation and abuse. But in 1922, it was already clear that prohibiting Americans from drinking spirits and beer would only make them want the booze more. Enforcing such an unenforceable law was already a nightmare. The only workable solution was what Manitoba and a few other provinces soon came up with: government control and the promotion of moderate drinking. In the summer of 1922, the details still had to be hammered out but even someone as skeptical as Klein thought this was the right approach to take, though the prospect of a group of politicians and bureaucrats devising regulations for the proper consumption of liquor concerned him and a lot of Manitobans.

At the same time, there was much sympathy for Reverend Vivian. The evidence proving his collusion with Piccolo was inconclusive and testimony by Joannie Smythe, George Dickens, and Adam Cole was unconvincing. They were dismissed as disgruntled and disillusioned disciples. The Crown failed, too, to convict Vivian on the charge of threatening Saul Sugarman with a weapon. He marched out of the law courts on Broadway a free man, promising to continue the battle against liquor and immorality.

Joannie Smythe, who left Vera to live with her sister in Toronto, did not doubt him. Klein made a point of being at the railway station to see her off and wish her well. "Jack was not a wicked man," she had told Klein, "only a troubled and misguided soul."

Klein also bid farewell to Hannah Nash, who, once the case was wrapped up, returned to Calgary to continue the fight against bootlegging along the Alberta-Montana border—as futile as that might prove to be. Before she left, Allard and McCreary even hosted a dinner in her honour that Klein had attended. No one on the force had ever witnessed such a gesture from McCreary, but he took the ribbing in good humour. He assured everyone that his respect for Mrs. Nash's skills as a policewoman in no way meant he had changed his attitude about immigrants, women, prostitution, or any other social problem. And funnily enough, no one questioned that declaration.

There was a connection between Klein and Hannah. Both of them felt it, but neither of them addressed it. Some things were definitely best left unsaid. What had happened between them three years earlier was a fleeting moment to be remembered but not acted upon. If anything, the last few weeks had shown that Klein's life was with Sarah and his children and Hannah could not have been happier for him.

Before the end of the summer, there were two wedding proposals. Lou Sugarman asked Rivka to marry him and Alec Geller finally worked up the courage to ask Shayna Kravetz to be his wife. Klein was to be Alec's best man and soon Sarah was immersed with both Rivka and Shayna in wedding plans.

One evening in August, Klein sat on the steps of his house,

having a cigarette, watching his three children play, and glancing at the newspaper. A story on the third page of that day's *Tribune* caught his eye.

> *Frankie Taylor, who provided testimony in the recent trial of Saul Sugarman in exchange for a more lenient sentence in his own trial of attempted murder, was discovered dead in his cell last night at Kingston Penitentiary. Taylor had been transferred to the Ontario institution as part of his plea deal. Prison guards questioned said they have no idea yet as to what had caused Taylor's death.*

That had to be the work of Rosen and Katz, thought Klein as he re-read the article. They probably paid off a few guards. No one crossed Rosen and lived to talk about it.

"Shailek, you have funny look on your face. What are you reading?" asked Sarah, sitting down beside him.

"Nothing important. Look how much fun they're having. Honestly, I don't know what I would've done or how I would've survived if something had happened to Niecee."

Sarah interlocked her arms with his. "But she came back safe and that's all that matters. Besides, deep down, I had faith that you'd get me through the ordeal. Like you always have, like you always will."

"I know you won't use his name and don't want to speak of this, but greed was Saul's undoing. He had an appetite for money, and for you, which could never be satisfied. In many ways, he's a more tragic figure than Jack Smythe."

"Well, as you say, I'm not going to talk about it. But there's something I should probably tell you," she said with a grin.

"What is it?" he laughed.

"Let's see … if it's a boy, I think we should call him Daniel, and if it's a girl, Sharon. I always liked that name. So say something," said Sarah, giving him a hug and a kiss on the cheek.

Sam Klein was momentarily speechless. After a minute or two, he stood up and kissed Sarah. "All I can say is, thank God there's no prohibition here because I really need a stiff shot of whisky."

Acknowledgements

It had been my intention for many years to reboot the Sam Klein Mystery series. For making this possible, I would like to thank Jamis Paulson and Sharon Caseburg of Turnstone Press. Both were enthusiastic about this new Klein adventure from the start. Sharon, as the editor of the novel, was an enormous help in particular in shaping and improving the manuscript. And Sarah Ens of Turnstone did a great job as copyeditor.

Thanks also to Hilary McMahon, my stellar agent and friend for her continued support. I am most grateful to my wife, Angie, who once again was my sounding board and offered excellent advice about all aspects of the novel, as well as for the support from our expanding family: Alexander and Shannon and their precious daughter, Liliana, and Mia and Geoff.

In this Klein story, as in the previous ones, I have used the names of my mother, Bernice, and her parents and siblings as the names of the main and very fictional characters. It is fitting, therefore, that this book is dedicated to my mother. Recently, she has been through a terrible health ordeal. Yet, she has faced this adversity with great courage and good humour that I and everyone in my extended family can only admire.

Allan Levine
Winnipeg, August, 2016

Allan Levine is an award-winning internationally selling author and historian based in Winnipeg. He has written thirteen books including the Sam Klein historical mystery trilogy. Winner of the Alexander Kennedy Isbister Award for Non-Fiction, the McNally Robinson Book of the Year, the Best History Book Award at the Canadian Jewish Book Awards, and the co-winner of the JI Segal Prize in Canadian Jewish History. His most recent books are: *King: William Lyon Mackenzie King: A Life Guided by the Hand of Destiny* (2011) and *Toronto: Biography of a City* (2014). A freelance writer since the early 1980s, his work has appeared in the *Globe and Mail*, *Maclean's*, *Toronto Star*, the *National Post*, and *Saturday Night*. A columnist for the *Winnipeg Free Press* since 2010, he explains the history behind current events.